Summer on Dune Road

A novel

Rachel Cullen

Published by Lime Street Press

ISBN: 978-0-578-28058-5

For Cocoa and Graham
And everyone lucky enough
to have a dog in their lives

Prologue

Megan

No one ever intends to fuck up their lives. I firmly believe this. I must admit that I've unfairly judged many people over the years for poor choices, bad behavior, dishonesty, or pure stupidity. But a few months ago, as a moral, studious, over-achieving college senior, I found myself in a predicament of epic proportions and realized that disaster could happen to anyone.

Chapter 1

Megan

As I throw yet another armload of papers into the massive recycling bin in the hall, a feeling of immense sadness washes over me. I'm the last one left in the dorm, and it's unnaturally quiet. Even at three in the morning on a Wednesday, there's always some movement. Whether it's someone pulling an all-nighter in the lounge or stumbling down the hall after one too many drinks, it's never quiet in a dorm. But I had the privilege, and often misery, of being the Resident Advisor (usually known as an RA) for the freshmen dorm this past year, and the students all packed up and left yesterday. I was looking forward to time by myself to sort through all of the crap I've accumulated in my time at Stanford, but it's far more depressing than I could have imagined.

I'm not sure what to do with most of my belongings. I feel guilty throwing them away, but I don't need them anymore. After numerous calls to area homeless shelters and housing agencies, it appears the residents of Palo Alto don't need my junk either. It's even more complicated because I'll be back here in the fall for graduate school. I planned to put everything in storage for the summer and retrieve it when I move into my new place in September, but Hope had other plans. She moved off campus after the winter quarter, claiming that she "couldn't take the squalor of the dorms for one more day." I'm not sure why I was surprised, but she leased a massive apartment in a brand-new building in downtown Palo Alto that no one under the age of thirty-five could ever afford. And within a week, she furnished the entire place with help from her father's decorator – including every item in my soon-to-be bedroom.

It's not that I'm ungrateful to have my living situation taken care of, and I recognize that most graduate students would kill to be in my position. But it still feels weird to be twenty-two and going from Container Store crates to Stickley bedroom furniture. I've known Hope since the first week of freshman year, and the only thing I could possibly be surprised about is that she didn't do something like this sooner. She's always been unapologetic about her status as the child of a Silicon Valley tycoon, and she never seemed to care what anyone else thought of her. Having come from a private school in Manhattan and a highly dysfunctional family with guilt money of my own, I was used to rich girls. But back on the East Coast, where I come from, they flash their generational wealth in a different way.

I walk back into my corner room to gather another pile of memories and find Hope sprawled on my unmade extra-long twin bed, clutching a photograph in her hand. "I can't believe you still have this," she groans, but through her wide smile, it's evident she's delighted.

"I'm going to have it framed and hang it on the wall of our apartment," I threaten, and then immediately wonder if I'm allowed to use the word "our" or if I need to call it *hers* since I'm only paying for the utilities.

"Don't you dare," she laughs as she holds the four-by-six photograph closer to her face to examine it more carefully. "Why did you ever let me have bangs?" she asks, without looking up from the picture. "Or wear that much camo?"

"You can't blame me for either of those," I reply while rifling through stacks of papers on my desk. "That was our first day of freshman year; you made those choices without any help from me," I tease her.

"We look like babies," Hope says, rolling over onto her back and crushing one of my many piles. The sounds of paper crunching like leaves are muffled beneath her t-shirt, and I say a little prayer that it's not one of the few piles I'm planning to keep.

"Speak for yourself," I retort, but I know that she's right. That's one of the things I love most about the picture – how young and naïve we were four years ago when we were just starting our college journey. I know that we are *still* young by most standards, and as our professors have reminded us daily for the past three months, we have our entire lives ahead of us. However, I would still give anything to go back to the beginning of freshman year and have this experience again. There are definitely things I would do differently, but I try to shake away the thought of Mateo, as I know it won't end well.

"Are you going to be done soon? I want to go get something to eat," Hope complains, rolling her narrow hips in the other direction to sit up and crushing more of my undergrad memories as she goes.

I try to stifle a sigh, but it escapes anyway. "Does it look like I'm going to be done soon?" I ask, gesturing to the disaster that surrounds us. "Everything has to be out of here by tomorrow at noon when they come to close up the dorm."

"Do you really need to keep any of this?" she asks, looking dismissively around the room. "We have everything you need at the new place," she adds confidently.

I take a deep breath and remember how lucky I am to have my living situation taken care of, before I reply. "I probably won't bring most of this with me, but there's some stuff that will go in storage, and then I have to figure out what I'm taking with me this summer," I remind her.

"I can't believe you're leaving me all alone!" Hope cries, flopping down on her stomach in a dramatic fashion, so all I can see is her long black hair cascading down the side of the bed.

"You're hardly going to be alone," I laugh. "Almost everyone you know is going to be in the Bay Area this summer, and your cousin is coming to stay with you for an entire month," I remind her.

"I know," Hope giggles, sitting up. "But it's not the same as having *you* here," Hope smiles. She knows exactly what to say to make me feel good, just as all best friends should. "Tell me again why you have to go to New York for the summer?" she asks.

I hesitate to reply because I've asked myself the same question at least a dozen times over the past few days, and I'm not sure I have a good answer. My original plan was to go to Vietnam and Thailand with my college boyfriend, Alex, like all good millennials, and then go home to New York for a few weeks to see my family before grad school starts in the fall. But that was before everything with Alex went to hell a few months ago. I was almost able to convince Tasha and Liz to come with me, but Google wanted Tasha to start right after graduation. Liz was already worried about her student loans and the cost of the trip. Once she got the numbers for med school tuition at Columbia, she decided that she had to work every available hour this summer. So, in the absence of any other plan, and with a strong desire to put three thousand miles between Alex and me, I panicked a couple of weeks ago and decided to go home for the summer, or at least to Danielle and Ted's house, the closest thing I have to a home.

I expected Danielle to be thrilled when I told her I would be coming back east for the summer, as she's always begging me to come back for breaks and to see my little sisters, but instead, she grew quiet, and I knew instantly that something was off. That's when she told me that they finally decided to sell the apartment in Manhattan and move to Westchester. I didn't understand the problem until she divulged that there would be a few months between the apartment sale and the house completion in the suburbs, so they rented a small two-bedroom condo for the summer to close the gap. Danielle assured me that I was welcome to stay with them no matter what, but I knew that none of us wanted that.

Danielle's excessive ex-step-motherly guilt is how I ended up with a free guest house for the summer in Westhampton Beach. Yet again, I am a bit of a "charity case," but I'm out of options. Danielle assured me that I would never even see her friend, Nora. She's the recently divorced, recently "retired" CEO with a fabulous Hamptons beach house, and for some unknown reason, she's letting me squat in her fancy guest-house for the summer. At that point, I decided I had nothing left to lose.

Realizing that my thoughts have left an excessive pause in my conversation with Hope, I reply, "I just need a change of scenery."

"Okay," she shrugs. "The Hamptons were super lame the last time I was there," and then she throws in, "I don't remember having to clean out *my* room when I moved out of the dorm."

As much as I love Hope, there are times such as these when she drives me crazy. She doesn't remember cleaning out her room because her parents sent a moving crew to get her packed up, and she didn't lift a finger. At the time, I wondered how they knew what to keep and what to toss, and I worried she would miss valuable trinkets from college by not combing through her belongings on her own. But now I'm just jealous that she left the dorm one morning for class, and when she got to her new apartment that evening, everything was ready for her, as if by magic. Come to think of it, I bet there's a storage room somewhere in her parents' massive house that holds every stray paperclip and term paper from her room, just in case of emergency nostalgia.

It's not her fault that she's this sheltered, and she's surprisingly well adjusted for growing up the way that she did. But occasionally, when I'm stuck handling mundane issues like packing four years of my life into a few cardboard boxes, she's not the easiest person to be around.

"I'm probably going to be here the rest of the day - sorry," I apologize half-heartedly. "If I finish in time, maybe we can get a drink tonight?" I offer.

"Fine," Hope relents, pulling herself to her feet and turning back to search under the folds of my worn tie-dyed comforter for her phone. She removes her hand triumphantly and tucks it into the side pocket of her designer leggings before giving my room a once-over and holding up both hands in surrender as if it's all just too much for her. "I'll text you later," she calls out as she walks down the hall. I can't help wondering how she's acting so nonchalant when today may be the last time she's ever in this dorm, but Hope doesn't seem to have the same connection to student housing or many aspects of everyday life that I do.

Chapter 2

Courtney

I knew there wouldn't be anyone here to meet me at the airport, but still, a wave of disappointment washes over me as I make my way to baggage claim at JFK airport. Of course, it wouldn't make sense for Alyssa to come to the airport, and from what she's told me about New York, people just don't do that here, but it still feels lonely to get off the plane alone in a new city.

Maybe if I had gone to school more than forty minutes away from home, I would have had more experience with this, but Northwestern was just down the road from the small North Shore suburb where I grew up. We never traveled much as a family. In school, I traveled to college basketball games with the team, primarily by bus, and occasionally we flew together. I'm embarrassed to admit that I'm twenty-two years old, and this is the first time I've flown by myself. I don't think the thought ever occurred to Alyssa since she's a seasoned world traveler - when Alyssa was in elementary school, she used to fly by herself to visit her mom when she was filming on location.

I elect to feign confidence in the hopes of deterring the creepy-looking guy on my left from taking yet another step in my direction. While I wait for my colossal duffel bag to emerge onto the baggage carousel, I pull up the text from Alyssa with the address and detailed instructions on where to go to meet my Uber driver, and I stare intently at my phone until the strange guy backs up.

After an agonizing delay (where I automatically assume the airline has lost my bag), my oversized duffel with the purple ribbon tied to the handle is unceremoniously spat out. It comes crashing down the ramp with a giant thud. I rack my brain to remember if there is anything in there that could have been damaged in the fall, but the worst I conclude is that my conditioner could have exploded, and although unfortunate, it is fixable with a few loads of laundry.

Almost ninety minutes after touching down at the airport, and five hours after leaving Chicago O'Hare early this morning, I am finally on my way to "The Hamptons." I've heard and read so much about this place that I find it hard to believe it will live up to its reputation. I guess I'll find out soon.

I'm settled in the backseat of a maroon Kia Sorrento, flying east on some Long Island highway with all the windows down. My driver, Nils, is singing along to the radio with a halfway decent voice, and it's the first time in the last month that I've felt able to relax, or at least take a moment to pause and reflect on what's going on around me – every second until now has felt like a race just to get here.

When Alyssa first suggested I spend the summer with her at her parents' place in East Hampton, I thought it was an absurd idea. Since the year before sixth grade, I have spent every summer either at some type of basketball training camp or working, and more recently, both. But with college *and* my basketball career behind me, law school starting in September, and my parents finally taking the two-month-long trip to Australia that they've been planning for years - I couldn't think of a single reason to say no. Of course, it still feels extravagant and ridiculous to spend an entire summer lounging by the beach and partying, but Alyssa assured me I'd adjust quickly.

My phone buzzes, and I assume it's Alyssa checking on my progress. Unfortunately, I can't read the tiny font on the driver's GPS app, but the traffic has slowed to a crawl, so I can only imagine that what was supposed to be a two-hour drive to East Hampton will take quite a bit longer. I'm already thinking about which emoji would best convey my feelings about the delay to Alyssa when I notice that the text is from Preston.

PRESTON: HOW ARE YOU?

It's three tiny words, and my stomach is doing summersaults. We dated for the past two years and practically lived together all of senior year. But then, in April, when his dream came true, and he got drafted by the NFL to play for the Denver Broncos, we decided to break up after graduation. We parted ways eight days ago, and my heart is still in disbelief that my brain would agree to something so stupid. It seems Preston is having a great time reuniting with friends at home in Houston and is beyond excited to leave for summer camp in Colorado in a couple of weeks, so it's clear that he isn't weighed down with regret. Honestly, this was the final tipping point that led to me spending an opulent summer mooching off Alyssa; at least I'll be grieving in a mansion on the beach.

Courtney: Good. You?

Preston: I'm good. I forgot how hot Houston is in the summer.

Courtney: Soon, you'll be in the mountains – it will be cool there.

Preston: Haha – guess you're right.

Courtney: gotta go – almost at Alyssa's. It's so beautiful here!

Preston: Okay. Have fun!

Courtney: I will!

I shove my phone back in my bag, feeling deflated. I have no idea where we are, but we're no longer on the highway, and I can glimpse the sparkling water out the window to the right. I know it's immature, but I'm already thinking about what bikini I want to wear today so that I can post a selfie by the pool and Preston can see how much fun I'm having this summer.

Chapter 3

Nora

When I was little, my mother had a litany of expressions she used to throw at my siblings and me. When my younger brother's girlfriend moved to Florida, she told him that absence makes the heart grow fonder. When my sister wanted to invite the meanest and most popular girl for a sleepover, my mother said that a leopard doesn't change its spots. When my older brother and I used to fight, she would admonish that it takes two to tango. She seemed to have an expression for every possible situation and lived by them as if they were gospel. But the one that always upset me most was when she would say, "Nora, you can't have it all," and shrug, as if I was supposed to accept that and be okay with it.

From a young age, I *knew* I was going to have it all. It sounds like an absurd thing to understand as a child. I knew enough not to tell my secret to others, but I knew I was right. My life wasn't perfect, but it was damn close. From as far back as I can remember, I was beautiful, popular, and intelligent. Parents liked me, teachers liked me, girls wanted to be friends with me, and boys wanted to date me long before I was old enough to be going on dates. Looking back on it now, the pre-pubescent attention from boys was alarming, but at the time, I was flattered to be the "it" girl in my town and smart enough to want to get out of there the second high school was over. I expected things to change in college, but the spell continued. I aced four years at Duke while dating a string of hot guys and working on my business plan for a line of women's fitness clothing.

After college, my picture-perfect life continued when I left Richmond, Virginia, moved to Manhattan, and miraculously secured funding from a venture capital firm for my clothing line. I met Mason a couple of years later, and despite being a bit of a stereotypical investment banker, he was my dream man. He spent months wooing me to an inevitable engagement on New Year's Eve in Paris.

My mom passed away five years ago after a devastating battle with uterine cancer, to which she often remarked, "the show must go on." With my accomplishments over the past few years, I've often wanted to show her that I do have it all, and her proverb is wrong. After all, I was just named to Fortune's Fifty Most Powerful Women in Business List, I sold my company for a record amount this spring, I've already been offered six different CEO positions, and the custom oceanfront dream home I've built on Dune Road in Westhampton Beach is finally completed.

Sitting on a chaise lounge next to my heated pool, staring out over the empty white dunes to the glistening Atlantic

Ocean, I can pause reality and tell myself that "I've won." Although, I can't let myself stop there, no matter how hard I try. I can't forget that Mason is already living with his new girlfriend in *our* old apartment in Tribeca, and I'm here all by myself. I can't forget that no one depends on my opinion or insights for the clothing brand I painstakingly built into an empire over the past fifteen years. And I can't forget that I've been so busy having it all that I haven't given enough time to my real friends or my family, so I have tons of people who want to use me for connections or kiss my ass, but no genuine people in my life. At the age of thirty-nine, I might finally realize what my mom meant when she said that I couldn't have it all.

Chapter 4

Megan

"This place is ridiculous!" I squeal to Danielle while giving her a FaceTime tour of the guesthouse, unable to contain my excitement.

"Wow!" Danielle says, her eyes opening wider as she scans the all-white living room and view of the ocean, which is visible over my shoulder. "Is it wrong that I'm insanely jealous?" Danielle sighs, and I can hear screaming in the background.

"Not at all," I reply with a laugh. "Sounds like Abby and Tory are getting along well," I joke.

"Don't get me started," Danielle says. "They were great until about five minutes ago. They were sitting quietly, and Abby was helping Tory with a puzzle. Then Abby was helping *too* much, and Tory lost it," Danielle tells me.

"Do you have to go?" I question as the screams get louder in the distance.

"In a minute," she says. "I cannot wait until the house is

ready. We are going to kill each other in this tiny space all summer," she laments.

"Sorry," I say. I feel slightly guilty that I'm not there to help out with my sisters, but if the apartment is cramped with the four of them, it would be disastrous if I was there camped out on the sofa.

"Don't worry about it," Danielle assures me. "Quick, show me the rest of the place before I have to rescue Abby."

"Abby?" I question. Abby is six and a half, and Tory just turned four, so she must have misspoken.

"Yes, definitely Abby. Tory has turned into a nightmare. She bit Abby last week when she didn't get her way!" Danielle tells me.

"Oh shit!" I exclaim and try not to laugh at the image of precocious little Tory sinking her teeth into Abby's delicate arm, which was likely clad in a princess dress at the time. "Here's the kitchen. This is the dining room. And this is my bedroom," I say, repeating what the housekeeper said when giving me a tour of the guesthouse earlier today.

"I think we may need to come to stay with *you*!" Danielle says, and I hope she's joking.

"How do you know Nora again?" I ask Danielle. "And why haven't I heard of her before this?" I laugh.

"Nora was one of my roommates for that year I lived in Manhattan before law school. There were four of us in a two-bedroom apartment in Murray Hill. Nora's a few years older than me, and she had already rented it with one of her friends. That meant that they each got the real bedrooms, and I got a windowless corner of the living room that was made into a bedroom with temporary walls," Danielle laughs as if picturing the setup now. "Honestly, I think it might have been bigger than the place we are renting for the summer," she moans.

"How did you find that apartment?" I ask.

"Oh gosh, I can barely remember. I think the other girl was someone I knew from the restaurant. That was the year I waitressed while deciding if I wanted to go to law school," she tells me. "That girl must have been the connection to Nora. But honestly, it's all such a blur now. It feels like a lifetime ago," she says wistfully.

The screams in the background hit a disturbing pitch, and I know our call is going to end. "Sorry Megan, I've got to go," she apologizes.

"Of course," I say, but she's already gone.

I wanted to learn more about her relationship with Nora and why I didn't know, until two weeks ago, that Danielle was friends with one of the country's most successful women. It's clear *that* discussion will have to wait. It's times like this when I'm reminded of how unique (and bizarre) my relationship is with Danielle and with Abby and Tory. At this point, I've refined the story to a relatively concise paragraph. It's the elevator speech of my fucked-up family background, but it comes in handy to hit all the highlights – especially when I'm just getting to know someone.

My parents divorced about seven years ago, and then my dad almost immediately married a much younger lawyer who worked for him (Danielle). When I first met her, I couldn't stand her, but that was only because I didn't give her a chance. Then she got pregnant, and my dad cheated on her and wanted nothing to do with another baby, so she moved out and divorced him. That was about the time I realized I liked Danielle, and my dad was the real asshole. Shortly after the divorce, my half-sister Abby was born, and my dad showed his true colors by sleeping with our nineteen-year-old au pair and declaring that he didn't want me living at home anymore. That was when Danielle took me in and let me live with her and Abby, and shortly after that, her fiancé Ted moved in, and it was like I got a whole new family. Tory was born my freshman year of college, and although I can't claim any genetic link to her, I feel that she is just as much of a sister to me as Abby.

We're not a "typical" family, but it seems that the traditional family is less common these days anyway. We still got weird looks at parents' weekend at Stanford. Danielle is only fourteen years older than me, making her about fifteen to twenty-five years younger than the other parents, and then we added to everyone's confusion with Tory and Abby as most of my classmates' siblings were already in high school.

My brother never makes it into the short version of my story. People have enough trouble digesting my life with my ex-stepmom and half-sister; I can't expect anyone to understand why my biological brother doesn't play much of a role. Kyle is three years younger than I am, and he stayed with Dad after Danielle divorced him. At the time, it felt like Kyle was choosing Dad over me; but after a while, I forgave him. He was only thirteen and still reeling from Mom and Dad's divorce and couldn't handle any more change. They moved to London when he was in high school, and Dad sent him to boarding school over there since he wasn't cut out to be a hands-on Dad. Thankfully, Kyle and I worked through our issues, and we're much closer now. He decided to stay in Europe and just finished his sophomore year at St. Andrews in Edinburgh. I'm not sure he'll ever move back to the States, but we have a strong texting relationship, with the occasional FaceTime call for good measure, and that will have to be enough.

Chapter 5

Courtney

The party had already started when my Uber arrived at Alyssa's *estate*. That's not a word I have ever used before, but it was immediately clear that it was the only word suitable to describe this place. On second thought, the word *compound* might also work. There are multiple structures on the property, in addition to the obligatory pool and tennis courts, and the whole place sits on a sprawling emerald green lawn that gradually transitions into a football-field-size private beach abutting East Hampton's pristine Main Beach.

I didn't know that Alyssa was planning to have people over, and I would have preferred to have a quiet day by the pool, but Alyssa certainly had other ideas. She greeted me at the door in a tiny, ruffled, string bikini that showed more of her skin than I'd ever seen living on her floor in the sorority house in two years. Then, after whisking me to my designated bedroom and demanding that I change into my bathing suit, she brought me out to the pool to meet a dozen of her closest friends who had also grown up with summer homes in East Hampton.

I've finally extricated myself from the raucous group at the outdoor bar and escaped to a partially secluded chaise lounge chair on the far side of the pool. With sunglasses on, it's easy to pretend I'm looking at something on my phone while I get the chance to study Alyssa and her friends from a distance. Alyssa lived on my hall sophomore year at the Kappa house, but we didn't know each other very well. I spent almost all of my time playing basketball or hanging out with the team. In my *free* time, I hung out with my roommate Kerry, who is now home in Georgia for the summer, and of course with Preston.

Even though we were in the same sorority and pledge class, I didn't get to know Alyssa until the end of junior year, when we had a philosophy class together. Alyssa was a theater major, and I double majored in economics and women's studies, which meant that we never had any overlap in coursework. But we both needed this class to fill a requirement, and neither of us knew anyone else in the seminar, so we started sitting together and studying together and became friends.

Kerry and Preston thought it was weird that Alyssa invited me to East Hampton. Although we *had* become better friends over the past year, they both insisted that we weren't the caliber of friends that should spend the summer together. I was also surprised when she initially suggested it, but after Preston decided that he wanted to break up, and it was clear that the rest of my friends and family had plans lined up for the summer, it didn't seem like such a bad idea to do something out of the ordinary for once.

I hate to admit when I'm wrong, and I hope it's just a case of first-day jitters, but I'm starting to wonder if Preston and Kerry were right. I'm watching Alyssa dance half-naked around the pool, so drunk that she's not aware that she's spilled half of her daiquiri down her arm. She's taking turns pressing her body against the bare chests of her male friends – presumably the summer playmates of her youth – and *threatening* to untie her bikini top if they don't put on the song she's requesting. Alyssa and I ran in different circles at school. Still, on the few occasions, we did overlap, I swear I remember seeing her with her theater friends in the corner of a party, usually with vape pens or cheap red wine, looking slightly superior to the rest of us. At other times, she would be up in the common room night after night, preparing for an audition and surviving on hot water with honey to preserve her voice. But nothing I've seen would have prepared me for the "Girls Gone Wild" side of her that I'm seeing now in my first hour of what promises to be a very long summer.

"Courtney, get over here," Alyssa hollers and motions furiously with her hand for me to come to join her.

"I'll be there in a minute," I reply with a wave and a half-smile.

Just then, Alyssa appears to follow through on her threat, and her skimpy triangle top is off her body and flying through the air, landing gracefully on the surface of the pool. The display is followed by loud cheers and whistles. Then, as if on cue, the biggest of the guys picks her up and puts her over his shoulder, and carries her across the patio and into the house, while everyone laughs and someone yells, "Don't forget a condom." As soon as they're gone, the rest of the group resumes the party, and no one so much as glances in my direction. My finger hovers over the screen as I debate whether to text Preston. I'm desperate to tell him that Alyssa's house is actually an episode of MTV spring break. Just as I'm figuring out what to write, a text pops up from Preston:

PRESTON: HOW'S THE HOUSE? HOW'S EVERYTHING WITH ALYSSA?

I start to type and then erase my words and try to find the best way to capture the insanity I've seen this afternoon, but I can see he's still typing, so I wait to see what he says.

PRESTON: IS IT WEIRD?

And with that, I delete everything I was going to say. I don't need Preston to have the satisfaction of knowing he was right. Especially not if he's going to go off and have his dream summer.

COURTNEY: IT'S NOT WEIRD AT ALL! IT'S AMAZING!! WE ARE HAVING THE BEST TIME. ALYSSA IS HAVING A PARTY TODAY SO THAT I CAN MEET ALL OF HER FRIENDS. I HAVE TO GO NOW – IT'S GOING TO BE THE BEST SUMMER EVER!

PRESTON: TALK TO YOU LATER – HAVE FUN

I contemplate going over to the group and re-introducing myself, but I'm already about six drinks behind everyone else. I grab my towel and head toward the sliding glass doors without attracting attention from any of the guests. Maybe tomorrow will be better.

Chapter 6

Nora

I should have predicted this, but that doesn't make it any easier to see. The picture of Mason and Priya is front and center on *Page Six*. They are at a restaurant opening in Chelsea, and they look overjoyed to simply be standing next to each other. My ego wants to remind everyone that Mason wouldn't even be worthy of *Page Six* if it weren't for me – he would just be another balding banker dating a stunning girl half his age. It's somewhat validating that the caption only refers to him as "Nora Bradley's ex-husband." However, he's the one who's moved on and is getting photographed at restaurant openings, so the validation only goes so far.

Dating is so much easier for men, especially for those with money and power. Initially, Mason claimed that he thought my success was sexy, but it became clear that once my paychecks were bigger than his, it wasn't sexy anymore. We were barely separated before women started throwing themselves at him (honestly, it may have started long before we were separated, but I pretended not to notice). He's forty-three, which I've learned is quite youthful for men, in decent shape, makes a good living (especially when you include the money he got from the divorce), and he doesn't have pesky baggage like children.

On the other hand, I am a thirty-nine-year-old, self-made multi-millionaire. Except for a bit of cellulite on my upper thighs, I look just as good as I did when I was twenty-five, but I have zero prospects – I might as well have leprosy when it comes to dating.

That last thought might be a little unfair, given that I've only attempted one conversation with a single man since my divorce. However, it was so catastrophic that I can't imagine trying again. Just thinking back to that night at the bar at Ophelia makes me cringe. I'd been having such a nice conversation with the cute guy next to me. He bought me a Caribbean old-fashioned, and we were casually flirting - the way you do with a stranger when you start to think about how his lips would feel if you kissed them. I was in the middle of telling a funny story about my brother when one of his friends tapped him on the shoulder and whispered something in his ear. I knew it was bad news when I saw the look on his face. He looked as if he'd been slapped and then asked the question to which he already knew the answer, "You're Nora *Bradley*?!"

"Yes," I sighed, as though this was something to be ashamed of.

"Holy shit! Why didn't you tell me?" he asked angrily.

"You didn't tell me *your* last name," I countered.

"Yeah, but that's different. I'm not famous. I'm just some graphic designer," he said.

"Why does it matter?" I asked.

"Are you serious?" he asked, looking at me like I was crazy. "Of course, it matters. Were you just messing with me? Do you get off on average guys buying you twenty-dollar drinks?" he accused.

"Of course not; what are you talking about? I was having a good time talking to you," I tried to explain.

"Yeah, right, lady," he said. "I'm going to go spend my hard-earned money on someone else," he scoffed and pushed back his stool and stormed out of the bar.

By that point, we had attracted attention from most people on our side of the bar, and people weren't even pretending not to stare. My friend hadn't even arrived, but I left the bar with my head down to very loud whispers:

"*Did you see who that was?*" and "*She looked a lot better on the cover of Fortune!*" and "*How sad that she has to come to a place like this to pick up guys.*" Needless to say, I haven't been back to a bar since.

I was genuinely frantic right after the divorce; in addition to the logistics of splitting assets and moving to Westhampton, the deal to sell the company happened simultaneously. There weren't enough hours in the day to get everything done. The few friends I had left reached out to offer sympathy over dinner or drinks, but I didn't have the time.

I looked forward to the halcyon days of beachside bliss when I could take a walk on the dunes without the fear of a missed call. But after the first week of paradise, the novelty wore off, and now I'm restless, and the offers of support have dried up.

I've invented a new game where I scroll quickly through the contacts on my phone and then make myself stop and select someone at random. The point of the game is to make myself call (or text) this person and say hello, as a way of rekindling connections. So far, I've only followed through twice. One text was to my cousin, Jane, and the other was to my hairstylist, Fleur. As of now, I wouldn't call this project much of a success.

I wonder for the hundredth time this week if Eva is out here for the summer. I drove by her house the other night, and all the lights were on. In the past, Eva rented it out for the month of July, so that could still be what she does. I'm ashamed of how long it's been since I've been in touch with her. The first year Mason and I rented a house in the Hamptons we were fortunate enough to rent down the street from Eva and her wife, Chloe. I was worried that Mason might feel outnumbered by three women, but back then, my company was still hemorrhaging money as I tried to figure out the secret to retail success. Mason loved the attention that came with being the only man, even if two of the women never looked at him in *that* way. The four of us spent every night together that first summer, and when Labor Day rolled around, we planned to book the same houses for the following year.

Obviously, there were changes to our dynamic over time as Eva and Chloe had kids and then bought their own small house. Then we bought a slightly bigger house a few blocks away, and my career took off. However, up until about five years ago, we kept up our summer traditions and spent countless nights drinking wine, playing cards, and laughing as we watched the sunsets over Moriches Bay.

Their house is only a mile away. I could walk over and see if Eva is home. Or maybe I could even bike past the house and try to catch a glimpse to ascertain if it's even them or if it's merely July renters. It feels ridiculous to give this so much consideration, but I can't imagine what I'll say if I *do* see her. How can I apologize for my absence these past years? How do I insert myself into her life when we barely know each other anymore? I find myself without answers to these questions, so just like every other day, I decide to remain in my sanctuary, all alone.

Chapter 7

Megan

I try to remind myself that practically anyone would kill to be in my position. Sitting by the pool with a stack of books and nothing to do is essentially my dream, so I can't believe this is something I even have to tell myself. But oddly enough, after five days of lounging in luxury, I'm starting to get bored. I'm ashamed to even have this thought. I force myself to think back to how stressed I was this past fall when I was studying for the GREs or writing my senior honors thesis, and I was in desperate need of sleep. Then, I would have done anything for a nap under an umbrella while listening to the sounds of waves crashing two hundred feet away. So why can't I be thrilled to have it now? Is it just an inability to be satisfied with what I have?

A rustling sound by the pool gate disrupts my thoughts, and my head snaps up from the chaise to see what's making the noise. The iron gate swings closed, and the latch clicks neatly back into place before I can see who was there. It could have been one of the few household staff that Nora appears to employ. Although the only person I've seen more than once is the housekeeper who gave me a tour the first day. I have an odd feeling that it was Nora at the gate, but I don't know why. I also have the awful suspicion that Nora was on her way out to the pool and then saw that I was here and decided against it. I still can't believe that I haven't seen Nora again since the day I arrived, and even then, she greeted me quickly and disappeared! I know Danielle said that it would be like having my own place, but this is ridiculous. In case it was Nora, and I was the reason she didn't want to use the pool, I decide to go back to the guesthouse. I grab my book and dial Hope's number as I walk, hoping it isn't too early in California for her to be awake.

"Hey! How's the beach? Miss me yet?" Hope chides, thankfully answering her phone on the second ring.

"I do," I reply. My voice starts to crack, and I swallow and squeeze my eyes shut to keep from crying.

"Are you okay?" Hope asks.

"Yeah, I'm fine," I say quickly. "I haven't found a good routine yet."

"A routine?" Hope questions. "You sound like my grandma," she laughs.

"You know what I mean," I say, but I'm not sure that she does.

"I told you the Hamptons are lame," Hope reminds me.

"They aren't lame," I protest, although I'm not sure why I'm defending a scene I know nothing about.

"What have you done so *far*?" Hope asks, and I can tell

from her voice exactly what she's doing right now. Both of her eyebrows are raised, her chin is lowered and tucked in slightly to her chest, and she has one hand on her jutted-out hip.

"Not much," I admit. "I've walked on the beach and gone to the pool. I walked into town. I got some really overpriced food at a local deli because I couldn't find the grocery store," I tell her while eyeing the fourteen-dollar jar of olives that's now sitting on my counter.

"Well, you gave it a try. Now, come back," Hope pleads. "We'll have the best summer – I promise!"

I don't reply right away because my instinct is to say yes. I know I had a reason for coming all the way out here, but now it seems crazy that I came here by myself. Other than a place to live, I didn't have anything else planned. It's only been five days, and each one has been longer than the day before.

Hope must take my silence as a good sign because she continues her campaign. "And...you'll never guess who I saw the other day," she says, drawing out her words to create the proper level of intrigue.

"Who?" I question, my interest piqued.

"Someone who was asking about you," she teases.

"Who was it?" I ask again, growing slightly impatient.

"A certain gorgeous swimmer," Hope says, laughing now, as she's sure she's given it away.

However, my entire body has gone rigid, and I'm having trouble catching my breath. "Alex?" I ask, in what comes out as almost a whisper.

"Yes, of course, Alex," Hope giggles. "And he looked good," she adds.

"Where did you see him?" I manage to ask.

"Actually, he was right outside the building. I practically ran into him when I was on my way to Flywheel."

"Alex was at our apartment?" I squeak, attempting (and failing) to keep my cool.

"He was just walking by," Hope says. "I think he misses you," she says, and to my dismay, she actually makes a kissing noise. "I still don't get why you guys aren't spending the summer together," she says.

I feel awful about what I'm about to do, but I do it anyway. I rap my knuckles loudly on the dining table. "Hope, I'm so sorry, there's someone at the door. It's probably Nora. I've got to go see what she wants. I'll talk to you later!" And I hang up before she can reply.

Any thoughts I had about flying back to Palo Alto have vanished. It may be boring here, but just the idea of Alex wandering outside our apartment and asking about me is enough motivation to keep me tucked away on the East Coast for the summer. It *is* strange that he's still out west since I know he's starting work at The Blackstone Group in Manhattan in September, *and* his family lives in Connecticut. He has no reason to still be in California. Although I've been ignoring his calls and texts, so I guess it isn't that strange that I don't know where he is.

It feels weird that Hope doesn't know what happened with Alex, and therefore doesn't know why I'd find this so disturbing. I wonder, yet again, if the deal I made with Alex was worth it, especially now that I'm coming dangerously close to breaking my end of the bargain. But looking backward isn't going to help anything. I'll stay here for the summer, and Alex will be all the way out in California, and then in September, we'll switch coasts, and with any luck, he'll come to his senses, and I'll never have to see or hear from him again.

Chapter 8

Courtney

It's embarrassing how easily I've adjusted to my summer schedule—sleeping past ten and strolling into the kitchen to pour myself a cup of piping hot coffee and fix a bowl of homemade granola and berries. All of this is simply waiting for me on the counter as if I'm staying at a posh hotel rather than Alyssa's "little beach house," as she likes to call it.

"Good morning, sleepyhead," Alyssa calls out as I walk into the sun-drenched kitchen. She's sitting cross-legged at the twelve-foot-long bleached oak kitchen table, with four different types of drinks arranged in a semi-circle in front of her: green juice, water, coffee, and something that looks like sludge.

It feels unnecessary to point out that this is the first morning all week that *she's* been awake (or at least out of her room) before noon, so I simply reply with a cheerful wave and say, "Morning."

"Do you want to try the beach this afternoon?" Alyssa asks cheerfully.

"Haven't we gone to the beach every day this week?" I ask, visibly confused by her question.

"No, silly. I mean Main Beach, not *our* little beach. It will be fun to see people," she adds.

I can't help but laugh at Alyssa's viewpoint. We've spent every afternoon and most evenings at the pristine private beach just past her family's rolling green lawn. I don't know much about The Hamptons or about the beach scene here in general, but I already know that owning a property like this is about as exclusive as it gets, and people would sell a kidney for the opportunity to sunbathe here. Alyssa's house also operates like an all-day party, and she has friends coming and going at all hours of the day and night, which is why it's somewhat ridiculous that Alyssa views a day at East Hampton's largest public beach (only public to East Hampton residents, of course) as an exciting change of pace.

"Sure," I reply. "I'm going to go for a run again this morning. Do you want to come with me?" I ask her.

"Outside?" Alyssa asks, looking puzzled.

"The last couple of days, I've just run through the neighborhood until I hit about two and a half miles, and then I trace the same path back, so I don't get lost," I admit. "It's a beautiful area," I add.

"There's a group of us going to the Soul Cycle class at eleven. Renaldo teaches that class. He's so hot. You should totally come," Alyssa says.

I've never really liked biking, indoors *or* outdoors, and I've never understood the spinning craze, especially with these classes where it seems to be more about the clothes and the instructor's playlists. However, I can tell that my opinion won't be very popular. "I'm going to stick with the run. But I'd love to go to the beach later."

"Sounds good," Alyssa says. She takes a huge gulp of the thick, brown drink, and I'm dying to ask what it is, but I also don't want to know. "By the way, Chad is probably going to be at the beach today."

"Who?" I ask. As soon as the word is out of my mouth, I regret it because I'm sure that I'm supposed to know who he is after spending the past week with Alyssa's friends.

"You know, *Chad*," Alyssa repeats as if saying his name a second time and slightly louder is what will make the difference.

"Oh right," I say. I might as well have added the word "duh" to convey the absurdity of my forgetfulness, although, in all honesty, I still have no idea who she's talking about.

Alyssa beams at me with her pearly white teeth, clearly pleased that my memory has come back. "*And*...he likes you," she adds, thrilled to share this juicy piece of gossip.

"What? How can he like me? He doesn't even know me," I protest. At this point, I am finally putting in the effort to go through my mental rolodex and trying to put names to faces of the thirty or so guys I've met this week to figure out which one is Chad.

"He said you were really hot. And he loves tall girls," Alyssa adds.

I feel like I'm back in middle school with a friend whispering that some boy likes me when he's never even met me.

It clearly wasn't my witty conversational skills that got his attention.

"I'll be back around one, and we can drive over to the beach then. Make sure to wear a cute bikini, not that grandma-looking one-piece you wore the other day," Alyssa says and laughs.

I laugh along with her because it feels uncomfortable not to join in, even though I'm the butt of the joke. I wonder again if the Alyssa that I thought I knew at school the past few years was the real version, and the girl I see now is just her over-privileged summer personality. *Or*, if this is what she's really like, and in Evanston, it was all an act to fit in with her edgy theater friends. Whichever it is, I'm increasingly aware that 'Summer Alyssa' isn't quite who I bargained for.

Chapter 9

Nora

Peering through my bedroom curtains, I see Megan reading her book by the pool. She finished the spy novel she was reading over her first two days and then moved on to a hardcover literary fiction novel that's been on the bestseller list all summer. It looks like she's finished that one as well because today, she's reading the new biography by that South American activist I keep hearing about. I'm quite impressed with her reading choices; I know that I wasn't reading anything like that when I was twenty-two. In fact, I'm not even reading the same caliber of books right now – I still stick to the comforting romances and beach reads that I've always loved.

Megan glances up and adjusts her sunglasses, and although I know there's no way she could have seen me, I still recoil as if I've been caught with my hand in the cookie jar. Although this is probably far worse than sneaking cookies, I'm spying on my friend's daughter, who's supposed to be a guest in my home, and I haven't even properly welcomed her or introduced myself! I'm so embarrassed at my behavior on the day Megan arrived that I'm not sure how to recover. I was so upset about the stupid photo on *Page Six* that I barely said hi to her and then I shut myself back in my room. I'm sure she thinks I'm some crazy recluse, but then it hits me that it's pretty much the truth.

I turn my attention back to my phone and the emails that came through last night that I chose to "mark as unread" and save for later. The first one is from a previous investor. He made a fortune on the sale of my company, so it's not a big surprise that he's reaching out, if not just to say 'thank you.' I quickly scan the message and see that he has an opportunity he wants me to consider that he thinks would be a "great fit." I move the message to the mailbox with the rest of the emails I've received just like this one and move down the list. The next few are all more of the same; previous contacts who have heard I'm now available, and they want to help me find my next big thing. I know that everyone means well, at least most people — sprinkled in with some self-interest, but I just lost my *baby* — doesn't anyone understand? I put my blood, sweat, and tears into building my company at the expense of my entire personal life, and now everyone expects me to pick up, move on, and do it all again?

The last email would ordinarily have gone straight into the trash because I don't recognize the address, but the subject line piqued my curiosity, so it was spared. The subject line reads, "Bridget gave you this gift." I suppose it could be spam, but it feels unlikely that someone would get my sister's name correct in the subject line of an email without having any legitimate connection. And if it is fake, then I'll give them credit – hackers and spammers are getting better and more creative every day.

It must be boredom or perhaps depression that prevents me from deleting the email after reading the first line.

Dear Nora,

Your sister has hired me to help you. My name is Zadie, and I'm a matchmaker.

I can't believe that I don't delete the email straight away, or slam the computer shut, or throw it across the room (I have done that before, but only once, and it was justified.) But the perfect storm of my emotional discontent drives me to keep reading.

If you're still reading this, I'm going to consider that a victory! Your sister warned me that this wouldn't be an easy sell. I've never taken on a client before who didn't hire me themselves, and in your case, who may not even be interested in my services. However, your sister was very persuasive, and I'll admit that I've followed your career and your personal story for years, and I think I can help you find your match.

I'm sure this is a lot to absorb, but if you've read this far, it must mean something... Please reach out when you're ready, and I'll tell you all about myself and how my service works; I think you'll find it's different than anything else out there.

All the Best,

Zadie

I read through the email again and try to decide how to deal with Bridget. I could just wait for our family Zoom call this weekend and confront her in front of our brothers. But as I'm thinking through what obscenities to yell and how best to murder Bridget, the strangest thing happens. It almost feels like I'm hovering above and watching myself type the words rather than doing it myself. However, the result is that I send a reply to Zadie that says:

Dear Zadie,

Let's find a time to talk.

Nora

Chapter 10

Megan

Nine straight days of sunbathing and sleeping late have left me with a perfect, golden tan. I've also finally gotten rid of the dark circles under my eyes, which I've had since freshman year of college, and I assumed by this point I would have forever. But even my sun-kissed skin and de-stressed mood can't compensate for how bored I am.

I've watched groups of people my age on the beach all week, and although I'm far from shy, I can't imagine going over to any of them and introducing myself. Their reactions would likely range from polite tolerance to outright rejection, and although I'm eager for company, I'm not *that* desperate. Instead, I've decided to look for a job. It seems like the logical way to meet people, and it wouldn't be terrible to enhance my savings account before graduate school starts in the fall.

Other than Hope and maybe one or two friends from school, I don't know anyone who was as lucky as I was to finish college without any student loans, *and* I'm also fortunate enough that I won't have to take on any debt for graduate school. My jackass of a dad created a trust for me when he abandoned me that provided for all of my education, living expenses, and some extra. Even though I'm beyond lucky to have this money, I've realized recently that it's not the endless fund that I thought it was when Danielle told me about it in high school. When I was fifteen, and she gave me a glimpse at my trust account, it looked like an absolute fortune, and I'm embarrassed to admit that I thought it meant I was set for life. What I've come to understand over the past couple of years is that this money has set me up for a great debt-free start in life, but it certainly isn't a bottomless account, and if I don't watch how I spend it, I won't have anything left after grad school.

With this objective, I borrow one of the bikes from Nora's garage that the housekeeper told me I was welcome to use, and I set off for the ten-minute ride to Westhampton Beach's adorable little main street lined with shops, restaurants, and more real estate offices than anyone could possibly need. I'm not familiar with any of the stores, but I imagine that some of the stores are hiring. I think my first choice would be working in one of the cute clothing shops; I feel like I could fold clothes, make idle chit-chat, and meet people in town. I couldn't easily bike in a sundress, so I'm wearing white linen shorts and a black Club Monaco crop top that looks fashionable (I hope) but also makes me look experienced. I printed out twenty copies of my resume on the printer in the guest house; although my past work experience ranges from summer nanny to dorm RA to public policy research assistant, I'm shamelessly hoping that they are impressed with my three-point-eight GPA from Stanford and decide to overlook my lack of relevant work experience.

It's three hours later and abundantly clear that all the stores have already filled their positions for the summer, and the coffee shop did not share my opinion that I could learn on the job for the one open barista position. Admitting defeat, I decide to treat myself at the Beach Bakery and drown my sorrows in iced coffee and a black-and-white cookie. On my way out of the shop, I notice a message board with ads for local concerts and housecleaning services, and at the bottom of the board, there is a flyer advertising a need for SAT tutors. I scan the ad, which boasts an alarmingly high hourly wage paired with flexible hours, and I snap a picture with my phone to ensure I have all of the details.

On my ride back, I pretend to debate the pros and cons of SAT tutoring, but I already know I'm going to call about the position as soon as I get back *home*. It's funny that I already refer to this guesthouse mentally as home. I guess that's a normal tendency and trap people fall into; even when they are only on vacation for a few days or a week, they call the hotel or rental house their home. *Home* has been such a challenging subject for me ever since my parents' divorce. I will be forever grateful to Danielle (and Ted) for taking me in and including me in their family and their lives, but in some ways, I still don't really have a home. Wow - okay, that's way too deep and sad of a thought for me to process right now. I shake my head as if the physical activity will also clear the miserable thoughts from the inside.

I store the bike in the shed, next to four identical Trek bikes, and lock the digital keypad the way the housekeeper showed me on my first day. I don't even put my tiny backpack down when I get inside; instead, I dial the number from the flyer and hope that this will be the positive momentum I've been seeking.

"Hello?" someone says, answering on the third ring, without any additional introduction or mention of a tutoring company.

"Hi," I falter. I wonder if I have the wrong number, but even so, it seems I have little to lose. "Hi, my name is Megan. I saw your ad at the bakery in Westhampton Beach. I'm interested in SAT tutoring?" I hate that my voice goes up at the end, and it sounds like a question.

"How old are you?" he asks.

"Twenty-two," I reply.

"College?" he demands.

"Stanford."

"What did you get on your SATs?" he asks matter-of-factly.

"Combined or math and verbal separately?" I reply, although I can tell by his breathing that my question annoys him.

"Math and verbal," he huffs.

"Um, seven hundred-forty math and seven hundred-sixty verbal," I reply.

There's a pause, and I'm suddenly desperate for him to reply. I don't even know this guy's name, but I'm eager for his approval for something that I've been wildly confident about until sixty seconds ago.

"Alright, I still need one more tutor. Come by tomorrow.

You can take the test, and then we'll see if this will work," he says.

After a day of rejections and over a week without much human contact, I'm inappropriately relieved that this stranger wants to let me take some sort of test. "Great, thanks so much. Where should I meet you?" I ask, feeling annoyed that his bravado has shaken my confidence.

"Oh right," he says, revealing a hint of compassion. "I'll text my address. Is this the best number?"

"Yes, this is my cell phone," I reply.

"Okay. I'll see you tomorrow. Ten o'clock," he says, and it isn't a question.

He hangs up before I can reply, but seconds later, my phone beeps with a text providing an address for our meeting tomorrow. He didn't even include his name, and I consider replying and asking for it since it's already a little suspicious that I'm meeting some guy who advertises on handwritten flyers in coffee shops, but based on his clipped tone, I decide not to risk it. This whole thing may not be one of my best ideas, and I can just imagine what Danielle would say if I told her, but it's certainly the most interesting thing that's happened since I've gotten here, and I'm strangely excited for tomorrow.

Chapter 11

Courtney

At first, I don't understand any of the excitement surrounding Main Beach. It looks exactly like Alyssa's private beach, except here we are surrounded by screaming children, and we are sitting on flimsy folding chairs instead of sturdy teak loungers with the option of raising matching umbrellas if we decide we want shade. But then people keep showing up to say hello or drop off bottles of beer and hard seltzers disguised in neoprene covers, and I recognize this for the clandestine party scene that it actually is. At Alyssa's, she always knew who was coming over and played hostess for the group, but here she's delighting in running into people outside of her usual circle and blending in (to the best of her ability).

I don't love many of Alyssa's summer friends, but there are a few who don't seem too bad, especially in one-on-one conversations. I'm looking for either Serena or Natasha, but I don't see them anywhere. They are the two people that I've related to most, of all the people I've met so far. I can see the party side of them as well and how they fit into Alyssa's crowd, but I feel like I have a lot in common with each of them, especially before they have their fourth or fifth drink.

A large group has gathered over by the volleyball net, and I can't tell for sure, but I'm pretty sure the brunette in the purple bikini is Natasha. I turn to tell Alyssa that I'm going to go check out the volleyball game, but she is sitting on some guy's lap, who I've never seen before, and she is laughing hysterically as he tickles her ribs, and he grazes the side of her boob every time she gives him a chance. "I'll be back," I call over my shoulder to the small group that has gathered around our beach chairs and blankets, but I'm sure no one heard me.

Unfortunately, the girl in the purple suit doesn't turn around until I'm a couple of feet from the net, and then it's clear that it isn't Natasha. The ball lands out of bounds a few inches from my feet, and everyone on both sides of the net looks expectantly in my direction. I smile awkwardly and toss the ball back to the bald guy who motions for me to throw it to him, and then I turn to leave, hoping the game resumes without anyone wondering what I was doing there.

"Hey, you," a voice calls out before I get more than a couple of steps away from the game. I could pretend to ignore it, but I'm one hundred percent sure it's directed at me, and it will only make it worse if he has to yell again.

"Yeah?" I question as I turn around.

"Do you want to play?" the bald guy asks.

"Oh. Um, no, that's okay," I reply. I'm surprised and relieved by his benign question.

"C'mon, we're down a player. And you look like you can play," he adds.

I guess I shouldn't be shocked that he noticed my size. I was one of the shorter players on the women's basketball team at Northwestern, but compared to the average woman, I'm still pretty tall. "I'm more of a basketball player. I don't play a lot of volleyball," I reply, but I'm already inching toward the court.

"You'll be great," he replies. "I'm Tucker," he says and extends his long, muscular arm and enormous hand in my direction.

"Courtney," I clumsily reply while shaking his bear paw.

The next hour flies by, and it's easily the most fun I've had this summer. For the first few plays, I didn't exert myself, but my athletic nature and competitive drive took over, and before I knew it, I was all-in and invested in every point as if it was an NCAA playoff game. I'm laughing and dripping in sweat when Tucker announces that he has to leave for work, and the rest of the volleyball players all agree that they should get going as well. Before I know it, the group is disbanding, and people are heading toward the parking lot in pairs and trios. Tucker has pulled a grey t-shirt over his impossibly muscular chest, and I chastise myself for being disappointed.

"Are you sticking around?" Tucker asks as he leans over to grab his threadbare backpack.

"My friend is still here," I tell him. I point to the area where Alyssa and I had been sitting before with a handful of her friends, but now there are at least thirty people sprawled all over beach towels and folding chairs in a wonky circle, and

I can tell that most of the group is drunk, even though there are signs all over the beach clearly prohibiting alcohol.

"Oh," Tucker says, sounding surprised. Then he gives me a disapproving look that tells me he knows that crowd and isn't a fan.

I met this guy an hour ago, and the only things I know about him are that he has an impressive spike and a ridiculous body, but I'm desperate not to let him down. "Those aren't really my friends," I say.

"No?" He asks, but there's a glint in his eye and a hint of a smile when he looks to me for an explanation.

"I'm friends with one of the girls from college, but I don't know the rest of them. I'm visiting her for the summer, but she's totally different here than she was at school in Chicago," I tell him, feeling ridiculous for over-sharing.

"The Hamptons will do that to people," he says, nodding his head.

"I guess so," I confirm, but I don't actually understand how a sliver of real estate can have such an impact on someone's personality.

"I do have to get to work," Tucker says apologetically.

"Oh, right. Of course," I say, blushing as I realize I've kept him here.

"You should stop by sometime," he offers.

"Oh. Where do you work?" I ask.

"I'm a bartender at The Huntting Inn," he replies.

I have no idea what or where that is, and it sounds like it's cute and cozy. I respond, "Maybe I will." I'm unexpectedly nervous and excited at the prospect of visiting this stranger at work. Suddenly, I feel almost naked standing this close to

Tucker in my tasteful but very small black bikini, even though I've been diving around in the sand in front of him for the past hour.

"Hope to see you around," Tucker says and gives me a little half-smile that makes my stomach do summersaults. Then he reaches out for me, and I think he's going to give me a hug, which seems bizarre, but this whole day has been bizarre, so I go for it and reach for him as well. Tucker staggers back, clearly surprised by my abrupt action, and I almost fall over.

"Sorry, there was a bug on your arm," he says and gives me a little grin.

"Oh my God," I say, and I know my face must turn a thousand shades of red at the same time. "Thanks," I mumble and turn around to walk back toward Alyssa and her friends, too embarrassed to even look at Tucker before I go.

As I approach the group, Alyssa practically tackles me in a hug; although she is a fraction of my size, she is fueled by White Claw. "Chad is pretty upset," she says, but she's laughing.

"Chad? What do you mean?" I ask, momentarily confused, but then I remember that he's the guy who was supposedly interested in me.

"He seems to have gotten over it," Alyssa says, and she points to a couple lying on a blue and white striped beach towel, who should certainly be locked in a bedroom somewhere and not on a public beach.

"I guess he did," I laugh and turn away, so I don't have to watch.

"It looks like you found someone too," Alyssa prods.

"Oh no," I protest. "I was just playing volleyball," I tell her.

"That's not what it looked like from here," she says and raises her eyebrows.

"I promise, that's all it was."

"What about the crazy hot bartender from The Palm?" Alyssa asks.

"Oh, Tucker?" I say before thinking better of it. "He said he works at some inn," I reply.

Alyssa gives me a look that's worth a thousand words and shakes her head as if to say, 'You're so naïve, and I told you so,' at the same time.

"Trust me; he's the guy from The Palm. The bar and restaurant are inside this old hotel on Main Street. Everyone's dying to fuck him," Alyssa adds casually.

"It's nothing. It was just volleyball. I think he felt bad for me," I reply, but the butterflies in my stomach know I'm not being completely honest.

"*This* doesn't look like nothing," Alyssa says deviously and shows me a picture on her phone. I don't know how she took it at the exact moment when I thought Tucker was trying to hug me, but from this angle, it looks like we are alone on the beach, about three inches apart and reaching for each other – oh, and I'm basically naked.

"I promise, it was nothing," I say, but the crack in my voice betrays me.

"If it was nothing, then you won't care that I posted it," Alyssa says, smirking and waving her phone side to side.

"What do you mean?" I squeal, although I know *exactly* what she means.

"You look super-hot, don't worry," she says, and she pivots and goes back into the epicenter of the unofficial party.

I grab my phone and open Instagram as quickly as I can. Alyssa has thousands of followers, so the three hundred fifty-four likes that she's gotten in the past fifteen minutes are surely a reflection of that, rather than the picture of Tucker and me with the caption, "Courtney isn't wasting any time getting the lay of the land in the Hamptons." I expand the area that shows who "liked" the photo and scroll until I find what I'm looking for – Preston27 liked the post. Fuck.

Chapter 12

Nora

I'm sure this is one of the many signs of my age, but I despise video calls. I used to do them for work if necessary, and I've adjusted to the weekly Zoom call with my siblings because it's simply more practical than the conference call or three-way-calling we had to utilize in the past. With my brothers and sister, I don't care what I look like, so I don't have to spend half of the call staring at my own image and fixing my hair or adjusting my neck to the most flattering angle. Therefore, when Zadie sent me an invite for a Zoom call today, I replied and told her in no uncertain terms that I would prefer to just speak on the phone. Then she told me that the reality of being a matchmaker is that this call has to be on video – no exceptions. Zadie said after today, she would be happy to skip the video, but the introduction is non-negotiable. I suppose I could have replied and told her that I'm interested in what's on the inside, and I think the men she represents should be as well; however, I know that's total bullshit since I've spent hours poring over profile pictures on dating apps (under an assumed name) and swiping left for trivial flaws.

"Can you hear me? Can you see me?" Zadie asks.

"Yes. I can hear and see you," I reply, resisting the urge to roll my eyes. I wonder how many years we will have to use this technology before we no longer begin each and every one of these Zoom calls like it's our first. I'm now curious if, for the first decade after Alexander Graham Bell invented the telephone, every phone call began with confirmation that the other party was, in fact, at the other end of the call.

Zadie's voice interrupts my daydream. "Thanks so much for taking the time to meet with me today. I know it was tricky to find a good time for this call," she reminds me.

"Yes. Sorry about that," I apologize. Although I jumped on her initial email, once I slept on it, I lost my nerve, and it took several phone calls from my sister to convince me to follow through.

"I'd love to start by telling you a little bit about how my service works," Zadie begins.

"Sure, that sounds good," I tell her. I try to focus on what she is saying and try especially hard to look at her instead of my own image on the screen. I wish I remembered to hide my own picture, but it always takes me a few tries to recall exactly what I need to click. Instead, I concentrate on Zadie's unique combination of wavy, dark hair, caramel-colored complexion, and violet eyes. I know it isn't relevant, but I'm instantly curious about her background and the ancestry that led to her features. The best word to describe her is "striking," and I wonder further about Zadie's relationship status, as well as her age. She doesn't have a single line on her face, but her voice sounds like that of an older woman, and I don't know if there is a standard job description for a matchmaker, but I feel like youth isn't an advantage.

I think I missed a bit of her introduction, but I snap back to attention and swear to listen to the rest of her speech. "After finishing my Ph.D. in psychology, I practiced for a few years, but I knew I wanted to specialize in couples counseling, so I went back to school to get my master's degree in family therapy. I practiced as a marriage counselor for five years. I loved helping couples work out their issues, but during that time, I found that I had a knack for setting up friends and finding connections for people in my life, and that was my true passion," Zadie says. "You look pretty skeptical," Zadie adds with a laugh.

I'm not sure what expression I made, but I must have lost my poker face, and my emotions were clearly displayed on my face because I *am* completely skeptical. On the one hand, I'm pleased with all of her higher education, but on the other hand, it sounds like she threw all of that away because she liked setting her friends up on dates. I don't know what I was expecting, but I think this is a waste of time for both of us.

"Sorry," I apologize.

"Please, don't worry about it. You certainly aren't the first cynic I've come across in my years as a matchmaker," Zadie assures me.

I smile in an attempt to ease any tension and decide that I like her better than I did a moment earlier.

"Maybe that's enough about my background; let me tell you more about how this works, and we can see if it's something you want to pursue. Sound good?"

"Sounds good," I reply.

"I've worked with all types of people, but at this point, my most typical clients are prominent men and women over the age of thirty, who are looking for real connections, but find it difficult to date and meet people due to their high profiles," Zadie says.

Without thinking, I nod my head in agreement, and Zadie smiles in response. I must admit that she's growing on me by the minute, and the description of her customers sounds incredibly relatable.

"There are others in my field who operate solely with male customers, and the men pay the matchmakers an exorbitant fee to control the process and evaluate tons of women based on their detailed specifications," Zadie tells me.

"And the women?" I can't help but ask

"For these matchmakers, the women aren't the clients; they are the merchandise." Zadie must see the horrified look on my face, and she raises her hand to let me know that I should let her keep going before I interject. "However, the way I run my business is *completely* different. I believe that all of my clients should have an equal stake in the relationship search and that everyone's needs and desires should be considered *equitably*."

"That sounds fair," I agree.

Zadie presses on while she senses an opening. "I've never been in your shoes, but from my experience working with public figures like you, it's virtually impossible to meet someone through any of the normal channels. It's not like you can meet a nice guy at a bar or try your luck on Bumble, am I right?" Zadie winks at me.

"Oh my God, you won't even believe what happened to me," I start to say, having dropped my guard completely. Then I come to my senses before I share my most embarrassing night ever with a total stranger. "Yes, it's hard to meet people," I say, regaining my composure.

If Zadie is intrigued by my slip, she doesn't show it. "That's where I come in. I have a vast network of fascinating men and women just like you – looking to find their soul mate or just someone to have dinner with," she says.

"Hmmm," I say, unwilling to give a firm commitment.

"How about this; I'm going to send you a couple of pages of questions. It's not like a traditional dating questionnaire, I promise. You can answer as few or as many as you like and then send it back to me, and we'll see where that takes us," Zadie offers.

"Okay," I concede. "That sounds manageable."

"Great. I'll email it to you when we end this call. Oh, by the way, just so I can get a sense of your type – who would be your ideal date or "celebrity crush," I think some people call them?"

"Oh gosh, I don't know," I laugh. Just when Zadie starts to sound remotely credible, she asks something like this. "Um, Ryan Gosling," I say, unable to come up with another name.

"Interesting," Zadie says. "I make it a practice not to break up my former matches. So, I don't think I can set you up with Ryan but I'll see what I can do," she says with a mischievous grin.

I think she must be full of shit, but before I have a chance to reply or ask any questions, she ends our call.

Chapter 13

Megan

According to Google maps, it should take seventeen minutes to bike to the address where I'm supposed to go for this sketchy tutoring interview. To be safe, I planned to leave thirty minutes early, but I changed my outfit six times, so by the time I'm finally out the door and on the bike, it's nine forty-three – Google better be right!

Sixteen minutes later, I'm pulling up to an enormous contemporary farmhouse on a quiet street just south of Montauk Highway. I double-check the address on the stone mailbox against yesterday's text message to make sure I have the correct house, and then dismount and walk my bike up the gravel driveway. As I'm looking for a convenient place to park my bike, a guy, who looks about my age, appears from the side door of the house.

"Are you Megan?" he asks.

"Yes?" I reply, although it comes out as more of a question than a statement.

"I'm Joel," he says. He doesn't offer any additional information or even offer to shake my hand, but I guess I should assume that this is the person I texted with yesterday and who I'm supposed to be meeting today.

"Nice to meet you," I reply.

"Follow me. I'll get you set up back here," Joel says, and he starts walking toward the back of the house.

"Set up for what?" I ask as I quicken my pace to keep up with him.

"To take your test," he says, sounding slightly annoyed as if this was something I should have already known.

I open my mouth to ask what kind of test I'm supposed to be taking, but based on his frosty attitude, I think twice and decide I'll wait and see what happens. He leads me to the backyard and down a bluestone path to a beautiful patio, set up as an outdoor living space. One half is designated as the living room with multiple couches, coffee tables, and even an outdoor rug, while the other half has been reserved for dining with a long rectangular table and twelve chairs, covered by a fourteen-foot-long cantilevered umbrella that looks like a spaceship mated with a racing boat. On the table, there are multiple piles of paper, fresh legal pads, and a neat row of pens and pencils sitting next to a pitcher of ice water and one tall glass. *I* may not be sure what's happening, but it's clear that Joel has it all planned out.

"Is this *your* house?" is what slips out of my mouth, even though I have tons of more pressing questions.

"Yes. I mean, my parents own it, but this is where I live in the summer," he replies, looking at me like I'm a complete moron.

I don't know what I expected him to say, but for some reason, I expected him to be older, and then I was thrown when I thought he wasn't old, but he still owned this house. Now I'm all out of sorts and clearly look like a crazy person.

"So, what's all this?" I ask, gesturing to the set-up on the table.

"It's your test," he states.

The blank look on my face must say it all because he sighs but thankfully elaborates. "I know you said you did well on your SATs, but I need to confirm for myself. I've devised a special test that detects good tutors and weeds out the bad ones. Just because you're smart doesn't mean you can teach other people," he says brusquely.

My initial instinct is to turn around and leave. This guy is a dick. I don't need to prove myself to him or to anyone. But I've already discovered that there are no jobs in Westhampton Beach, and I'm sure the other towns will be the same. Without a car, I couldn't even get *to* a job in another town. My only other option might be babysitting, and as much as I've loved doing that in the past, I am *not* doing it again this summer – I have a degree from Stanford, for God's sake.

As I take my seat at the long, teak table, I try to convince myself that I won't be working with Joel. I just need to pass his stupid test, and then I'll be working with high school kids and meeting their families; maybe some of the other tutors are normal, and we could make fun of Joel together?

"I'll be back in an hour," Joel says. "Do I need to take your phone, or can I trust that you won't use it?" he asks

I look up at him with disgust, incredulous at his question,

and he quickly gets the message. "Got it," I'll be back in an hour," he says again and backs away toward the house.

It takes me a minute to stop seething, and then I pick up a pencil and get to work. Schoolwork has always come easily for me, and I've never minded taking tests. The first few questions are unusual but thought-provoking, and by the time I'm at the bottom of the second page, I'm genuinely enjoying myself. I have the same feeling I had back in high school when the rest of my life seemed chaotic or downright miserable; I could always rely on my brain and the predictability of my classes. I also tried not to take for granted that even though I wasn't the most popular girl in school, I looked a certain way (and still do) and have always fit in, which made school a refuge of sorts, although I know that's not the case for a lot of kids.

I'm so engrossed in the test that I don't notice Joel's shadow start to creep over the table until he's practically on top of me. "Time's up. Pencil down," he announces. I think he might be attempting to be funny, but his shot at humor fails, and he's merely annoying.

"I'm finishing the last question," I tell him as I scribble the rest of my response to the short-answer essay question.

"Time's up," Joel says again.

I drop my pencil and make no effort to hide my eye roll when I hand him my packet. He doesn't say anything as he thumbs through my test, and although I'm confident in my responses, I'm unreasonably nervous about sitting here while he scrutinizes my answers.

"I'm going to go," I say. I'm unable to bear the awkward silence a moment longer; I push back from the table, grab my small bag, phone, and sunglasses, and start walking toward the driveway. Joel doesn't respond or even look in my direction, and I decide that this *was* a complete waste of time, but at least it's only eleven fifteen, and I can still be on the beach before noon and drown my sorrows with a good book and a Miller Lite.

As I'm closing the gate to the yard, Joel breaks his silence. "Can you start tomorrow?" he calls out.

"What?" I yell back. I'm not sure I heard him correctly, and if I did, it seems unlikely that I understood his cryptic language.

Joel walks down the path toward the gate, using his hand to shield his eyes from the sun. "You aced the test. You've got the job. I have a junior who is re-taking his SATs for the fourth time in a few weeks, and I want you to start with him tomorrow. I'll have more students for you shortly," Joel tells me.

"Oh," I say, unable to think of anything else. I was so annoyed with him a minute ago that it's taking me a second to re-group. I still think Joel's a pompous ass, but I'm perversely pleased that he's impressed with my test scores. And I *do* want a job. "How much does it pay?" I ask.

"We charge one hundred and fifty dollars an hour, and you take home one hundred and ten," he says.

"People pay that?" I ask.

"You're joking, right?" Joel asks, but the question is rhetorical. "I'm about to raise my rates because I can't keep up with demand. Parents will pay just about anything to help get their kids into college. And although there are tons of options for tutors in Manhattan and Westchester, these families don't want to give up their summers in the Hamptons, and there aren't many options out East," Joel says candidly.

"How long have you been doing this?" I ask him. I realize again that I don't know anything about him or about his tutoring business, and I should probably ask a few questions before accepting the job.

"This is my fourth summer. I started the summer after high school. My parents also *insist* on coming out here every year for the entire season," he says as if spending the summer here is a tragic punishment. "The summer before college, I was bored, and my parents' friends begged me to help their twins study for the SAT. You wouldn't believe how dumb those guys were," Joel adds. "Anyway, it wasn't hard to help them improve their scores since they were so low to begin with, but their parents were thrilled, and then a couple of other people asked for my help," he says.

"Then what happened?" I ask, trying to figure out when he went from doing a favor for a family friend to charging a massive fee and having a small business and more students than he can handle.

"When I came back the summer after my freshman year at Columbia, I decided to make a business out of it. Actually, it was part of an entrepreneurship contest. I won the contest," he brags. "But then I was making so much money that I decided to keep doing it," he adds.

At the mention of Columbia, my heart skips a beat, and I can't help but think of my ex-boyfriend, Ryan, who also went there. We broke up four years ago, and so much has happened since then, but he was my boyfriend through almost all of high school and my first love (and my first everything), and he will always hold a special place in my heart. I want to ask Joel if he knows him, but they would be at least three grades apart, and if by some chance he does know him, what will I say then?

"I'll take the job," I tell him, hoping it's a good decision and feeling that there is a minimal downside.

"Good choice," Joel says.

At his arrogant reply, I almost change my mind, but I would be the only loser in that scenario. Instead, I offer him a half-smile and try not to look as annoyed as I feel.

"I'll text you the details for tomorrow," he calls out as I'm getting on my bike.

"Thanks," I reply. As I pedal back toward Nora's house, I'm pleased with myself for getting the job because I always like to succeed, and I'm excited to have something to do other than go to the beach. I'm also hoping that I'll get to keep my distance from Joel – nothing good can come of having to spend more time with that pretentious jerk.

Chapter 14

Courtney

"I'm soooo hungover," Alyssa moans as she pads into the kitchen and flops down onto the couch. "Have you already been for a run?" she asks accusingly as she notices my outfit.

"Not yet," I reply. I did an hour of yoga with an app on my iPad, but it feels like I should keep this to myself. "I'm going to go try and find somewhere to shoot hoops," I tell her. "I think I saw courts when we were driving around the other day."

"You mean the ones near the senior center?" she asks, looking at me like I'm insane.

"Um, I guess so. Is that far away?" I ask, feeling embarrassed that I'm still so dependent on her for everything.

"It's not that far. But you can't run there. You need to drive," she tells me.

"That's okay. I'm fine to run there," I say.

Alyssa rolls over onto her side and groans as if the small

movement caused her significant pain. "Courtney, seriously, you have to drive there; it's like four miles away. I know you're going to play for like three hours or something ridiculous like that; please just take my car. The keys are over there," she says, motioning in the direction of the kitchen island.

"Thanks," I reply, acquiescing. "Do you want to do something when I get back? Can I pick anything up for you while I'm gone?" I ask her.

"I'm going to go back to bed," Alyssa mutters and pulls herself up from the couch, then she staggers back toward the south wing of the house where her bedroom suite is located.

"See you later. Feel better," I call after her, but I'm not sure she even hears me.

When we went to bed last night, the kitchen was in shambles. Alyssa invited a few friends over, and it quickly turned into a party. I switched to water after my second drink because it felt like everything was getting out of hand, but clearly, I was the only one who saw it that way. I tried to clean up before going to my room, but Alyssa insisted that I leave everything as it was. She even got to the point of physically restraining me from cleaning. Although I have at least seven inches and who knows how many pounds on her, it felt like a terrible idea to defy her in her inebriated state – and so I went to bed.

However, when I got up this morning, the kitchen, and the whole house, were spotless. I'm not sure what time the housekeeper arrived in the morning, but she must have gotten an early start. I'm glad that she was already in another part of the house when I came into the kitchen this morning. I feel terrible leaving that mess for her but having to look her in the eye would have been too shameful.

The keys to Alyssa's Porsche convertible are easy to spot in the center of the immaculate granite island. I know Alyssa also had a car at school; I can't exactly remember what it was, but I'm pretty sure it was a Prius or some other reasonable and practical car. This reinforces my belief that she led a double life for the past four years and the girl I'm spending the summer with is a virtual stranger.

I ease into the driver's seat and need to quickly figure out how to slide the seat back at least six inches, so my knees aren't touching my neck. I've ridden with Alyssa several times this summer, so the car is somewhat familiar, but it's quite different being the driver of a car like this. I'm not certain how much this car costs, but I'm sure it is the most expensive car I've ever driven; it may even be twice as expensive. With that in mind, I put the car in gear and inch down the pea-gravel driveway hoping that the gate automatically slides open the same way it does for Alyssa.

After several wrong turns, an almost catastrophic parking episode, and an incident with my handheld ball pump, I've found my rhythm on the court. It felt good to play volleyball the other day, but it was different than this. My body has craved the familiar cadence of the ball dribbling on the court and the delightful swish of the ball through the net. Suddenly I long for the agony of a grueling team practice, and I wonder what life will look like in the future with basketball as a hobby or a footnote on my resume. I try to push that thought aside, as well as the thought of Preston at the NFL Combine. Why does he get to make a lucrative career out of the sport he loves while I have to go to law school? I know all the answers to that question – the first being that even if I wanted to play professional basketball, I'm not nearly good enough for the WNBA.

I shake my head and return my thoughts to the task at hand – shooting as many free throws as possible in a row without missing. Right now, I'm at thirteen.

"You're pretty good," a voice calls out as number fourteen circles the rim and drops in.

I turn to look and see where the voice is coming from and can't keep myself from smiling when I see Tucker approaching with a ball under his arm. "So, it's not just volleyball, huh?" I ask. I know I have a stupid grin on my face and sweat stains on my grey tank top, but he's so cute that I can't help myself. I may not see eye-to-eye with Alyssa on much so far this summer, but I must concede that Tucker's appeal is hard to miss. He reminds me of a younger Jason Statham, the brooding hot bald guy with a few days' worth of stubble and an action hero's body.

"I'd rather play volleyball. I'd honestly rather be on the beach doing pretty much anything," he says wistfully. "But I only have a little bit of time and no one to play with, so thought I would shoot some hoops," he says.

I find it impossible to believe that Tucker couldn't snap his fingers and have a group of women and men lined up to accompany him anywhere he wanted to go, but the modest look is adorable too.

"Want to play some one-on-one?" he asks.

I'm instantly conflicted. As much as I like shooting layups and free throws, I would much rather actually *play* basketball. I know I'm a good player, but it's one thing to be a good former college player (whose last game was over four months ago) and another to play one-on-one with a guy at least six inches taller than me, who can spike a beach volleyball. I contemplate for a minute, and then the side of me that wants to play overrides the side that is worried about embarrassing myself.

"Let's go," I reply, rolling my ball off the court so that it comes to rest near my bag under a tree and indicating that we'll use his ball.

"Check," Tucker calls, passing me the ball, and I respond and pass it back with a solid chest pass, hoping I know what I've gotten myself into.

Almost an hour later, Tucker and I are resting under the tree, and I am trying to catch my breath. Technically, I won, but I think he may have taken it easy on me toward the end. Either way, I feel great about how I played, and I feel like myself for the first time since arriving in East Hampton.

"Are you sure you don't want some?" Tucker asks again, offering me his water bottle.

I can't believe that I forgot to bring anything to drink, *and* I'm dying of thirst, but it feels way too intimate to share his water bottle. "I'll be fine," I tell him.

"You look like you might pass out," he says, but not

unkindly. "I'll take off the top, and you can pour it in your mouth, so you don't have to get my germs," Tucker jokes.

The offer is too good to pass up, and if I'm being honest, I really have no issue with his germs. "Thanks," I say and gratefully accept the bottle.

"So, how's it going with your friend who isn't really your friend?" Tucker asks.

I'm surprised and flattered that he remembers this tidbit of information from our quick chat after the volleyball game. "It's okay. I'm not sure what I expected from this summer, but it definitely wasn't *this*," I tell him.

"It doesn't seem like there's much to complain about. Your friends know how to party; they have endless bank accounts and no responsibilities. I would have killed to have a summer like that at your age," Tucker remarks, and I detect a note of bitterness in his voice that wasn't there a moment ago.

"How old do you think I am?" I ask him.

"I don't think there's any good way to answer that," he laughs.

"I'm twenty-two," I reply. "How old are *you*?" I ask.

"I'm twenty-four," Tucker says. "But I think we come from very different places, and I'm an *old* twenty-four," he says warily, staring off in the distance.

"I'm not like *them*," I retort. "I didn't grow up like this. I went to school on a scholarship," I tell him. As soon as the words are out of my mouth, I wish I could take them back. Tucker looks at me with newfound appreciation and nods. I meant to say *partial* scholarship because that's the truth. And then the rest of the truth is that I came into a lot of money a few years ago when I found out about my real birth father (and my two sisters) when he died. But I didn't grow up with money, and I still haven't adjusted to having it. Mostly it just sits in an account somewhere earning interest, but I don't worry about money anymore — and probably the biggest adjustment is knowing that I won't ever have to.

"How did you end up hanging out with Alyssa?" Tucker asks pointedly.

"You know Alyssa?!" I ask, dumbfounded. I know that I never told him her name; I only referred to her as "my friend."

"*Everyone* knows Alyssa," Tucker replies.

"What? How?" I ask, absorbing this new information.

"She's made quite a name for herself out here. She's a regular at the bar – well, at all the bars," he adds with a grin.

"Huh," I reply, trying to let this sink in. "We haven't been to any bars yet this summer," I tell him. "Just some parties."

"How long have you been here?" Tucker asks, raising his left eyebrow.

"About ten days?" I reply.

"That makes sense," he says, nodding and licking his perfect lips.

"What makes sense?" I ask impatiently. I don't like it when I can't figure things out.

"She got kicked out of The Palm and Nick & Toni's about two weeks ago. That must have been right before you got here," Tucker says.

"What did she do?" I ask in amazement.

"I wasn't working that night, but it seems she had a bit too much to drink and got into a little argument with a waiter. At Nick & Toni's, I heard that something happened in the bathroom," Tucker says. I can tell there's a lot more he isn't telling me, but I decide not to push him. "She's been lying low, but I'm guessing she'll be back on the scene soon enough," Tucker says confidently.

"How long have you been a bartender there?" I ask, deciding to change the subject.

"A few years," he replies vaguely.

"I always wanted to try bartending," I say wistfully, unsure why I've said this out loud since I know how stupid it sounds.

"It's not like it looks in the movies – I promise," Tucker says.

"Do you know of anywhere that's looking to hire someone?" I ask. I don't think I realized I was going to say it until the words are out of my mouth.

"Someone who is looking for a bartender with no experience?" Tucker questions.

"No, no, of course not. But maybe a hostess? I've worked as a hostess before," I tell him, which is mostly true. Due to the time commitment that basketball required in college, I didn't have a chance to get much work experience. But I did work at a local restaurant for two weeks during the summer after my freshman year of college, and I feel like I have a good idea of what being a hostess requires.

"Hmmm," he replies as if seriously considering my request. "Summer jobs out here are hard to come by, and they are usually filled in the spring. But I may have a friend who knows someone who's looking," he tells me.

"That would be great!" I reply. I hadn't thought about getting a job until a few minutes ago. This was supposed to be my carefree summer, which did not include plans for a job. I'm sure Alyssa will think it's absurd, and she might even be angry about it, but it could be nice to have something to do other than party all the time. I'm about to ask for his phone number so I can follow up with him about the job when my phone rings. I pull it out of my bag and see that it's Preston calling. A giant photo of him appears on my screen with multiple hearts next to his name – I guess I haven't made any updates to his contact profile. We haven't texted in over a week, and we haven't talked on the phone in even longer. I'm debating about whether to send it to voicemail when it's clear that Tucker has also seen the image on my screen.

"You should get that," Tucker says, hopping up and swinging his bag over his shoulder in one quick motion. "I've got to go anyway," he adds.

Before I can protest or get his number, he's walking toward the parking lot. I hurry to answer the call hoping it will assuage some of my guilt, although right now, I'm not sure where my loyalties lie.

Chapter 15

Nora

It's a beautiful evening to sit on the deck and watch the sunset. I've brought a glass of wine with me and the damn printout of questions from Zadie that I've carried around for the past three days. I've successfully answered two questions and stared at the rest blankly for countless hours. I could easily forget about it and tell Zadie that I'm not interested or only send it back with a couple of answers completed, but I'm strangely intrigued about where this might lead. I suspect that part of me is simply curious to see if her clients are as famous as she suggested they might be, although I've never cared too much for that game. My goal would be to find a nice, normal guy who doesn't give a fuck about who *I* am or how much money *I* have.

Number three on the questionnaire asks me to list my five favorite words and my five least favorite words. How is this possibly going to help find me a date? I quickly fill in "Lasciv-ious and Fluorescent" on the favorite list. It's not about the meaning; although lascivious has some fun connotations, it's about how they feel on my tongue when I say them *and* that I'm unable to say them out loud without simultaneously spelling them in my head. On the least favorite list, I write, "Bulbous and Barf." I could easily add "Moist" to the list, but it seems too obvious – doesn't everyone hate that word? I go on to the next page and decide to come back later for the rest of my words – or not.

I still have a few blanks, but by the time the sun goes down, all the outdoor lights have come on, and I've refilled my glass one more time, I've completed most of the questionnaire. I'll sleep on it and determine whether I send it to Zadie as is in the morning or if I try to complete the rest. The lights are all on in the guest house, so I assume Megan is home. With each passing day, I feel worse about ignoring her, but it almost seems like it's too late at this point.

Inside, I rinse out my wine glass and leave it in the empty stainless-steel sink. I contemplate scooping myself a bowl of ice cream as a reward for my progress but then think better of it. My stomach rumbles slightly as I close the freezer door and turn off the kitchen lights, as if it's protesting my dessert choice, or maybe it's upset that I ate a late lunch and never got around to eating dinner. Either way, it's almost ten o'clock and seems like a total waste of calories to eat right as I'm getting into bed. I pat my taut stomach by way of apology and promise it I'll have something good for tomorrow's breakfast.

I slip under the heavy down comforter, which is a necessity considering how cold I like to keep the house at night, coupled with sleeping in tiny shorts and a tank top. Mason and I used to fight about the temperature; he argued that if we turned up the heat, we wouldn't need a giant goose-down comforter in July, but he always missed the point. The best way to sleep is when the room is freezing cold, but your bed is comfy and warm – trips to the bathroom are a nightmare, as are those first few steps out of bed in the morning, but other than that, it's perfect. Encouraged and shamed by Megan's reading prowess, I've been reading the past few nights before bed instead of getting sucked into an hour of garbage on Netflix. However, tonight I don't have the attention span for the biography I made myself purchase at Red Jacket Books, instead of the enticing beach read on the front table that was calling to me.

Just as I turn the television on and select an episode of a cheesy hospital drama I've seen many times before, the TV goes black. I reach for the remote and stab at the button for several seconds before I realize that it's not just the television that isn't working. Although I'd turned the lights off when I got into bed, it's not truly dark with the lights off. There's always the glow from the alarm panel and the soft light that peeks under my door from the hall, and the glimmer of the pool light that comes through the bottom inch of the roman shades. But right now, it's *pitch black*. It's not that I've never experienced a power outage – of course, I have. But usually, Mason was around, and for all of his flaws, he would always be the one in any sort of emergency to spring to action - whether it was gathering candles, or registering the outage with the electric company, or checking the fuse box. And of course, I've never been in *this* house for a power outage because I've only been here a few months. I remember something about a generator, but just as quickly as it comes to me,

I remember Mason telling the contractor that he didn't want it.

Megan!!

Suddenly I remember that I'm not alone! I have a young woman staying with me, and although I've been a terrible hostess so far, it would be unforgivable to let her sit in a strange place in a power outage without checking on her. In an instant, I've found my slippers and, blessedly, my fully charged phone, and I'm on my way to the guest house. The flashlight on the phone lights my path down the hallway and the stairs, but it doesn't keep the silence and shadows from being creepy as hell. I walk back through the kitchen, which only moments ago was humming with the quiet whir of the dishwasher, refrigerator, and air conditioner, and now it sounds like the scene in a horror movie right movie the main character gets killed.

On the deck, I should be able to get a good sense of the extent of the outage, but when I get outside and look around, it takes me a minute to figure out what's going on. The street-lights on Dune Road are out, but almost every house seems to have *some* smattering of lights. It's then that I realize I must be the only house without a generator – fucking Mason. One of the proverbs my mom would repeat pops into my head, and I can hear her saying, "An ounce of prevention is worth a pound of cure," and I curse Mason again. I walk over to the side gate where I can get a view of the north side of the road and the town of Westhampton Beach. Thankfully it looks like there is complete service only a few blocks away. I hurry back across the deck toward the guest house. I knock on the door and hold my breath while I wait for a response.

Chapter 16

Megan

The knock on the door scares the shit out of me. It's not like I'm scared of the dark or anything, but I've never been a huge fan, and when all the lights turned off unexpectedly a few minutes ago, I couldn't keep myself from screaming. Thankfully, no one was around to see or hear me. I've finally found my phone and started to adjust to my relatively new surroundings in the blackout when the sudden thwack on the door would easily have cost me one of my nine lives – that is, if humans were like cats.

"Who is it?" I timidly call out, wishing my voice didn't sound like it belonged to a ten-year-old girl.

"It's Nora," the voice replies, almost apologetically.

Of course, it's Nora – who else would it be? But then I remind myself that she's been hiding since my arrival, so perhaps it's not so obvious after all.

I quickly open the door and see Nora standing right outside in the door in a microscopic black tank top and shorts, which barely covers her boobs or her butt, and enormous sheepskin slippers. I can't remember exactly how old Danielle said she was, but however old that is, I hope I look as good as she does when I'm her age.

"Are you okay?" Nora asks.

"Yeah. Um, yeah, of course, I'm fine," I tell her.

"I'm so sorry we don't have a generator. My ex-husband said it was a waste of money, but it turns out he was wrong. I don't know why I'm surprised," Nora says, rambling on.

"It's fine," I tell her. I'm starting to feel awkward, and it's clear she is too. I think we would both prefer to be on our own, but I don't think there's a polite way to say it.

"Do you mind if I come in?" Nora asks. "Or maybe we can sit outside?" She offers, motioning to the lounge chairs with overstuffed Sunbrella cushions.

"Sure," I acquiesce, stepping out on the deck and closing the door behind me to signal that I've selected the second option. Although there are no lights at Nora's house, there are plenty of lights coming from other homes, and the moon is almost full. It's much lighter out here than it was in the guest house, and I must admit that it's a treat to enjoy the warm, beach air at night. Up until now, I've been on the couch either reading or watching TV every single evening, and I make a promise to myself to get out more.

The silence is slightly uncomfortable, but Nora is the one who asked if I wanted to sit out here with her, so I decide to let her be the one to break it. While we wait, I look up at the beautiful night sky and admonish myself for not taking advantage of my surroundings.

"I'm sorry I've been such a terrible host," Nora blurts out.

"What do you mean?" I ask, taken aback by her declaration. "It's so nice of you to let me stay here," I tell her.

"I should have done a better job of making you feel welcome," Nora says.

Nora must be around Danielle's age, so although she's not old like my mom or dad, she's still a lot older than I am, and it feels totally awkward having her apologize to me. Especially when I don't even think it's warranted. "Please, don't worry about it. It's *amazing* of you to let me stay here this summer. I'm not sure why you even agreed to it," I say with an embarrassed laugh. "But you certainly don't need to do anything else," I reassure her.

Nora is quiet for a minute as if absorbing this information and then replies. "So, what have you been doing?"

"Not too much. I went to the beach a lot and sat by the pool and read. Your house is stunning, by the way," I gush, hoping that I remembered to pay her this compliment on the first day.

"Thank you," she says. "It's not quite how I pictured it."

"Why not?" I ask.

"Oh, not the house. The house turned out better than I could have imagined. We bought the land several years ago. There was a smaller, older house on the property, and we tore that down. Then we worked with an architect to design our dream home, and amazingly it was finally ready," Nora says.

"That's great," I say.

"It is. I just didn't imagine that I would be living out here full-time all by myself." Nora pauses and looks around at the expansive deck, and then continues. "It was supposed to be our summer house. Our weekend retreat. Where we came to recharge after a grueling week of work in the city, but now I have no grueling weeks, and no apartment in Manhattan to escape from, and no husband to escape with," Nora says wistfully.

"Oh," I say quietly, completely unsure what else I should say.

"Oh my God, I'm so sorry!" Nora exclaims. "I cannot believe I just said all of that," she says as if snapping back from a trance. "You must think I'm insane!"

"No, no, it's totally fine," I try to assure her, but I'm not sure I'm very convincing.

"I don't know where that came from?!" Nora says. "I guess this is what happens when I don't have contact with other humans; I lose all of my social skills."

"Don't worry about it. I haven't had much contact with others the past couple of weeks either," I tell here.

"Seriously? This place is crawling with young people. You should be out partying!" Nora says.

"I know," I agree. "I haven't really met anyone yet," I offer and realize how lame it sounds.

"You don't *know* anyone here?" Nora asks. She sits up and turns her whole body to face me.

"Nope," I admit. "Well, I met this super annoying guy today when I went for my tutoring interview," I add.

"Why did you want to come to Westhampton if you didn't know anyone?" Nora asks.

"I thought Danielle would have told you."

"To be fair, she may have tried to tell me. I was quick to tell her that you were welcome to the guest house, but I didn't really listen for a lot of details," she explains. "God, I'm a shitty friend," Nora says to herself.

"My plans for the summer changed. Then I made other plans and those also changed. I thought about staying in Palo Alto with a friend of mine, but there's a situation with a guy that seemed like it would be better if I were three thousand miles away. So, I decided to go home and hang out with Danielle and Teddy and the girls, and that's when she told me that they sold the apartment and they were going to be in a small rental while they were waiting for the house in Westchester to be ready. She suggested the Hamptons because *everyone* loves it out here, and you were kind enough to offer me somewhere to stay, but that was my only connection," I explain.

"Now I feel even worse!" Nora says, lying back down on the chaise and putting her hands over her face. "I assumed you had friends here," she says.

"I'm sure I know some people here," I tell her. "I know that I have friends from high school who come out here, but I've lost touch with them over the last four years. And my college friends all seem to be from the west coast," I clarify.

"And what did you say about tutoring?" she asks, picking up on my earlier comment.

"I looked for a job in town the other day because I was looking for something to do. I thought I could meet people that way, but no one was hiring. Then I found this flyer advertising for SAT tutors, and I went and interviewed for that this morning, and I got the job," I tell her.

"Congratulations," Nora says. "Do you want to do that?" She asks.

"It's fine. The pay is good, and it's only a few hours a week. The guy who runs it is a total ass, but I don't think I'll see much of him. My first student is tomorrow, so I'll see," I tell her.

"Let me know how it goes," Nora says, sounding genuinely interested.

Before I can reply, there's a massive whooshing sound, and all at once, the whole house jumps to life. I hadn't noticed just how quiet it had become without the ambient noise, but the noise is jarring with the simultaneous hum of the pool filter and air conditioning condenser. Not to mention the flash of indoor and outdoor lights brightening the sky.

"I guess the power's back," I say, stating the obvious. "That wasn't out for very long."

"The benefit of losing power out here on Dune Road is that residents won't stand for it. There's enough money and connections out here that things get taken care of," Nora says.

"I guess we don't need to sit out here anymore?" I offer. Although I'd be more than happy to stay outside and talk, I don't want Nora to feel like she has to stay out here with me.

"Right, I guess not," Nora says, and I sense that she might also like to stay out here, but I don't want to push it.

Nora gets up and heads toward the sliding door to the main house, and I walk toward the other end of the deck that leads to the guest house. It's silly to think that Nora and I would be *friends*, but I'm a little sad to think that we'll go back to normal tomorrow.

"Good luck with tutoring! I'll see you tomorrow," Nora calls out as she walks into the main house and gives me a little wave. And just like that, the summer looks a little brighter.

Chapter 17

Courtney

I can't stop thinking about Preston after yesterday's call. We FaceTimed in the park for almost an hour, and it felt like old times. He told me funny stories about training camp and some of the crazy guys that will likely be his teammates – it sounds like the NFL will be quite a different experience than Big Ten football. In exchange, I regaled him with stories about Alyssa's opulent Hamptons lifestyle. We didn't talk about *us*. I think we both knew that it would be safer to avoid that topic. He didn't mention any girls; it seems that his days are filled with workouts, eating, and sleeping. I didn't say anything about Tucker either, but there really isn't anything *to* say. There was a teensy bit of harmless flirting, but the second he saw that I got a call from another guy, he lost all interest and ran away – which is probably for the best. Although, I *would* like to find a way to get in touch with him, just so I can ask about his connection for a hostessing job.

I decided to swim laps this morning to change up my routine, and to my surprise, Alyssa was sitting by the side of the pool when I finished – at eight thirty in the morning!

"You're up early!" I exclaim.

"The phone woke me, and I couldn't go back to sleep," Alyssa complains. She swings her bare slender legs into the water and wiggles her toes as if the feeling is unfamiliar.

"You sleep with your ringer on?" I ask, surprised that she would let anything disturb her slumber.

"It was my dad," she says as if that explains everything. Obviously, the confused look on my face tells her that I require additional explanation. Alyssa sighs softly but continues to clarify for me. "I can't block my dad's calls – *ever*. I use 'do not disturb' when I sleep or take a nap, or just don't want to be bothered, but in my settings, I always have to allow calls from him," she says, with a dramatic eye roll.

There are pictures all over the house of her parents, so I know exactly what her dad looks like, but I try to pull up the image of him in my memory from the one time we met in Evanston my junior year. Alyssa was in a play, I can't remember the name, but I know that it was super depressing. Her mom was shooting a movie in Greece and couldn't leave the set, but her dad came out to see it, and I met him outside the theater after the show. It's hard to get a sense of how tall and broad he is in the pictures, but in real life, he seemed like a giant. He didn't look like other dads that I had met, but I couldn't quite place what it was. Perhaps it was something about how he carried himself or how he spoke? I couldn't put my finger on it, and it wasn't like I spent much time with him. Although I grew up with a wonderful stepdad, I was always scrutinizing other people's dads as if there was something I was missing out on. (It turns out that I was, but I'm not going to think about it right now, especially since things are finally all on track with my family).

"What did he have to say?" I ask her.

"He's going to be in town tonight. He wants to take us to dinner," she moans.

"Oh wow!" I reply. I wasn't expecting this turn of events. When Alyssa asked me to spend the summer here, I assumed that her parents would be with her. It was only after I arrived that she informed me that her mother was cast in something last minute and would be in Vancouver the entire summer, and her father didn't want to spend the summer here without his wife, so he decided to stay in their house in Greenwich by himself. I'm sure he must have to go to work or do whatever it is that he does. I know Alyssa's mom is a movie star, but she's not the kind that makes ten million dollars for each movie, so I'm pretty sure that her dad must do something that pays well to afford this type of lifestyle.

"We're going to have to be on our best behavior," Alyssa tells me, as if this is going to be an issue.

"Of course," I reply, not sure exactly what's expected of me.

"I've got to go clean out my room and take a run over to the dump before he gets here," Alyssa says and pushes her petite body up off the bluestone patio.

I suspect she's joking, but then she says, "Occasionally, he likes to spot check, so I need to make sure there's no evidence."

I laugh uncomfortably as if this is something every

twenty-two-year-old does before their dad comes home – now that I think about it, it's probably not that unusual.

"How long is he here for?" I ask.

"Oh, just tonight. He's flying to Vegas tomorrow and then on to Vancouver to see my mom," she tells me.

I cannot comprehend the world that Alyssa lives in and certainly can't understand how I didn't realize any of this when I knew her back at school.

"I'm guessing he'll want to go to The Maidstone Club for dinner," Alyssa says. "Be ready by five. He'll want to be there for cocktails," she informs me.

"What's The Maidstone Club?" I question, since it isn't something she's mentioned previously.

"Oh, it's just our country club. It's kind of old and boring, but my dad likes it," she shrugs.

"Alright, off to clean," Alyssa groans as she heads back inside.

* * *

I almost do a double-take when I walk into the living room at four fifty-five and see Alyssa sitting on the couch across from her father in the upholstered wing chair. She is wearing a white sheath dress that covers her knees even when she is sitting. She has a soft yellow cardigan tied around her shoulders, and she's wearing a strand of pearls and matching pearl studs in her ears. I hardly recognize her! I'm so grateful that I heard her say country club and selected my only Lily Pulitzer item, a stylish and modest blue and pink romper, and Tory Burch flats.

"It's lovely to see you again, Courtney," Mr. Winters says, hopping to his feet to greet me.

"Thank you so much for having me. It's so beautiful here," I say, gesturing at our surroundings and fumbling for the right words to describe his astonishing compound.

"We like it," he humbly says as if referring to a small mountain cabin.

"You ladies look lovely. I'm quite the lucky man tonight, aren't I?" he asks rhetorically. "Who's ready for dinner?" he adds.

"That sounds great, Daddy," Alyssa says, smiling up at him. I'm glad I haven't just taken a sip of something because I would surely spit it all over the living room. It now appears that there are three versions of Alyssa! I didn't see her interact with her father for very long on that night back at school, so I can't remember how she was with him then, but this is certainly not the mellow, artsy, theater girl from Northwestern, and it's a far cry from the scantily clad girl who parties all night long and has slept with a different guy almost every night since I've been here. It seems dramatic, but I want to yell, "Will the real Alyssa Winters, please stand up?!" But of course, I don't do that. Instead, I smile at her dad and tell him that I also cannot wait for dinner.

The Maidstone Club is certainly not my scene, but it's hard to deny the spectacular location, views, service, or food. I follow Alyssa's lead through cocktail hour and the entire meal. Soon it becomes clear that she's a much better actor than I ever thought. Unfortunately, I'm not nearly as skillful at it as she is, but luckily, her dad is much more focused on Alyssa than on me.

"What are your plans for the fall, Courtney?" Mr. Winters asks as we finish our main courses. I've been adding the occasional comment throughout the meal, but mostly the two of them have talked about people I don't know, and that suits me just fine.

"I'm going to law school in New York. At NYU," I say, with a hint of pride.

"Good for you!" He says enthusiastically.

"You'll be right near Alyssa then, won't you?" he says.

"Um," I reply, suddenly flustered. When we were at school, Alyssa told me that she was going to move to Los Angeles in the fall and start auditioning. But then I heard her tell someone the other night that she was going to take a gap year (or two) and go bum around Southeast Asia. Neither of those scenarios involves her being "right near me."

"I know she'll be on the Upper West Side, but still, you'll both be in Manhattan," he clarifies.

"Right," I reply, taking a sip of my wine as I try to catch Alyssa's eye.

"Should we get dessert?" Alyssa asks. Other than when she's been stoned, I haven't seen Alyssa eat anything with flour or sugar in it all summer.

Unfazed by Alyssa's attempt at distraction, Mr. Winters continues. "Do you know where you'll be living? Will you have to be in a dorm?" he asks, visibly disturbed at the thought.

"Yes, I'll be in a dorm this year; it's right by the school. I thought it would be easier to meet people that way. But I hear that most second and third-year students live in apartments, so I guess I'll do that," I tell him.

"It's good to get real-world experience," he says, but it's unclear who he's talking to. "Not everyone has parents who happen to have a spare apartment just blocks from Juilliard," Mr. Winters says, finishing his own glass of wine.

"You're going to Juilliard?!" I practically yell, unable to control my surprise. Both Alyssa and her father look at me like I've gone mad, although for completely different reasons. "Oh, right. Of course," I say, trying to laugh at myself. "Must be too much of this," I add, indicating my wine glass, although I'm just starting my second glass of Sauvignon Blanc.

If Alyssa's dad suspects something is amiss, he doesn't say anything. Instead, he shakes his full head of salt-and-pepper hair as if trying to rid himself of an unpleasant thought and plows ahead. "Alyssa will be getting her Master's in Fine Arts from Juilliard. She didn't want to study there for her undergraduate degree, which we accepted, but just like her mother, she will be a Juilliard student," he says with pride.

Alyssa's smile is tight, and it's the first crack in her armor I've seen all night. "I didn't *get in* to Juilliard for undergrad," she says quietly.

"Either way, it's clear they saw the error of their ways," Mr. Winters says. "Let's see about some dessert, shall we?" he asks as he snaps his fingers to summon the waiter.

Alyssa smiles at her dad as if this is the best idea he's had all night, but I can tell she's just holding herself together until she can run wild. I wonder if she'll be able to hold out until tomorrow morning when her dad leaves?

Chapter 18

Megan

"Explain to me *again* why you're doing this?" Hope asks. I can hear bewilderment in her voice, in addition to the whir of the hot tub in the background; she must be up at her house in Lake Tahoe.

"I was getting bored. And it's easy money," I tell her.

"I cannot believe that you are spending your carefree summer at the beach teaching stupid teenagers how to answer multiple-choice questions," Hope sighs.

"It's not like that," I say, defending myself. "And the kid today was pretty cool. And he definitely wasn't stupid. Honestly, I'm worried I won't even be able to help him improve his score. Joel made it sound like the kid had failed four times, and that's why he was taking the test again, but it's really because his parents have insane expectations," I tell her.

"That's harsh," Hope says. Although, I happen to know

that she got a perfect score on the math section of the test and only ten points shy of perfect on the verbal portion.

"He seems pretty smart, but he's so stressed about the score that I don't think he can focus on anything else," I tell her.

"Hmm," Hope replies, and I can tell she's lost interest. "Tell me about Joel," she demands.

"Oh God, he's the worst!" I tell her. "He's so pretentious and full of himself. And he's just plain weird," I add.

"Is he cute?" she asks.

"What?" I ask.

"What does this pretentious weirdo look like?" she asks.

"Oh, gosh, I don't know," I say.

"What do you mean, you don't know? You met him – you said you went over to his house, and he gave you some crazy test," she reminds me.

"I barely noticed what he looked like. I was too busy noticing what a jerk he was," I tell her.

"Oh, come on, give me something," Hope insists.

"I guess he isn't terrible looking," I tell her.

"Ha!" she laughs accusingly. "Do go on."

"He has light brown shaggy hair, as in, he could use a haircut. He has a nice, strong chin – I did notice that. He wears glasses – I think they might be fake, just to make him look smarter," I say unkindly.

"What about the body?" Hope pries.

I humor her because I know she won't give up until she's gotten what she wants. "He's tall. He was wearing baggy khaki shorts and a loose t-shirt, so I have no idea what's going on under those clothes. His legs weren't *terrible*. It looks like he might do some form of physical exercise. But I'm guessing he mostly just sits around and tells people how smart he is and how dumb they are," I say.

"I think you secretly want to fuck him," Hope casually says.

"What is wrong with you!" I yell at her. "I just told you that I hate him!"

Hope is laughing so hard that it takes her a minute to respond. "I know, but it would be angry sex. I promise I won't tell Alex about it," she says.

"You're the worst," I tell her, but of course, I don't mean it. I miss having her close by and miss having her outlandish personality to shake things up. My conversation with Nora last night was the closest I've had to "girl-talk" since I left Palo Alto, and that's sad. "Guess who I finally talked to last night?" I ask Hope, in an attempt to change the conversation.

"Alex?" she guesses.

"Oh, um, no," I quickly reply. I now regret that I made this a guessing game. "Nora! Danielle's friend - the one who owns the house. There was a blackout for an hour or so, and we hung out. She's pretty cool," I tell Hope.

"She's the one who owns Limestreet Athletics, right?" Hope asks. "Can she get you tons of free clothes?"

"She used to own it. Danielle told me that Nora sold it a few months ago. But, yes, I'm sure she still has access to free clothes. Or at least a good discount," I assure her.

"When are you going to start doing anything *fun*?" Hope whines.

I want to protest, but I know that she's right. "Should I ask Nora if she wants to go to a bar with me?" I joke.

"There are worse ideas," Hope says. "Wow, she's pretty hot," Hope adds.

"What? How do you know?" I ask her.

"I just googled her," she says, and I realize this should have been obvious. "There are like a zillion pictures of her. Is this what she looks like in real life?" Hope questions.

"Hold on," I tell her while I grab my laptop. Just as Hope promised, my screen instantly fills with images of Nora. There are pictures of her in Limestreet clothing, pictures of her in business suits, pictures of her in a ballgown receiving some kind of award, and the list goes on and on. "Yeah," I admit. "This is pretty much what she looks like. Obviously, she's wearing a lot of makeup in most of these, and she's pretty dressed up, but she looks like her picture," I assure Hope.

"You should definitely go out with her!" Hope demands. "She could pass for your older sister! I bet she's fun," she adds.

"How can you possibly tell that?" I ask her.

"It's just a feeling I have," Hope says, and she laughs.

"Maybe you're right. But in the short time I talked to her last night, I didn't get the impression that she was a hard-core partier. She made a comment about her ex-husband that made me feel really sad for her," I confide in Hope.

"See!!" Hope exclaims. "You guys can go out together and drown your sorrows.

"Any*way*," I say, drawing out the second part of the word for emphasis. "Anything going on with you?" I ask.

"Not really. I came up to Tahoe for a few days. It's beautiful here in the summer," she gushes.

I try to imagine the view that Hope has right now from her hot tub – looking over the lake and the vast mountains with the snow-capped peaks even in the summer. But I'd still take the view from Nora's deck any day – the ocean waves and the iconic dunes; every beach view from this point on will pale in comparison.

"I forgot to tell you!" Hope says excitedly. "I ran into Alex again yesterday when I was packing up the car."

"Oh," I reply. My heart starts beating rapidly, and I desperately hope that's all there is to the story.

"He asked about you," she says.

"Really? What did you say?" I ask her. I'm trying to keep the panic out of my voice, but I'm not sure it's working.

"He asked how you were doing," she says.

I breathe a tiny sigh of relief when she tells me this. The thought of Alex wandering outside my future apartment is still disturbing, but at least he's three thousand miles away.

"I told him that it was all one nonstop party for you in the Hamptons," she laughs.

"You didn't?!" I practically scream.

"Don't worry. He knows you too well – he could tell I was lying," Hope laughs again. "Hey, I actually have to go; I'm supposed to meet my neighbor, so we can go out. This is what people our age are supposed to be doing!" She reminds me.

"I know, I know," I tell her, but my mind is racing with thoughts of Alex, and I feel like I'm going to be sick.

Chapter 19

Nora

When I see Zadie's name pop up in my inbox, I'm both nervous and excited. She replied immediately the other day after I sent back the questionnaire and said that she would "get right on it." So, when I see her email this morning, I assume it will have information about a potential date. However, the email is succinct and merely says, "I'll be sending along the rest of the details later today. Plan on meeting your first date tomorrow night at Dockers at seven."

My first reaction is to write an indignant reply. How dare she assume I'm free tomorrow night and that I'm going to go out on a date before I even see this guy's profile. But then I take a deep breath and remind myself that I'm choosing to take this leap. Although my sister was the one who got the ball rolling, I could have said no at any point after that, but I decided to give it a try, and that means playing by Zadie's rules. Then, before I can change my mind, I walk out onto the deck and ask for Megan's help.

"Good morning!" I call out to Megan as soon as my bare foot lands on the warm mahogany plank.

"Good morning!" Megan calls back as she looks up from her book. I can't quite make out the cover of this one, but it looks like she finished what she was reading yesterday and has started something else – I wonder how many books she brought with her?!

"Do you have any plans tomorrow night?" I ask her as I make my way over to her lounge chair. There isn't a cloud in the sky, and I raise my hand to shield my eyes from the brilliant but blinding morning sun.

"Sadly, no," she replies. "But I promise I'm going to ask that other tutor to hang out – if I see her again," she adds.

"I'm not giving you a hard time," I assure her. "I was hoping you could do me a favor," I say nervously.

"Sure. What is it?" Megan asks.

"I have a date tomorrow night," I say.

"That's great!" Megan replies, and she even claps her hands to show her excitement.

"I think it is. Well, it may be. Honestly, I have no idea. It's kind of a blind date," I confess.

"Ohhh," Megan says and wrinkles her adorable nose.

"It's not quite a blind date. Ugh, this is so embarrassing," I tell her and then wonder if it was a mistake to even bring it up in the first place. "My sister thought I should stop sitting around acting sorry for myself, and it's not easy for me to meet regular guys, so she hired a matchmaker," I say, feeling my cheeks turn red as I say the word.

"A matchmaker? Like from *Fiddler on the Roof*?" Megan asks as she starts to laugh, but not in a mean way.

"I know, right?!" I agree with her. "I guess this is how it's done now, or at least that's what the matchmaker says," I laugh.

"What do you need me to do?" she asks, thankfully returning to the initial topic.

"This may sound crazy. And please feel free to say no. But I was wondering if you would come with me?" I ask. The shocked look on Megan's face is priceless. I quickly realize that I need to do a much better job of explaining myself before this poor young woman runs away and never comes back. We've "hung out" a couple of times over the last two days since the blackout and even had lunch together yesterday, but I cannot assume that she still doesn't see me as a crazy person.

"Sorry! That didn't come out right," I quickly say. "We are going to a restaurant that isn't too far away. It's just at the end of Dune Road; it's called Dockers Waterside Restaurant. I was hoping that you would come with me and just hang out at the bar for the very beginning of the date – I'll buy you dinner and all your drinks! And then if the guy doesn't seem like he should be on the Ten Most Wanted list, you can head home," I say hopefully.

"Sure, "she shrugs. "I'm not doing anything else," Megan says casually.

Relief floods through me with her nonchalant response. I would never have pictured a twenty-two-year-old recent college grad as my new friend this summer, but I guess life works in mysterious ways.

* * *

Emboldened by thoughts of my upcoming date and my conversation with Megan, I make the decision to stop by Eva's house and attempt to make up for lost time. I pull one of the bikes out of the garage and notice that it's been used recently. I assume that this must be how Megan is getting around town, so I put that one back and grab a slightly dirtier model from further back in the garage – it feels rude to alter the settings on her bike. Even though I'm temporarily delayed due to a lack of air in the tires, I instantly feel lighter as soon as I'm pedaling down Dune Road with the wind in my hair. It occurs to me that I should probably be wearing a helmet, especially considering the way some people drive around here, but I don't want to turn back.

On the short ride over, I try to think through what I'll say if Eva *is* home. I test out multiple excuses for my absence over the past few years, and each one is lamer than the next. The truth seems pretty pitiful, but as is the case with most things, it's the best and simplest option.

There aren't any cars in the circular driveway when I arrive. I'm tempted to turn right around and bike home. Although they have a one-car garage, in all the time I've known Eva and Chloe, they have never parked in it. I probably need to accept that I don't know a lot about their lives now – maybe they've become the type of people who park in the garage?

Just as I'm about to ride through the empty half-moon driveway and return home, I hear laughter and splashing that sounds like it's coming from the backyard. I ease off the seat and walk my bike to the back gate to peer into the yard. I feel like a trespasser, and my heart starts beating rapidly as I worry idiotically that someone will catch me here.

I guess the thought isn't too idiotic because seconds later, a large black dog comes bounding toward the gate, barking wildly. A woman's voice follows quickly, yelling, "Penny, get back here!" I turn to run back to my bike. I can't believe how stupid this was! It's been four years – Chloe and Eva don't even live here anymore, it's some new family with a black Labrador retriever who parks their car in the garage! I can't believe I've been this out of touch that I didn't even realize one of my best friends moved away. I'm the worst!"

"Nora, is that you?" the voice calls as I'm swinging my leg over my bike.

I turn my head to see Chloe's puzzled face over the top of the gate. I want to die of embarrassment but also of relief. "Yes, it's me," I say sheepishly. "You got a dog?" I ask.

"Ha, yes. It seems you've already met Penny. Don't worry; her bark is worse than her bite," Chloe says. My face clearly shows that I don't believe this for a second because she presses on. "No, really. She barks like crazy, but she wouldn't hurt a fly. She's only eight months old, but she's already eighty pounds. We're hoping she's going to stop growing soon! We probably need to invest in some training, so she looks more like a friendly family dog and less like an attack dog," she laughs.

I laugh along with her and feel the tension in my shoulders start to ease. I don't deserve this, but it feels so natural – almost like old times. I wonder what it will be like with Eva... that will be the true test.

As if she can read my mind, Chloe says, "Eva's out at the grocery store, but she should be back soon. Come sit down and have a drink with me." Chloe motions with her hand, waving me over to the backyard. "The kids are in the pool. Between the pool and the dog, they barely notice me anymore," she chuckles.

The last time I saw the kids, they couldn't have been left alone for a second, even on the side of the pool, and now they are swimming by themselves. Wow. I hesitate one last time but then walk determinedly toward the back gate. This is why I came here, right? If I've learned anything about life – especially this past year, it's that you can't rely on anyone else to make you happy.

Chapter 20

Courtney

Last night was surreal; I'm still trying to convince myself that it wasn't a dream. Other than a tiny slip during dinner, when it appeared like she might lose her temper, Alyssa acted like the prim and proper daughter her dad seems to think she is, for the entire evening. She even went so far as to tell her dad that we'd started a book club with a few of her local friends, but other than that, we'd stayed in most of the summer. I expected her father to call her on the act at some point, but he simply nodded and sipped his wine as if it was what he expected to hear. I tried to catch Alyssa's eye a few times during the meal, but she refused to make direct eye contact. When we got back to the house, I was sure I would be able to grab Alyssa to figure out what was going on, especially with Juilliard, but she said goodnight to her dad and me at the same time and went straight to bed.

I'm almost positive that her dad left first thing this morning, but just in case, I prepare myself for the innocent version of Alyssa that might greet me in the kitchen. Instead, I discover the Hamptons model sitting at the island in a white string bikini, drinking what appears to be a bloody mary (the bottles of vodka and bloody mary mix are the key giveaways).

"Good morning!" Alyssa says enthusiastically.

"Hey, good morning," I reply, with far less enthusiasm.

"I guess your dad is gone?" I ask.

"Thank God, right?!" she replies.

I walk behind her to grab a glass from the cabinet, taking a minute to formulate my response. I pour some of the spicy tomato juice into my glass but opt to skip the vodka at this hour. "What was going on last night?" I ask Alyssa.

"My dad's just really weird," she says with a wave of her hand.

I don't think this even begins to cover what transpired at dinner, but I may need another tactic to get her to talk about it. "What was he saying about Juilliard?" I venture.

Alyssa takes a generous sip from her drink and then pauses as if considering if she wants to answer my question or not. Then she sighs as if it's an enormous effort and offers a brief explanation. "My mom went to Juilliard. As far as she's concerned, that is the *only* school for serious actors. Once I said I was interested in acting, it was a foregone conclusion that I would also go to Juilliard. I didn't want to stay in New York for college, but my parents didn't care. But then I didn't *get in* to Juilliard," Alyssa says and pauses to take another mouthful of bloody mary.

"Northwestern isn't such a bad school," I offer, trying to make a joke.

Alyssa looks at me and raises her eyebrow. "Try telling

my mom that. People would literally do anything to get a spot in the theater program at Northwestern, and my mom was still like, "It's not Juilliard..." it was absurd," Alyssa says.

"So, you're going to go there now for your master's degree?" I ask her, trying to put the pieces together from last night's dinner.

"No. But they think I am," Alyssa says.

"Oh," I reply, nodding slowly, but I'm just as confused as I was before.

"I want to go out to LA after graduation and start auditioning. My mom thinks that it's *beneath* me to wait tables and go on hundreds of auditions for bit parts in sitcoms. She pulled some strings and got me into the MFA program at Juilliard, even though she claims that I got in on my own. I never filled out an application, so it's pretty hard to believe *that* happened," Alyssa says.

"So, where are you going in September?" I ask her.

"I'm going to LA. I just have to figure out how to do it without losing my trust fund," Alyssa says casually.

"Gotcha," I reply because what else can I say? Until a few years ago, I would also have judged her for being worried about a trust fund and even *having* a trust fund, but after coming into my own surprise inheritance two and a half years ago, I find that I now have a bit more sympathy.

"Let's go out tonight and celebrate," Alyssa says, which feels like a non sequitur.

"What are we celebrating?" I ask her.

"My dad is gone!" She says. "Where should we go?" she asks me. This is the first time she has asked my opinion. Previously, she has made all the decisions on our ventures. Perhaps she thinks I'm finally getting a feel for the area. But before I get a chance to reply, she says, "What about the bar at The Palm?"

"Oh sure," I say, though I don't think she cares about my response.

"They make the best martinis. And the bartender there is so hot! I haven't been there for a few weeks. That's perfect!" It's obvious that she's forgotten about my encounter with the hot bartender on the beach, and I will do her the courtesy of pretending that I don't know why she hasn't been there recently.

* * *

Alyssa makes the surprisingly responsible suggestion to take an Uber to The Palm before I even think to propose it. On the ride there, she tells a few hilarious stories from past evenings at the bar, although she leaves out the one from earlier this summer, when she got kicked out. I'm expecting something quite different when we walk into a fancy steak restaurant with white-haired men in blue blazers sipping three-hundred-dollar bottles of red wine. Alyssa greets the beautiful blonde hostess with a kiss on the cheek and then heads straight for the open stools at the carved wooden bar.

"It's not quite how I pictured it," I say to her.

"What do you mean?" Alyssa asks.

"I don't know," I reply, sensing that whatever I say will be the wrong thing. "I guess I thought it would be busier?" I offer.

"Wait thirty minutes," Alyssa says knowingly. "We're so

lucky to get these seats," she says and nods at me. "It will be packed here soon. And then it closes pretty early too – it all happens quickly," she assures me.

"Okay. What are you going to get?" I ask her as I point to the elegant drink menu.

"The Lemon Drop," she replies. "Ooh, Tucker's working tonight," she says excitedly.

I try to contain my own excitement at this news. I'm not sure why I care if Alyssa knows that I ran into Tucker at the basketball court, and then I remember her Instagram post and remember exactly why I care.

"Hi, ladies. What can I get for you?" Tucker asks as he appears in front of us and slides thick cocktail napkins on the bar in front of each of us.

"I'll have a Lemon Drop," Alyssa says in a syrupy sweet voice.

"I'll try the Paloma," I say.

"Coming right up," Tucker says as he walks back toward the middle of the bar to begin making our cocktails. I'm pissed off that Tucker didn't even say hi, but I can't share that with Alyssa, so I have to sit here and pretend that everything's fine.

"See, I told you so," Alyssa says, tapping me lightly on the shoulder.

"What do you mean?" I start to ask, but then I turn to look over my shoulder, and I understand. We've only been here ten minutes, and already the bar area has doubled in capacity.

"Just wait – it will be packed soon," she tells me.

The bar crowd is at least half the age of the wealthy steak lovers seated in the restaurant, and although I don't recognize anyone, I can tell that this is certainly a place where people come to be recognized. Tucker brings the jewel-colored drinks and places them down expertly in front of us before he disappears to assist one of the dozens of thirsty new arrivals. The Paloma is delicious – bitter and refreshing at the same time, with just a hint of sweetness; I guess Tucker is as good at making drinks as he is at basketball. I take another sip of my drink and turn around to ask Alyssa how hers is, only to find that she is engrossed in a conversation with a petite redhead and a somewhat familiar-looking attractive olive-skinned guy, who I must recognize from one of Alyssa's house parties.

Tucker reappears with the furtiveness of a cat, slips me a folded-up piece of paper, and gives me an adorable smile. I glance at Alyssa to see if she's paying attention, but she's definitely not. I can't remember the last time I received a handwritten note. I open it in my lap, since the cloak and dagger routine seems important to Tucker.

Sorry about this. It's easier for me not to have any interaction with Alyssa. Here's the contact info for my friend at Docker's. No guarantee that she still needs a hostess, but it's worth giving her a call.

Elena – 631-325-4315

And here's my number if you want a rematch on hoops sometime soon – 631-465-7685

I fold it back up and shove it in my jeans pocket, but Alyssa is still laughing with her friends, and I'm sure she hasn't noticed anything. However, Tucker does catch my eye and gives me a smile that causes all sorts of butterflies to flutter in my stomach, and somehow, I manage to smile back and mouth the words, "thank you," without looking like a total loser.

"Let's get out of here," Alyssa says, finishing off her drink and pushing it forward on the bar.

"Already?" I question.

"Yeah, it's dead here tonight," she says. I look around at the throng of people behind us but decide not to argue. "I just heard about another party. We're going there," she informs me.

It seems pointless to argue, so I finish my drink and reach for my wallet.

"It's already covered," Alyssa says.

I don't know if that means she already paid for the drinks, or if one of her friends paid, or if she has some sort of old school tab here where everything gets put on an account, but I know to trust her when she says something has been taken care of. I try to get Tucker's attention to let him know that I'm leaving, but he's deep in conversation with a group of women at the other end of the bar. I grab my purse and follow Alyssa and her friends out of The Palm toward the next adventure of the evening, but I touch my pocket as we go to reassure myself that I got what I came for, and perhaps my summer will soon be changing for the better.

Chapter 21

Megan

I'm not sure what the appropriate attire is to accompany my ex-stepmom's friend on a blind date, especially when I'm supposed to be sitting at the bar by myself for the evening. I thought about calling Danielle to ask her opinion but based on her texts from the past few days, she is swamped at work and busy with the impending move, so I don't think I should bother her for fashion advice.

It rained last night, and when I woke up this morning, it was barely sixty degrees. Once the sun goes down tonight, it will be even cooler – quite the change from the low ninety-degree temperatures of the past week. I already have goose-bumps standing here wrapped in my towel, which means that any of my little sundresses are out of the question. I grab a pair of white jeans that have a couple of small rips in them, but hopefully, the expensive label means they're still appropriate for this restaurant. I decide on a black cropped tank top because it seems the most innocuous of my "fancy" tops, and it will give me the widest range of options for finding something to bring to go over it in case I get cold.

I know I'm not the one going on a date, but I put extra effort into my hair and makeup. I take a last look in the mirror before I go to the main house to meet Nora; my skin has a healthy golden color from my time in the sun, and there are new blonde streaks in my hair that somehow never appeared in the California sun. I've blown my hair completely straight, and without the natural waves, it reaches well beyond my bra strap – I think the last time my hair was this long was at the beginning of high school. I used brown eyeliner to highlight my eyes, and they look bigger and brighter than usual. I used to resent when people told me that I was girl-next-door-pretty because I thought it was a backhanded compliment, but I've come to appreciate it, and I've decided that it means I'm approachable. I had an ex-boyfriend who took it several steps too far and was crass enough to tell me that I was perfect because I was the girl that everyone wanted to bring home to meet their parents *and* still really wanted to fuck – he claimed that was a rare combination. Putting thoughts of all ex-boyfriends out of my mind, I grab my phone and my wallet and leave to meet Nora for what is sure to be a unique evening.

Nora doesn't say much on the short car ride down Dune Road to the restaurant, and I assume she is nervous about her date. I'm taken aback when she grabs my arm as we walk up to the hostess stand. "Is this crazy?" she asks, sounding terrified.

"No," I reply, hoping I sound convincing. "But you can leave whenever you want," I remind her.

"Right. That's right," she says again, more to herself than to me.

When we get to the host stand, Nora gives them the name of the guy that she's supposed to be meeting, and the host assures her that the gentleman has already arrived and is waiting at the table. I'm not sure Nora is ready to be separated so quickly, but she is whisked away by the uniformed man in the white shirt and black pants with the double eyebrow piercing. Suddenly on my own, I walk over to the bar and am pleased to find several open seats. Before I'm fully seated, a bartender materializes right in front of me and asks what she can get me to drink. It's at this point that I realize that I've never been at a bar by myself. I've arrived a few minutes early and waited for a friend or a guy to meet me, but I've never gone out knowing that I'll be spending the evening alone – it feels oddly empowering and terrifying.

I request a vodka with club soda and lime because I can't think of anything else to order. I'm actually in the mood for something fruity, like a banana daiquiri; however this doesn't seem like the place to get a frozen drink, even though it's a stone's throw from the beach.

"Is anyone sitting here?" someone asks.

I turn to see a tall, sandy-haired girl, who looks about my age, with her hand on the barstool next to mine, waiting expectantly for my answer.

"No. I'm here all by myself," I reply. I feel like a moron

as soon as the words are out of my mouth. She wasn't asking about my status for the evening, she just wanted to know if she could use the chair, but now I look like a total loser.

"Thanks," she says and takes a seat next to me.

The bartender brings my drink and quickly disappears before I can ask if I should pay now or offer my credit card; I suppose this isn't the type of place where people duck out on their bills. I take a sip and quickly notice that my drink is about seventy percent vodka and thirty percent club soda, not quite the ratio I'm accustomed to, but also not too bad – maybe it will make the evening pass more quickly.

"Do you think it's weird if I have a drink while I'm waiting for an interview?" the tall girl next to me blurts out.

"What?" I ask, startled at the sound of her voice.

"Sorry," she apologizes. "Hi, I'm Courtney," she says, introducing herself.

"Hi, I'm Megan," I reply.

"I'm supposed to be here to interview for a job as a hostess, but the woman I'm meeting with is running late, so they told me to wait at the bar for her to show up," Courtney explains.

I nod in acknowledgment and silently wonder how she managed to get an interview when I couldn't find anyone hiring at this point in the summer. So far, tutoring has been relatively easy, and I don't know that I'd want to work here, but I'm still slightly jealous that she successfully found an open position.

"That's why I asked what you thought about having a drink while I'm waiting," she explains. "I guess I'm just nervous. Sorry if I'm bothering you or if this is weird," she apologizes.

"Not at all," I try to assure her. "Nothing could be any weirder than why I'm sitting here right now," I tell her.

Courtney raises her eyebrows and looks at me expectantly as if to say, 'now you have to tell me.'

"I'm staying right down the road in the guesthouse of one of my ex-stepmom's friends this summer, who I just met when I got here two weeks ago." I pause for effect, but she doesn't give any hint of alarm, so I continue. "She's here in the restaurant on a blind date tonight and asked me to come with her and sit at the bar in case she needs to make a quick getaway. Naturally, I said yes, because I don't really know anyone else here and have nothing else to do," I divulge almost like a confession.

Courtney laughs loudly and subsequently, looks far more relaxed than she did when she sat down. "Thank you. I needed that," she says. "That's hysterical and almost makes me feel better about my hot mess of a summer," she says.

Now it's my turn to give her an expectant look, and it's clear that she agrees that it seems fair for her to provide some additional explanation after I over-shared; after all, we won't see each other after tonight, and it's therapeutic to share your troubles with a stranger, right?

"To make a long story short — I'm staying with a friend from school for the summer, honestly, she's more of an acquaintance — but she's an entirely different person here than she was at school. She has a ton of crazy, partying friends just like her, which is not what I expected," Courtney says.

"Sorry," I say, although I wonder to myself if it's worse to have crazy friends or no friends.

"It's okay," she says as a reflex. "I didn't initially plan on getting a job this summer. It was supposed to be a big vacation after my senior year of college before I start school again in the fall," Courtney says.

"That's exactly what I was doing this summer!" I exclaim foolishly as if this is an amazing twist of fate. I'm sure a ton of people are spending their summer vacationing in the Hamptons between college and graduate school; it's just that I haven't met any of them yet.

"No way, really?!" Courtney replies.

Her response instantly makes me feel better – it seems that she is also impressed with this coincidence. "What are you doing for graduate school?" I ask her.

"I'm going to law school in New York. You?" she asks.

"I'm going back to California for my master's in public policy," I tell her.

"That's great," Courtney says. "I continue to pick schools where the weather is way too cold. You're smart to stay in California," she comments.

"I'm from New York, but I don't know that I could ever move back here. After four years of California winters, I don't ever want to wear a hat or gloves again," I say.

"I should have thought of that," she laughs. "I'm from the Chicago suburbs..." she starts to say, but before she can say anything else, Nora comes rushing out of the dining room and runs up to me.

"We have to go," Nora says urgently.

"Oh, um, okay," I say, trying to figure out what transpired.

"What happened?" I ask Nora as I fumble in my bag to find my wallet.

Nora, obviously in a hurry to get out of here, throws two twenties on the bar and then says to me, "That should cover it. I'll tell you about it on the way home."

"Bye. Nice meeting you," I say to Courtney as I hop off the barstool. "Good luck with your interview."

"Thanks. Nice meeting you as well," she says.

As I follow Nora out to the car, I'm anxious to hear about whatever it was that went so badly on the date. It was obviously so bad that she had to leave shortly after it started, but I'm also a little sad that I didn't get to stay and hang out longer with Courtney. I know it seems strange after only talking to her for a few minutes, but I had a funny feeling that we could have been friends.

Chapter 22

Nora

It's been three days, and I can't stop thinking about the blind date. I've drafted multiple emails to Zadie, but I've deleted each of them, and I've also ignored her emails. It's worse every time I think about it, especially my overreaction. However, my pride keeps getting in the way of admitting my mistake.

I felt bad about dragging Megan out of the restaurant and avoiding her questions, but I had already dug the hole, and I didn't know how to climb out of it. Now I realize it's time to start making apologies. I've never been good at apologizing; it's something that Mason and I used to argue about. Even when I did apologize, he would find fault with the way that I did it and accuse me of not being sincere enough or making excuses within my apology. I'm guessing after the way I acted, I'll never see this blind date again. Although he certainly deserves one, I don't think he'll even want to hear an apology from me. But I do need to address the issue with

Zadie and Megan, and it's not going to get easier if I keep putting it off.

I find Megan reading out by the pool, in the shaded lounge bed that has become *her* spot. "Hey, do you have a minute?" I ask her.

"Sure," she says, putting her book down on the towel next to her. "What's going on?"

Megan may be almost twenty years younger than I am, but now that I've gotten to know her better, it feels like I'm talking to a friend my age. I don't know if that means she's very mature, or that I'm not so mature, or that once you pass a certain age, age difference becomes less relevant. Whatever it is, it's comforting and a bit disconcerting at the same time.

"I wanted to talk to you about the other night – about what happened at the restaurant," I begin to say.

"Okay?" Megan says, giving me a puzzled look.

"I think I owe you an apology," I say to her, and I immediately admonish myself for using the word 'think' – what's wrong with me?

"No, you don't. It's totally fine," Megan says.

I love the idea of being let off the hook so easily, but I know I need to push through. "I haven't been on a date in a long time. That is not an excuse, but I was really on edge the other night, and I overreacted. I should have given my date a chance to explain and shouldn't have pulled you out of the restaurant. Especially when it looked like you were having such a good time," I say to her.

"Don't worry about it," Megan says, but from her tone, I feel like she appreciates my effort. "Are you going to see him again?" she asks.

"Oh God, I don't think so. I'm sure he thinks I'm a complete nightmare," I laugh awkwardly. "But I do need to let Zadie know what happened. I've been avoiding her," I explain.

"Are you going to let her set you up again?" Megan asks.

"I don't think so," I reply. "This may have proven that I'm not fit to date," I say, trying to make a joke out of it.

"Oh, come on, you should give it another chance," Megan says, looking at me hopefully.

Our age difference feels quite stark suddenly, and there's so much I want to tell her. I want to tell her to enjoy her twenties but not to squander them. I want to tell her that she shouldn't settle down with the first guy she meets, but if she finds the right guy, she shouldn't let him go. Oh, and also not to wait, or it might be too late to have babies – if that's something she wants. But of course, I don't say any of these things. Instead, I change the topic. "Who was that girl you were talking to at the bar? I was so absorbed in my own issues that I didn't even ask!"

"She was waiting to interview for a hostess position. We only talked for a few minutes, but she seemed nice. Her name is Courtney. I didn't get any info for her or anything," Megan says.

"You know where to find her," I say.

"Huh?" Megan says, looking confused.

"She'll be at Dockers. She was interviewing to work there, right?" I ask.

"I guess so. It would be weird if I just showed up there," Megan says.

"It's a bar. It wouldn't be weird at all. You could ask the

other tutor to go with you?" I suggest. The look Megan gives me tells me that this is a bad idea.

"I met the other tutor a couple of days ago. She came to pick something up when I was meeting Joel. I don't really see us hanging out a lot," Megan says.

"Why not?" I ask. I'm sure I should stop pressing the issue, but I'm curious.

"It's hard to explain. I got the feeling right away that she wasn't looking to meet anyone new. Joel said that her family has come here every summer since before she was born, and she didn't give off a friendly vibe," Megan says.

"You never know if you don't try," I say to Megan, and I cringe as I hear the lame words come out of my mouth.

"I guess," she replies half-heartedly, not looking convinced. Then she looks at her Apple Watch, "I have to go get dressed now. I'm tutoring twins this afternoon," she sighs.

"You're tutoring them both at the same time?" I question.

"Honestly, I would prefer it that way. The parents didn't want back-to-back sessions and wanted individual sessions for their identical twins, so they hired Joel and me to come at the same time," she says.

"Is that the guy who runs the company?" I ask.

"Yes. And he's such a pain in the ass," Megan moans.

"Sorry," I say gently.

"It's okay. It's only ninety minutes. It can't be that bad. Although it's a bit of a long bike ride, so Joel's driving me there and back. I'm not looking forward to that," Megan says as she gracefully stands up and wraps a towel around her body.

"Good luck!" I call after her as she walks to the guest house.

"Thanks," she calls back.

Before I can lose my nerve, I pick up my phone and dial Zadie's number. One down and one to go.

As I bike over to Eva and Chloe's house, I replay my conversation with Zadie from earlier this afternoon. Zadie was understanding, although I'm not sure I deserved her compassion. After she'd been so nice, I couldn't say no on the spot, so I agreed to look at a few more profiles, but I can't imagine actually going on another blind date.

Eva and Chloe have also been incredibly understanding, and I'm not sure I'm worthy of their forgiveness either. In the past week, we've quickly fallen back into some of our old routines, and I'm desperate to ask Eva why she's cutting me so much slack when I've been such a terrible friend. Although, I'm worried that if I open that can of worms, I won't like what I find. As my mom would say, "It's best to let sleeping dogs lie."

When I arrive at their house, I pull my bike up to the back gate and take the bottle of wine I've brought out of my basket. Eva insisted that I didn't need to bring anything, but I feel terrible showing up empty-handed, especially since this is the third time they have hosted me this week, and they haven't been to my house once. I know it's easier for them to be here because of the kids, but I'm starting to feel like a freeloader.

"Hello?" I yell into the backyard to announce my presence. Penny is the first to welcome me, and I bend down to rub her soft black head, and she nuzzles my leg appreciatively.

"Nora, is that you?" Eva calls out.

"Yes, it's me," I reply as I walk past the hedges and see Eva on the deck wringing out a pile of clothes and hanging them over the railing.

"Is the dryer broken?" I ask.

"Oh no," she laughs. "The kids pushed Chloe into the pool, and then Chloe pushed me into the pool, and then we all ended up swimming in our clothes. I'll put them in the wash later, but I didn't have anywhere to put a pile of sopping wet clothes right now." She doesn't look remotely upset about this turn of events; in fact, she looks positively amused. I think I would be so pissed off if I got pushed into the pool, especially right before my friends were coming over for dinner. However, Eva is taking it all in stride – I guess that's part of motherhood.

I don't know what Eva was wearing previously, but now she has on a loose-fitting yellow shirtdress, and her damp, auburn hair is hanging down her back, and it's left a wet patch on her dress. As usual, she isn't wearing any makeup, but her olive skin is glowing from days in the sun, and she looks radiant – happy.

"How did the date go?" Eva asks excitedly. She takes the bottle of wine from my hand and expertly opens it with a corkscrew that was lying on the table. She pours us each a glass and looks at me, waiting for my reply.

"It could have been better," I say, taking a seat in the rattan side chair.

"What happened?" she asks, sitting down next to me.

"It's embarrassing," I say.

"Ooh – that's the best kind of blind date story," she laughs.

I bury my face in my hands, so I don't have to look at her, but at the same time, I remember how much I love swapping stories with Eva and her uncanny ability to see the funny side of everything. I cringe as I think about what a bad friend I've been and how lucky I am that Eva hasn't held it against me.

I drain my glass and then begin to tell the story. The beginning of the date is boring, and I quickly gloss over that. The guy was a lot older than I would have liked. He wasn't unattractive, but certainly not someone I could ever picture myself dating. He made fine small talk over appetizers and told me that he retired early after making his fortune at a hedge fund and now sits on multiple boards and makes even more money.

Eva listens intently. "This sounds like a boring first date. Get to the good part," she insists.

"He ordered a gin and tonic, or at least I think that's what it was. Anyway, it came with a lime. He squeezed the lime, and some of it got in his eye," I say.

Eva is looking at me, and I know she wants me to hurry through these boring details, but I think they're important for the story. "I got some lime juice on my cheek as well, and I grabbed my napkin from my lap to wipe it off. There was a waiter walking by, and I turned around to ask for an extra napkin to help my date since it looked like he was having some trouble. The next thing I know, he rubbed his hand right across my boob and then stuck his whole hand into my lap, right between my legs!"

"Holy shit!" Eva says. "I don't understand – why did he do that? Did he just decide to grope you? Did he get really drunk, and it suddenly hit him?" Eva questions, clearly trying to figure it out.

"I didn't stick around long enough to find out," I tell her.

"Huh?" she asks.

"I screamed "pervert" very loudly, then accused him of assaulting me, grabbed my bag, and ran out of there," I tell her.

"Wow!" Eva says. "That's awful and possibly traumatic. But I'm not sure I would say it was embarrassing," she says thoughtfully.

"That's because I haven't told you the rest of it," I tell her.

Eva doesn't say anything but motions for me to continue.

"As I was running away, I heard him say, 'My contact lens! I lost my contact! That's my only good eye! I can't see anything!'"

"Oh my God!" Eva says as she starts to put the pieces together.

"Yup. He got lime juice in his eye, and his contact lens came out, and he's blind in his other eye, so that meant he literally couldn't see anything. He was just wildly moving his arms in search of his contact, or maybe in search of anything – he was totally panicking." I tell her.

"So, what did you do then?" She asks.

I look down at the ground because it's too mortifying to make eye contact. "I was already a couple of steps from the table when he said it. And I had just accused him of molesting me, and everyone heard me say it. I had to leave," I admit shamefully.

"You left him there? Totally blind?!" Eva asks, but I can tell she's about to laugh, even though it's all so awful.

"There were several waiters helping him and the people from the next table. He wasn't *alone*."

Just then, Eva starts giggling, and then it shifts to a full-blown belly laugh, and I can't help it, but I start laughing right along with her. "That could be the worst first date story I've ever heard," she says when she finally catches her breath.

"I know, I know," I reply. "That's why I'm never dating again," I say solemnly.

"Oh no. Totally the opposite. You have to go on another date as soon as possible. You've got to cancel this one out. Get back on the horse – all that bullshit," she tells me.

"Sorry, not going to happen," I tell her.

"You have to do it," Eva says, suddenly more solemn.

"What do you mean?" I ask her.

"You owe me," she says.

"What?" I question.

"For disappearing these past years. You owe me," Eva says, shooting me a look that appears surprisingly serious.

I'm only a little bit surprised that she brought it up. I'd been expecting it, but after we hung out a couple of times and she didn't mention it, I thought maybe she'd let it go – not that I deserved to be let off the hook so easily.

"You want me to pay you back for being a shitty friend by going on a date?" I ask her.

"No," she says.

"Okay. Then what?" I ask.

"I want you to repay me by going on lots and lots of dates and telling me all about them," she says with a sneaky smile.

Chapter 23

Courtney

"Did you seat that couple at table six?" Leslie asks, sounding incredibly annoyed.

"Yes?" I reply, but my voice goes up at the end as if it were a question, and I can already tell that it's the wrong answer.

"That section is closed," Leslie huffs.

I look over toward the back where the older couple is slowly getting settled at the table, and the man is putting on his reading glasses to get a good look at the menu. I don't see anything about that part of the restaurant to indicate that it's closed. I give Leslie a look that conveys my total ignorance.

"The waiter in that section is on a break. So, you can't seat anyone there," she explains, rolling her eyes and pushing me out of the way at the podium to make adjustments on the computer.

"Sorry," I apologize. I almost ask if I should go move the older couple to another table, but thankfully I realize before I say it that this would be a bad idea. Today is my first afternoon as a hostess at Dockers, and it's becoming increasingly clear that I'm not capable of doing this job. I don't know what Tucker said when he called his friend, but I barely had to answer any questions in my "interview" and they gave me the job without asking questions about my experience. At the time, I was thrilled, but two hours into my first shift, I'm starting to think that whatever favor Tucker called in is not going to be very helpful in the long run.

"Can you take these to table eleven?" a harried waiter asks, as he runs by me, practically throws a plate of calamari into my hands, and doesn't stay to hear my answer.

I'm not sure if I'm even supposed to deliver food to the tables or if there's a certain way that it should be done, but I'm pretty sure the worst possible outcome would be if I just stand like a statue holding an appetizer watching it get cold. I desperately try to remember which is table eleven as I wander through the restaurant. A kind-looking woman must sense my confusion, and as I approach her table, she helpfully calls out, "I think that's ours." I slide it onto the center of their table, tell her that it's my first day, and then hustle back to the front before I get in trouble for something else.

The next four hours continue in about the same way, and by the time I'm untying my silly half-apron at eleven o'clock, I can't decide if I should just quit or wait to be fired, which I'm convinced is inevitable.

"Good job tonight," a voice calls out as I'm walking out the door. I turn around out of habit because I'm quite certain I'm the only person around, but if I'd let the words register, I'm sure I would have kept walking – those words certainly weren't intended for me. When I turn, I see the waiter who passed along the plate of calamari at the beginning of the night.

"Hardly," I reply.

"I'm serious. It takes a while to catch on. You did great for your first night," he says. "I'm Brian, by the way."

"Courtney," I reply. "Thanks for saying that. I felt like it was a disaster. Glad to hear it didn't seem too bad. I'm only working two nights a week, so I won't be back for a few days. Hopefully, it will give me some time to recover," I say to him.

"Have a good night," Brian calls after me.

"Thanks. You too," I call back.

I'm not even thinking about guys because every time I do, my thoughts go straight to Preston, but it's hard not to notice that Brian is really cute in a traditional way. Thankfully, he also appears to be incredibly nice. He's totally not my type, but he's the kind of guy that most of my friends would fall for. He's shorter *and* trimmer than I prefer, although I could see from his bare arms that he is muscular, just the lean, ropy kind of muscle. And he has floppy coffee-colored hair that reminds me of a puppy but also makes me feel like he would be right at home on a surfboard or the cover of a Hollister catalog. I'm sure Alyssa would be all over him if she got the chance, but I should probably do this seemingly-nice guy a favor and keep her far away.

I slide behind the wheel of Alyssa's car, and I'm about to drive off when my phone rings. I should be able to drive and talk at the same time, but I haven't figured out how to pair my phone with the Bluetooth in her car, and I'm too embarrassed to ask. I'm desperate to get back to Alyssa's, take a shower and crawl into bed, but I see Preston's name on the display and realize that if I don't answer, it could be days before I get the chance to speak with him again.

"Hey, you!" I answer and instantly feel awkward about my greeting.

"It's Preston," he says.

"I know," I reply.

"Oh, sorry," he says.

"How are you?" I ask.

"Exhausted," he says, and he definitely sounds that way. "The practice sessions are brutal. And now that we've done the initial weeks of training, it seems like someone is always having a party," he says.

"Sounds fun," I reply awkwardly. I miss him so much that my heart physically hurts. It was fun to flirt with Tucker but Preston is still the only guy for me. It's painful to pretend to talk to him as a friend instead of a boyfriend, but I don't want him to think I can't keep up my end of the bargain, and Preston was quite clear about how he wanted to handle this. Our last FaceTime call was surprisingly great, especially considering the ongoing tension, but other than that, we've only had a few uncomfortable text exchanges, and it seems like we are both struggling for things to say.

"It's not too bad. It's weird to be playing football and partying and not having to worry about going to class or studying. It's like I'm doing the same thing I was doing in college, only now there's no classwork, and I get paid," he says.

"Sounds pretty great," I reply.

"*You* don't seem to be missing too many parties. Anything you want to talk about?" Preston asks.

"What? I don't think so," I reply. I know that I mentioned a couple of Alyssa's parties because I didn't want him to think he was right about this summer being a mistake, but I have no idea what he means.

"Don't worry about it," Preston says. "I'm glad you're having such a good time. It looks like things are going well for both of us. Hey, I've got to go," Preston says abruptly and ends the call.

I have no idea what just happened. I stare at the silent phone and try to make sense of our conversation, but I can't figure it out. I'm beyond tired, but I'm so disturbed that I'm almost shaking, so I decide to sit and wait for a minute before driving home on the dark, unlit Hamptons roads. Out of habit, I open Instagram to mindlessly scroll through posts while I wait for my body to feel normal again; however, based on Alyssa's posts, I experience the exact opposite reaction.

At first, I can't even figure out where these pictures are from, but then I realize that the collection of images is from The Palm the other night, as well as the party from the following evening. She seems to have a knack for capturing me doing something completely innocent that looks entirely different in the split second when she takes her picture. She's posted at least ten pictures from the past few days highlighting her amazing summer. I'm only in the background of a few of the photos, but it seems like an unfortunate coincidence that I keep getting caught on film. In the first picture, it looks like I'm whispering dirty secrets in Tucker's ear (when I'm really asking if we need to settle the bill.) In the second picture, it appears that I'm tightly hugging one of Alyssa's friends (he was about to fall over, and I grabbed him to keep him on his feet.) And in the third picture, I'm asleep on the couch with a boy I've never seen before, sleeping right beside me. (Even *I* can't explain what's happening here, but I recognize my outfit, and I had too much to drink that night and fell asleep on the couch – it looks like someone fell asleep next to me.)

I know exactly what I'm going to find, but I insist on confirming it. Preston27 has liked all the photos, and for the last one, he even left a comment, "looking cozy."

Chapter 24

Megan

Danielle and I have been trying to find a good time for a phone call for the past several days, but it seems like we are never free at the same time. I know she's overwhelmed with the move and the girls, and I feel bad bothering her again, but I miss talking to her, especially when I still feel so unsettled. There only seem to be a few people in my life who truly understand my relationship with Danielle – especially once they learn that both of my biological parents are alive and healthy and not in prison or impaired or living on a desert island. Although, as far as providing comfort or advice or kind words, they might as well be all those things. Danielle has really been the only one in a parental position since my sophomore year of high school. I wish I had a better way to describe our relationship than calling her my "former stepmom" since that doesn't come close to describing what she is to me, but sometimes the truth is the most succinct. I send her another text to check on her availability.

Megan: Is this a good time to talk?

Danielle: Hi! How are you? I can't talk right now because I'm on a work call – but I'm barely even needed on the call – we can text if that's okay?

Megan: sure

Danielle: How's tutoring going?

Megan: It's okay – the kids are actually better than I thought they would be

Danielle: What about the other tutors?

Megan: I only met one other girl, and she's not very friendly. And then there's Joel...

Danielle: Oh no

Megan: It's not how I thought it would be. I was doing this to meet people, and the only people I've met are high school juniors and Joel

Danielle: Joel is really that bad?

Megan: He's a pompous ass! And now I have to see him at least twice a week! We are tutoring twins together, and it's a bit of a hike, so he drives me there and back.

Danielle: I hate to say this, and I know this isn't enlightened thinking but is there any chance that he likes you?

Megan: ew, gross! And definitely not!

Danielle: Okay – just asking. You can always come crash with us And you can go back to Palo

Alto whenever you want – you have lots of friends there.

Megan: No, that's okay. I'm fine here – it'll be okay.

Danielle: Just a suggestion

Megan: I did meet this one girl, and she seemed like someone I would want to hang out with, but I don't have her phone number or anything.

Danielle: Sorry about that ☹ Where did you meet her?

Megan: Long story – I would have to go back to the bar where she's working to find her, and that makes me feel like a stalker. I feel like it's harder to meet a friend than it is to meet a guy

Danielle: Don't underestimate the importance of a good friendship or the work that it may take to find a friend or keep a friendship going – I think girls spend far too much time worrying about romantic relationships and should spend more time nurturing female friendships

Megan: This is getting really deep for a text exchange

Danielle: Sorry!

Megan: It's okay – I'm just kidding. Would it be weird if I went back to the bar to try and find this girl and see if she wants to hang out?

Danielle: What do you have to lose?

* * *

Joel comes to pick me up later that day, and I give a passing thought to what Danielle texted me as we drive to the twins' house for our session, but I dismiss it almost as quickly as the thought pops into my head. We drive in silence out to the house in Quogue, and when we arrive, I take twin A out to the covered patio to review math, and Joel works with twin B in the kitchen. An hour later, we get back in Joel's midsize BMW to return to Westhampton Beach.

The quiet hum of the air conditioning is the only noise in the car. Although I don't want to engage in conversation with Joel, the silence is unbearable, and against my better judgment, I decide to break it. "Do you mind if we listen to music?" I ask him.

"What kind of music?" Joel asks.

"I don't know, just music," I reply.

"It makes a difference," Joel says. "I'm very particular when it comes to music," he says bluntly.

I sigh and sit back in my seat, thinking to myself, 'of course, he's particular when it comes to music,' but then Joel surprises me by elaborating.

"I don't do well with loud noises. So, I've found that country music and classical are what I enjoy most. However, it doesn't seem that a lot of people like those genres, so I usually don't listen to anything when I'm with other people," he explains.

I turn my head slightly to the left to get a better look at Joel in the driver's seat. He is staring straight ahead at the road, with his hands at ten and two; I feel like I'm seeing him for the first time.

"I'm good with classical or country," I offer. "And we could listen at a low volume – or we could keep the music off – that's fine with me too," I tell him, and I mean it when I say it.

Joel must press a button on the steering wheel because I don't see his hands leave their ten and two positions, but a faint sound begins to emit from the speakers, and it takes me a second to recognize that it's some type of country music. Other than a couple of old Shania Twain songs and maybe something by Kenney Chesney, I wouldn't recognize a single country artist or song, but whatever it is that's playing in the background is surprisingly pleasant.

"Is this okay?" Joel asks me, and it's the first time I think I've ever heard him sound unsure of himself.

"Yes, it's great. Thanks." I reply.

I don't know why I decide to push it, but something about Joel's attitude makes me feel like there's an opening. "Is it just music, or are there other loud noises that bother you?" I ask.

At first, it doesn't look like Joel has even heard the question, and then I worry that he's heard the question, and it's annoyed him, and he's choosing not to answer me. It's not like I care what he thinks, but I mentally kick myself since we still have fifteen minutes until we reach Nora's house on Dune Road, and so far, this was the least awkward it's been.

Joel keeps his eyes trained on the road, but he responds quietly after a moment. "It's not just music. I'm bothered by a lot of loud noises. I also have tactile issues, and I'm bothered by certain scents. It's generally referred to as a sensory processing disorder, but oddly enough, even with my issues, doctors said I never quite fit the mold for sensory processing disorder."

I'm not sure how to respond or if I'm supposed to respond at all, but thankfully Joel continues speaking, which lets me know that I should simply keep listening.

"They had me tested for everything. As you might have guessed, I didn't fit in very well with the other kids," Joel laughs, but I don't laugh along with him. "When your parents have a lot of money, and you aren't the kid they hoped you would be, then they just keep testing you to try and figure out what's wrong. But the doctors said I wasn't autistic and didn't have Asperger's, which is bizarrely what they were hoping for because at least it would have been a label they could have given to their friends," Joel tells me.

"Oh wow," I say because it seems like that deserves a response. I can't believe that Joel is telling me all of this – it's like I've uncovered an entirely different person on this car ride.

"Anyhow, the team of psychiatrists told my parents that I was really smart and had some sensory issues that I could learn to deal with, and I needed more practice with social cues, and then they sent me on my way," Joel says.

Joel has made the turn onto Dune Road, and instead of being thankful that I am moments away from escaping the car, I find myself wishing we had more time to continue the conversation; it feels disrespectful to run off after he's shared this personal information, especially when it explains so much.

"That sounds like a lot to deal with," I say to him, hoping that it's the right thing to say.

"High school wasn't a lot of fun," Joel says, and from the way he raises his eyebrows and the slight lift in his voice, it appears that he is making an attempt at humor – the first one of its kind in all of our interactions.

"Probably not," I reply.

"I liked my time at Columbia, but I don't think I had what most people would think of as the 'typical college experience,'" Joel says.

At this point, Joel has pulled the car into Nora's driveway and shifted into park. I'm trying to determine if it's more awkward for me to stay in the car now that we've reached my destination or for me to leave at this point in the conversation. Before I can give it any more thought, Joel answers the question for me. "I'll pick you up Thursday afternoon," he says, and it seems clear that the car ride and the connection are both over.

"Great, I'll see you then," I say to Joel as I raise my body from the low-slung leather seat. "Thank you," I call out as I push the car door, and it closes with the heavy satisfying thud of an expensive German automobile. I've thanked Joel each time he's driven me home previously, but those have been through tight lips, and only because I know that's what I'm supposed to say, but today is the first time I mean it.

* * *

I'm not sure what to expect when Joel picks me up forty-eight hours later, but I'm surprisingly anxious. It's weird not to be dreading the car ride. I joked with Hope that I must be getting desperate for friends if I was looking forward to an awkward conversation with a weird guy that I previously despised. She automatically assumed that I have a crush on him. I admitted to her that Joel *is* cute, but I don't think of him that way, and I honestly just want someone to talk to other than Nora. I'm not sure if Hope believed me, but that's probably because she thinks of all cute guys as potential hook-ups, but I know that it's true.

When I get in the car, Joel greets me with a quick "Hello," and then we drive for the first few minutes in complete silence. I'm almost convinced that I imagined the entire conversation from the other day when Joel leans forward and switches on the radio. "Sorry," he says sheepishly. Soft piano music fills the car, and I know that I didn't make it all up.

On the drive back from tutoring, Joel surprises me by addressing me as soon as the car starts moving. "The students seem to connect well with you," Joel says.

"Oh, yeah. Thanks," I reply. I'm taken aback both by his observation and the compliment.

"I know all the material. Likely far better than you do, but the students don't respond to me in the same way," Joel says.

I decide to ignore the jab when I respond. "Everyone has different styles," I say.

"I'm fine with it," Joel says quickly. "I don't particularly care if they like me. I only care if the test scores go up the required amounts and the parents continue to hire me and refer me to their friends," Joel says bluntly.

"Got it," I reply.

Then Joel shocks me with his next comment. "I'm sorry if

that was rude. I didn't mean to be rude. Apparently, I do that a lot, but I don't intend it," Joel says.

"That's okay," I tell him, and then before I know what's coming out of my mouth, I say, "What are you doing later?"

"After I drop you off, I'm going to go home and go for a run. Then I'll have dinner and likely spend the rest of the evening working on the beta version of my app," Joel says.

"Any chance you want to come to get a drink with me at Dockers?" I ask him.

"Why?" Joel questions.

I'm taken aback by his response, but I suppose it is a reasonable question. Our limited interactions can barely be described as friendly, and suddenly I'm inviting him to go get drinks – especially since it doesn't seem like he spends a lot of time socializing at bars.

"This is kind of embarrassing, but I met a girl there last week, and I think she's working there now. I was going to go get a drink and see if I could find her." I say.

"I didn't realize you were a lesbian," Joel says matter-of-factly without a hint of emotion or judgment in his voice.

I replay what I just said to him and realize that this is the logical conclusion, even for someone who *doesn't* have an issue with interpreting social cues. "I can see how you would think that." I laugh as I continue, "But I'm only interested in meeting her as a friend."

"I didn't know people did that to find friends," Joel replies.

"You're probably right," I say, realizing that the whole idea is foolish.

"I'm rarely right about friends. What time do you want to

go? Do you want me to drive, or do you want to meet me there?" Joel asks.

"I'll meet you there. Is eight o'clock okay?" I ask him, marveling at the bizarre path my day is taking.

"That's fine," Joel replies, and we drive the rest of the way home in companionable silence.

Chapter 25

Nora

Keeping my promise to Eva, I told Zadie that I would be open to more dates. From the way Zadie hesitated on the phone, I was worried that she was going to drop me as a client after my terrible behavior on my first blind date, but she only asked me to give her a few days, and she would send over another match.

Now it's been three days since that phone call, and although I ran out of the restaurant saying that I never wanted to date again, I find that I'm feeling impatient to give it another try, or at least to get the next date over with.

I've always loved summer at the beach. When we were designing and building this house, Mason and I would talk about all the parties we would throw here once it was finished and daydream about our perfect future at our perfect house.

However, now that I'm here, and summer is in full swing, I feel like I'm trapped in an ivory tower watching everyone else fulfill their summer dreams.

I've touted the importance of being a strong, independent woman for the past twenty years, but what I failed to realize was that although I had my independence, I was also part of a team (at work and at home) and rarely on my own. Now I'm alone on both fronts, and more than anything else, it's lonely. I had no problem attending parties by myself when Mason couldn't attend or traveling the world on my own, but I knew there was someone at home waiting for me, and there was the added benefit that people weren't gossiping about me wherever I went.

Thankfully, before I sink any deeper into this well of self-pity, my phone rings, and my sister's chipper voice pulls me out of it.

"Hey, Bridget," I say as I answer the phone.

"Hi Nora!" she exclaims.

"How's it going?" I ask.

"Fine. Everything's fine. How are *you*?" she asks, drawing out the last word to make sure we both know that I'm the one we need to be concerned about.

"I'm okay," I tell her.

"You don't sound okay," she counters.

"I'm fine. I promise."

"When's your next date?" Bridget asks.

"I'm not sure," I say.

"Why not?" She asks.

I contemplate messing with her and telling her that I've fired Zadie and I'm not going on any more dates, but that seems unkind. "I'm waiting to hear about my next match from Zadie," I tell her.

"Hmmm, okay," she replies, sounding skeptical. "What else is going on?" she asks.

"Not too much. I promise I'm not complaining, but it's a little boring to be out here all summer with nothing to do," I say.

"I would kill to have a weekend with nothing to do!" Bridget says. As soon as the words are out of her mouth, I hear crying erupt in the background. I can't tell which of my nieces is bawling, but my money is on Colleen. At three and a half, she is quite the terror. Quinn is ten months older, but she is practically an angel. I find it somewhat ironic that a good Irish girl like Bridget ended up with "Irish twins," but she doesn't see the humor in her situation.

"Do you have to go?" I ask.

"Probably soon," she replies. "I gave Colleen my iPad, which should entertain her for about five minutes before she loses it again. Don't judge me," Bridget sighs.

"I would never judge!" I assure her. "You could come out here to visit," I say. I suggested this a few weeks ago, but Bridget was adamant that it would be too hard.

"Patrick has to work," she tells me.

"I know, but you can bring the girls. It will be fun! And I'm sure Megan could help out with some babysitting," I say. I haven't run this by Megan, but I know from Danielle that she has experience with kids, and I'm sure she would be willing to help out.

"That's a nice offer, but you just don't understand," she says.

I take a deep breath before I say something I'll regret. She lives just shy of four hours from here, and I know I don't have kids, but I can't imagine it would be impossible for her to put them in the car and drive out here – especially for a free vacation at the beach; with her sister!

Bridget is great when it comes to texts, emails, and phone calls. She's always been great at checking in on me, and then after Mason left, she went into overdrive – including her most recent effort in setting me up with a matchmaker. But I feel like we never see each other in person.

"Then I'll come to visit you," I say to her. I should have suggested this earlier. I was fixated on our locations — I'm in a house directly on the beach, and she's in a lifeless cookie-cutter Philadelphia suburb, but the venue shouldn't matter.

"That's nice of you, but it's too hectic here. I wouldn't really have time. Maybe in the fall? Things may calm down then," she offers. As if on cue, Colleen starts to scream hysterically in the background. "I've got to go. Keep me posted on your next date!" And with that, she's gone.

Chapter 26

Courtney

It's my third shift at work, and I'm finally figuring things out. I only made two mistakes on my second shift, and so far today, I don't think I've fucked anything up yet. My blood pressure is permanently elevated as I'm perpetually ready to be unprepared, which I know is an oxymoron.

It's shortly after nine, and the waitlist for table-seating has finally dwindled down to the last two couples that are standing in front of me. I know that it's good for the restaurant to have the tables booked weeks in advance *and* to have a long waitlist for the few tables they set aside for walk-ins, but it puts me in a constant state of panic. I felt terrible when I initially underestimated the wait time, so I changed my technique and exaggerated the times so guests would be pleasantly surprised. However, when Leslie overheard me and saw several customers leave because they didn't want to wait that long, she got really pissed off. Now I'm back to providing shorter estimates and subject to the wrath of hungry, angry women in sundresses coming up to me every five minutes to remind me how long they've been waiting.

A couple comes up to the stand, and before I can give them the good news that it will only be five minutes until a table is ready, the woman, who looks about my age, informs me that they want to sit at the bar. If I'm busy, I point people in the right direction and let them go on their own, but if I have time, I'm supposed to grab menus and walk them over. As I'm leading them over to the bar, I debate whether or not I should say anything to her. I'm not always great at remembering faces, but I'm almost positive that I talked to her last week, and then she had to run out when her boss had a blind-date emergency.

I hesitate as I place the menus on the top of the bar and then decide that I have nothing to lose. "Were you here last week?" I ask her. "I'm pretty sure we met the night I came in to interview," I say cautiously.

"Yes! Hi!" She replies enthusiastically. "I'm Megan. She's not my boss. She's my ex-stepmom's friend," she starts to say. "Sorry, that's not the point. Yes, she had an emergency, and I had to run out," she says. "It's nice to see you again."

"You, too!" I say, trying to match her level of enthusiasm. "I'm Courtney," I remind her.

"This is Joel," Megan says, indicating the man sitting beside her.

"I have to get back to work," I tell her.

"Oh right, of course," Megan says.

"I have a break in fifteen minutes. I'm not sure if I'm allowed to sit down at the bar while I'm working. If I can, I'll come back and say hi." And then I add, "If it isn't interrupting your date! I'm sorry, I just realized that I'm totally intruding," I say.

"Oh gosh, not at all," Megan says quickly. "This isn't a date. Come back whenever you want!"

I don't have time to go back to the bar during my break because Leslie makes me fold napkins. I'm about to protest that it's my break and I'm not supposed to be working during that time, but she doesn't seem to like me very much, and I don't think this will help my case.

By the time I get back over to the bar, it's after ten, and I'm certain Megan will have already gone home. To my surprise, Megan and Joel are still at the bar. Megan is looking at something on her phone, and Joel is staring off into the distance. Their glasses are empty, and the bill is in front of them sitting up neatly creased in a lowball glass, waiting to be paid. If this *was* a date, it doesn't look like it went well.

"I had to fold napkins," I apologize as I approach them.

Megan gives me a puzzled look, and then she seems to understand what I am trying to say. "Don't worry about it. Are you done now, or do you still have to work?" she asks me.

"I was supposed to work until ten-thirty, but the manager told me I could go home, so I guess I'm done for the night," I say.

"Do you want to sit down and have a drink?" Megan asks me.

"I'm going to go home," Joel says abruptly. He pushes back his barstool and stretches out his long arms as he stands up.

"Oh," Megan says. She seems disappointed as she looks up at Joel. "He gave me a ride here," Megan explains to me.

"I'm ready to go home," Joel says again to no one in particular.

"I can give you a ride," I offer. "You said you live close to here, right?" I ask her.

"Sure, thanks!" Megan says. "I'm staying at a house on Dune Road. It's about four miles. I suppose I *could* walk; I just wouldn't want to do it at night."

"I have to drive all the way back to East Hampton, so that's not a big deal at all. We can get one drink, and then we'll go," I say.

"Here's money for my drink," Joel says, handing Megan a crisp twenty-dollar bill.

"Thanks," Megan says as she accepts it from him. "You only had one beer; do you want change?" she asks. I'm pretty sure she's joking, but I don't know her, so it's hard to tell.

"I'll subtract it from your next paycheck," Joel says, and *he* doesn't seem to be joking. With that, Joel turns and walks toward the front of the restaurant.

Megan looks at me and says, "Don't even ask." And then we both start laughing.

One of the bartenders comes over to take our order, and he takes the bill from the empty glass and crumples it up in his hand to signify that we can continue adding to the tab. Tonight is the first time I've met him. Although he introduced himself earlier, I cannot remember his name. Instead, I give him a big smile and hope that it doesn't come up.

"What can I get for you ladies?" he asks.

"I'll have another vodka soda," Megan says.

"I'll have a margarita on the rocks, no salt. Please," I throw in at the end.

"Coming right up," he says, and he heads toward the middle of the bar to start making our drinks.

"How do you like working here?" Megan asks.

"It's okay so far. The people are pretty nice, and it's a fun place to hang out," I tell her.

"Are things any better with your roommate?" she asks.

I'm flattered that she remembered this detail from our previous conversation. I consider myself to have good self-esteem, but I'm generally still amazed when anyone other than my immediate family, or Preston, listens intently when I'm speaking – maybe I *do* need to reevaluate my definition of "good self-esteem."

"Not really. It's like she's single-handedly trying to bring back the *Girls Gone Wild* series," I complain.

"That sounds intense," Megan says.

"I must sound like such a loser. It's not that I don't like to party or have fun, but she's on a whole other level. I think what I really can't get over is how different she is here from who I thought she was at school. And that doesn't even begin to cover what she's like with her dad! I think she might actually have multiple personality disorder!" I exclaim.

"That sucks," Megan says.

"Sorry. God, I'm so sorry! I guess I just needed to vent. I'm sure you don't want to hear about this," I say. I pause to take a sip from my drink and give myself a chance to break eye contact.

"I do. Honestly, it's so much more exciting than what I've been doing all summer," Megan tells me.

"Are you still hanging out with your stepmom's friend?" I

tease her and then worry that we haven't established enough of a bond yet where teasing is appropriate.

Megan laughs out loud, and it seems that I'm in the clear. "It's actually my *EX*-stepmom's friend if you want to get your facts straight," she jokes.

"What about that guy you were here with tonight?" I ask her.

"He's technically my boss. I hated him up until a few days ago. Now I find him to be interesting in small doses," Megan says, raising her glass to finish the last swallow of vodka and ice.

"Where do you work?" I ask.

"I'm an SAT tutor. I didn't have any real plans for the summer either, but after the first week, I was so bored that I decided it would be good to have something to do and make some money. I was hoping I'd also meet people, but I seem to have struck out there," Megan says.

"Other than Joel," I say glibly.

"Exactly," Megan smiles.

I feel awkward cutting our conversation short, especially since Megan seems so normal. But it is getting late, and I still have a forty-minute drive on dark back roads. "I might need to leave soon if that's okay with you. I can't imagine that Alyssa is going to be in shape to drive anywhere tonight, and there are other cars at the house, but she *is* letting me borrow her car, and East Hampton feels like a long drive at night."

"Of course! Let me pay the bill, and then we can go. It was so nice of you to offer to drive me home. I wasn't quite ready to go yet, and I had reached my limit of topics to cover with Joel in one day," Megan says.

Megan signals for the bartender, but before she can take the bill from him, I signal for him to put it on my account. "You don't have to do that," Megan says. "We had drinks before you got here."

"Please, don't worry about it," I tell her. "You can leave the tip if you want?" I offer.

Megan slides the twenty that Joel gave her underneath her empty glass. "Thanks. I'll get drinks next time," she says as we walk out of the empty restaurant into the parking lot.

Megan wasn't exaggerating when she said that she lived down the road. It's a straight shot down Dune Road to her house, and then she signals for me to stop when we get to one of the massive gates that are presumably hiding an oceanfront mansion. It would be about a forty-minute walk, which might be nice during the day, but these roads are so dark, and this two-lane road has no shoulder or sidewalks, so I wouldn't think of walking home at night either.

"Thanks so much!" Megan says as she pops open the car door. She is about to get out, and then she turns toward me and asks, "Can I get your number? Is that weird?"

I laugh and feel some of the tension drain from my shoulders. I had been wondering the same exact thing. For a millisecond, I wonder if I should clarify that I'm straight and then immediately chastise myself for having the thought and feel terribly narrow-minded. Of course, it doesn't matter, and it's totally presumptuous of me to assume she would be interested in me if she *were* into girls. I try to think if she mentioned a boyfriend in either of our conversations, other than saying Joel wasn't her boyfriend, and I don't think that she did. But I don't think I said anything about guys either. God, why do I overthink everything?! She's a nice person; I like hanging out with her, and I need friends – it doesn't matter who either of us wants to sleep with – why is making friends so hard!

"It's not weird at all. I was going to ask you the same thing!" I say to her, and we quickly trade phones and exchange numbers. As I'm about to back out of the driveway, I hear the telltale chime from my phone and glance at it in the cupholder to see that Megan has already texted me.

There are a few extra cars parked in the driveway when I get back to Alyssa's. I know it was too much to ask for, but I was hoping that Alyssa would have gone somewhere else to hang out tonight, or at least that I was back late enough that everyone would have already left.

The marijuana smell is overpowering when I walk into the house. I have no problem with pot and honestly think it's a lot safer than alcohol, but it seems like they could have cracked a window or smoked on the deck rather than hotboxing the entire house. Because of basketball, I've never tried marijuana in any form. I was always terrified that it would show up on a random drug screening, and it never seemed worth the risk. There were certainly other girls on the team who felt differently, but not me. As I follow the smell to the game room, it occurs to me that my days of random drug tests for sports are over, and pot is legal in a ton of states now, so maybe it's finally something I can try. Although, I'm positive that Alyssa and her crew are not who I want to get high with for my first time.

It's hard to count exactly how many people are here because they are lying all over each other on the couches in the game room. The lights are dimmed, and Pink Floyd is playing in the background. I don't know if Alyssa and her friends like Pink Floyd or if they think that's what they should be listening to while taking bong hits.

I cross over to grab a seltzer from the mini-fridge, and that's when Alyssa notices that I'm back. "Heeeeyyyy," Alyssa says sleepily. "Come hang out," she requests as she leans her head back on top of the guy who's currently spooning her.

"I'm really tired. I'm going to go to bed," I tell her.

"Okaaay," Alyssa exhales, obviously not interested in pushing the discussion.

"I'll see you tomorrow," I say to her. I'm not sure if she heard me or not, but she doesn't respond as I walk out of the room.

I don't remember closing my bedroom door when I ran out for work, but maybe I did pull it shut behind me, and I simply forgot. I put my phone in my back pocket and use my free hand, the one without the can of seltzer, to turn the doorknob. I can't believe that it takes me as long as it does to figure out what the noise is; maybe that says something about the status of my life. There's panting and moaning, and it really does take my brain way too long to process these very familiar sounds. I instantly regret it, but I flip on the light switch and let out a scream when I see a naked guy lying on my unmade bed with a stark-naked woman holding her gigantic breasts and bouncing up and down on top of his dick like she's auditioning for a role in a porno. It's funny, but the first thought that occurs to me is that I didn't know real people had sex like that; I know that's definitely not what Preston and I looked like.

"Get out of here!" The woman yells at me, and I can now see and hear that although her physique is that of a full-grown woman, she's at least several years younger than I am and has the baby face of a younger teenager.

"This is my room!" I yell back at her. The situation is beyond absurd, because although they are both staring straight at me and the bouncing has stopped, neither of them has moved an inch. We are having this conversation while they are still actively having sex, naked, on my bed, five feet away from me.

"Dude, at least let us finish," the guy requests. I think I vaguely recognize him from one of Alyssa's many gatherings, and I assume he is in his early twenties like we are. It's not my issue, but I find myself hoping that the girl is at least of consensual age because that makes this slightly less horrifying

An involuntary laugh escapes my lips at his farcical request because I don't know how else to handle the situation. I back out of the room and even shut off the light. I guess that the interruption didn't kill the mood because as I close the door, I hear the moaning pick up speed, and it sounds like they are back on track.

Chapter 27

Megan

It's another picturesque summer day, and the biggest decision I must make is whether to sit by the pool or to walk a hundred yards over the dunes to Nora's private beach. I know the summer may not be all I imagined so far, but as I pull on my black bikini and white gauzy cover-up and grab my book for a day of sun-drenched reading, I remind myself that I'm damn lucky.

Nora is sitting by the pool, under the large navy and white striped umbrella, in a white one-piece with a section of the Sunday *New York Times* stretched open in front of her. "Are you going to the beach?" Nora asks.

"I'm not sure. I thought I would sit by the pool for now. If that's okay with you?" I quickly add.

"Of course," Nora says. "I'd love the company. Do you want to sit in the shade, or do you want sun?" she asks.

"I'm going to start off in the sun, but I probably should sit in the shade," I say.

"A little sun won't kill you. Although I'm mostly in the shade now because my dermatologist yells at me at every visit," Nora laughs.

I grab a fluffy white towel from the spa-like display next to the door and lay it out on a lounge chair close enough to Nora that it doesn't seem like I'm avoiding her, but also not too close that if she wants to read the paper and ignore me, she can do that too. I lay down, but I don't pick up my book right away. The temperature is somewhere in the low eighties without a trace of humidity, and I want to lie here for a few minutes and simply feel the sun's rays all over my body. I can't have been lying here for more than a couple of minutes when Nora yells, "No Fucking Way!"

I raise my body up with my left elbow and cup my hand above my eyes so I can see Nora better. "Is everything okay?" I quietly ask.

"That fucker is actually engaged," she says, only this time she isn't yelling, the way she says it sounds more like she can't believe what she's saying.

"Who is?" I ask her.

"My ex-husband. We *just* got divorced. And now it's one of the very few engagement announcements in the Sunday Style section of *The Times*, so everyone is finding out about it at the same time as I am," Nora says. "God, he's such a dick!"

"I'm sorry," I offer. I'm not sure if it's the right thing to do, but it seems like Nora wants to talk or at least vent, so I pick up my towel and move it closer to her under the shade of the umbrella.

"I should have known this was coming," Nora says, sadly shaking her head.

I think a lot of young women my age would be out of their depth giving marriage, or ex-husband, advice to an older woman. However, I have had more than my fair share of experience with Danielle and both of my parents, so I decide to dive right in. "You can't blame yourself. I obviously don't know your ex-husband, but if he's anything like my dad, which I hope he isn't, but if he is, then he won't think or act logically, and the only person he'll ever think about is himself," I tell her.

"Thank you," Nora says. "I never met your dad. He and Danielle weren't together that long, and I've been a pretty crappy friend when it comes to staying in touch," Nora admits.

"Don't worry; you didn't miss out on much," I laugh, trying to make a joke of a situation that is anything but funny.

"In catching up with Danielle more recently, I did hear that he wasn't the best of husbands," Nora cautiously says.

"That's an understatement," I reply.

"But...Danielle is forever grateful to him for bringing you into her life. And of course, Abby too," Nora says.

It's silly, but I feel a prickle of tears at the back of my eyes as Nora mentions this. I know how important Danielle is to me but hearing that she's told someone else the feeling is reciprocated fills me with unexpected joy. Of course, I *know* this deep down, but sometimes I forget, and it's exactly what I needed to hear right now.

"That's why you need to go on more dates. Otherwise, you won't get to meet your Ted. Danielle wouldn't have met Ted if she had never married my dad," I remind her.

"Didn't they meet in the park or something?" Nora asks.

"I'm pretty sure there wasn't some ridiculous matchmaker involved."

"Okay, fine. They literally met on a bench in Central Park, which seems too implausible to be true, but I'm not sure you will be able to replicate that," I laugh.

Nora looks away for a minute, and I wonder if I said or did the wrong thing. When she looks back at me, all of the fury and passion from moments earlier is gone; now, she just looks miserable. "But Mason wasn't like that. He was far from perfect, but he used to be kind and smart and funny. He was the biggest supporter of my company for years," Nora says wistfully.

I don't think there is anything that I can add that would be useful at this point. I don't think that bashing him further would be helpful, and I already gave my attempt at humor, and that fell flat. Instead, I nod in a way that I hope conveys understanding or sympathy.

"I don't know when it all started to change. I guess it was when my business really started doing well, and I was traveling more and constantly in meetings. He started to resent all of it and to resent me," she says. It seems more like she's talking to herself than to me. "I don't think there was anything I could have done differently, or maybe that's not true, maybe I could have worked less," she says, trailing off.

"I know marriage is hard. Alright, I don't *actually* know that, but that's what everyone says and what you read in books and see in movies and on TV. I'm sure this is naïve, but I feel like if he's the right person, then he should be willing to support you no matter how successful you are and shouldn't resent you when you become some crazy billionaire," I say to

Nora, gesturing toward her with my hands to try to make my point.

Nora laughs, and I feel good that I could make her laugh. "You're probably right. Although I don't know what Danielle told you, I'm not a billionaire – just so we're clear," she smiles. "Okay, enough about me. Let's talk about you. Are you seeing anyone?" Nora asks.

"You know that I don't know anyone here. Other than Joel," I say.

"I meant back at Stanford. Is there someone there?" she asks.

I feel anxious for the first time in weeks as I think about the mess I left behind in Palo Alto. My instinct is to tell Nora that there's no one special and move on; however, I don't want to do that. Sharing with Nora is almost like sharing with a stranger. She doesn't know any of the people involved, and she barely knows me – I can finally get this off my chest, or at least get some of it off my chest, and there won't be any consequences.

"There was someone, but we broke up," I say tentatively.

"Is that a good or a bad thing?" Nora asks.

"It's complicated," I reply.

"Isn't it always?" she asks.

"I guess so. But I never imagined it would be *this* complicated," I say.

"How so?" Nora asks, fixing her grey eyes on me as she responds.

I sigh and readjust myself on the firm lounge cushion as if the story I'm about to share needs physical preparation as well. "I've known Alex since freshman year. We lived on the same hall that first year and there were a bunch of us that were really close. The eight of us did everything together; we ate and studied and drank together, and we would even crash in each other's rooms instead of walking ten feet down the hall," I say wistfully.

"I miss college," Nora says and smiles at me.

"Alex was actually pretty shy that year. We kissed once during freshman year at a party when we were both really drunk, but that was it. Then we were friends for the next two years, but we didn't live near each other on campus. We weren't in any of the same classes, so I barely saw him until right before senior year."

"And then what happened?" Nora asks.

I try not to let the current situation color my memory because the beginning was great. "We were both RA's senior year, you know, Residential Advisors? Which meant that we came back to campus for training a week before everyone else moved in so we could be settled to help the freshmen. Alex used to be a swimmer, but he hurt his shoulder, so he wasn't swimming his senior year, and he didn't want to live with all the swimmers if he wasn't on the team. We saw each other at RA training, and we basically started dating that week," I tell Nora. I try to remember how much fun we had during the fall quarter and how I had even started planning for our cross-country long-distance relationship. It's almost impossible now to believe that I felt that way, but I know that I did at the time.

"So, what happened?" Nora prods.

"Fall quarter was great. It was almost the perfect relationship, although it wasn't particularly physical, if you know what I mean," I tell Nora.

"I think I do," Nora replies.

"Anyhow, at first, it was kind of refreshing that he was taking things so slowly, so it didn't bother me too much. Then we both went home for the December break. I went to New York to spend Christmas with Danielle and Ted and the girls, and he went to Connecticut to see his family; then I think they went to St. Bart's for New Year's or something. Anyway, we both came back to school in January for the winter quarter, and things seemed different. He was weird," I say.

"Weird?" Nora questions.

"I know that isn't very descriptive. He started acting super possessive and jealous when I went anywhere without him or when he couldn't find me, even though he was barely interested in touching me. To make it worse, he was convinced that I was cheating on him with the TA from my Justice in Public Policy class," I say. There must be something about the way I say this last part because Nora raises her eyebrow slightly as if to inquire further.

"He wasn't entirely *wrong* to be suspicious, but I would never have even thought about it if things were going well. *And* nothing officially happened with Mateo until after I told Alex that I wanted to break up with him," I tell her. I still feel like I'm on shaky ground with my side of the story because of how things have turned out, but it seems important to stress that I wasn't totally to blame.

"The plot thickens," Nora says, but she gives me a reassuring smile. "So, you broke up, and then you dated your TA?" she asks.

"It wasn't quite that clean. Alex was being so crazy. I tried to talk to him about it first, but that didn't work, so then I just started avoiding him. That didn't work well either, and he got more upset. While that was happening, I was taking this amazing class with a new TA from Argentina – Mateo. I had a bit of a crush on him because he was so smart and funny and ridiculously hot. I went to his office hours more than I needed to, but it all felt harmless."

Nora has both of her eyebrows raised now, and although she can't possibly know how this story ends, I can tell that she has a good idea about many of the pieces.

"Alex and I had a fight, and I told him that I wanted to break up with him. He said that he didn't want to break up with me, and I still remember trying to explain to him that only one person needed to want the break-up for it to happen. I knew that we were over, and although I know I wasn't supposed to date a TA, especially the one that was teaching my class, Mateo and I started seeing each other," I tell Nora.

"How did Alex take it?" Nora asks.

"Since Mateo and I weren't supposed to be sleeping together, I didn't plan to tell him. We didn't plan to tell anyone. But we were stupid, and I brought Mateo back to my room one night," I say. I haven't said any of this out loud before. It's hard to feel great about my side of the story, even though I know it all made sense at the time.

"In the dorm?!" Nora asks, and it's clear that she knows what a dumb idea this was.

"I wasn't thinking," I say, shaking my head as I remember the details of the evening. "I had my own room, and Mateo was a grad student with a roommate off-campus, and we had almost gotten caught by his roommate several times, so this seemed like a better idea. But of course, that was the night that Alex decided to use his key to slip into my room in the middle of the night, and he walked in on Mateo and me," I say, hiding my head in my hands, unable to maintain eye contact with Nora.

"No way!" Nora screams. I'm sure she isn't actually delighted with my misfortune, but she does appear to be enjoying the retelling. I suppose it *is* quite amusing if you didn't have to live through it.

"It's true. My luck is just that bad. Alex flipped out. I tried to get him to calm down and to remind him that we had already broken up, so I could date whoever I wanted. However, it really went to hell when he recognized Mateo as my TA..." I say, trailing off.

"What did Alex do? What about Mateo?" Nora asks. She is clearly enraptured with my tale, and I feel slightly better that I was able to get her mind off her own troubles, even if it means revealing mine.

I try to focus on what Nora is asking, but I keep getting lost in my own thoughts. I picture Mateo looking much younger than his twenty-six years, running out of my dorm room with his jeans barely zipped, wearing his sweater inside-out, and carrying his loafers in his hand. Alex stayed behind and sat on my bed as if he were claiming his territory. I obviously hadn't told any of my friends about Mateo, and I had been too busy to talk to most of my friends, so no one even knew that Alex and I had broken up at that point – or at least that I had tried to break up with him. I think back to Alex's face when he told me what he wanted in order to keep him from telling my advisor and jeopardizing Mateo's grant and my acceptance to graduate school.

Alex explained that all I had to do was pretend like nothing had happened. We would go back to being a couple, and he would keep my secret. I protested that there was no way I was going to start having sex with him now, and I remember exactly what he said to me, "This is just about appearances." I couldn't fathom why it was so important to him that people thought we were still dating, but at the time, faking a relationship seemed like the path of least resistance.

I know that my initial intention was to tell Nora everything, but now that I've started talking, I don't think I can. I don't think I can even tell her about Alex's initial bargain, let alone what came after that. I don't want to leave Nora in suspense after giving her this much, but suddenly I'm worried that if I tell her anything else, she'll feel obligated to call Danielle. I've been thinking of her as a benevolent stranger, but I must remember the potentially disastrous connection.

"That was pretty much it for Mateo and me," I lie. "And Alex was pissed off for a long time. In fact, he's still kind of mad. Thankfully, he'll be working in New York next year, and I'll be back in California, so we'll have three thousand miles between us," I say.

"That's it?" Nora asks, sounding disappointed. "Where's Mateo now? Couldn't you date him now that you've graduated?" she asks.

"It didn't really work out," I tell her. This part is true, but what I don't say is the main reason it won't work out is that his wife just got her visa and will be joining him in Palo Alto.

Chapter 28

Nora

I stare into the full-length mirror and try to see myself as blind date number four will see me when I meet him for wine tasting in forty-five minutes. Zadie told me that his name is Bob, but I've decided to mentally keep track of them by number, especially at the rate of bad dates I've had so far.

I suppose it's not fair to classify the last two as bad; they just weren't good. Number two was a nice enough guy but painfully boring. Zadie wanted me to give him a second chance, but I couldn't endure another evening discussing black holes and deep space. He made it clear that although he makes a living as a tax attorney, his true passions are physics and astronomy.

Date number three had promise until we got to the dessert course. He was attractive, smart, and polite. I thought we had good chemistry, and I was looking forward to a second date until he burst into tears when I ordered the pistachio gelato. Apparently, pistachio is his ex-wife's favorite flavor, and merely the mention of it was enough to set him off. He confessed that he wasn't over her, and he shouldn't have let his friend set him up with a matchmaker.

Neither Eva nor Bridget would hear of it when I told them I wasn't going on any more dates. "What about three strikes, and you're out?" I asked Bridget, but she told me that didn't apply to my situation. So here I am, getting dressed up to meet another potential disaster. Instead, I could be reading by the pool or reviewing prospectuses for potential investment opportunities. Or I could be working on my next big idea for a multi-million-dollar company, which might be the best use of time, seeing as I've come up with zero new ideas since selling Limestreet Athletics.

If Bob sees what I'm seeing, he'll see a thirty-nine-year-old woman, who could pass for thirty-three or thirty-four unless he gets within a few centimeters of my face where the faint crow's feet and laugh lines are visible. He'll see shiny chestnut hair cascading over my shoulders and intense grey eyes highlighted with too much eyeliner and mascara for an afternoon date.

If he's like most men, Bob will notice my cleavage before he notices the rest of my outfit or anything else about my body. I stare at the plunging neckline of the pale-yellow sundress and wonder if it's too much for a first date. I've had this dress for years, and it's one of my favorite things to wear in the summer because of the way it highlights my tan. I bought the dress in Montauk several years ago at one of the local beach shops for thirty-five dollars. On the hanger, there's nothing remarkable about it. But the simplicity of it and the way that it fits me perfectly and reveals enough cleavage to be sexy without being slutty, makes it one of the best items in my closet. I grab a pair of strappy sandals and a small Prada clutch that has seen better days, and I'm ready to go.

* * *

I call Bridget from the car on my way to the date. It's a twenty-five-minute drive, and this seems like an efficient use of time and a good way to quiet my nerves.

Bridget picks up on the fourth ring. "Hey Nora, is everything okay?" she says upon answering.

"Yeah, of course, it's fine. I just called to say hi. I'm on my way to meet another blind date," I say, rolling my eyes, even though she can't see me.

"Okay. I have to put you on speakerphone. It's dinner time here," she says.

I glimpse the clock on the dashboard and note that it seems way too early for dinner, but thankfully I catch myself before saying anything – she must mean dinner for the kids. "Why don't you use the Air Pods I sent you?" I ask her.

"I can never seem to find them when I need them," she says, sounding flustered.

"I put mine right on the counter with my keys," I offer.

"I don't think my counter looks like your counter," she retorts. I can't remember her ever snapping at me before.

"Got it," I say, deciding to change the subject. "Have you thought any more about coming up to visit? Or about me coming to visit you?" I ask.

"Not really," Bridget retorts. "I just don't think it's going to work with the kids," she says. As if Quinn can read the room, she starts wailing in the distance.

"Maybe Patrick could watch the kids for a weekend, and you could come by yourself?" I suggest.

"Nora. You just don't get it!" she explodes. "You have no idea what my life is like. And until a few months ago, you never even hinted at visiting or being involved or seeing your nieces. So, forgive me if I'm not bending over backward to try and make this work," she yells.

I am too stunned to respond. I focus on the car in front of me so I don't get in an accident and wait to see if Bridget is going to say anything else. When there has been a prolonged period of silence, minus Quinn's whimpering in the background, I decide to speak. "I had no idea you felt this way," I begin.

Bridget quickly cuts me off. "I'm sorry. I shouldn't have gotten so upset. I must be having an off day," she offers.

"It sounds like there's a lot more to it than that," I say. "I'm about to meet this blind date. Can I call you later so we can talk?" I ask.

"Seriously, don't worry about it," Bridget says. "I just kind of lost it a little bit. It's fine," she says.

"I want to talk about this. I don't think I've been looking at things from your perspective. I just want to give this the attention it deserves," I say seriously.

"Go have fun on your date. Have a few drinks for me! You deserve to meet a new guy and get over Mason, right?" she says, fighting to get back her usual light tone.

"Seriously, I want to call you later tonight or tomorrow – you tell me what works best for you," I say.

"You can call when you have a chance, but don't worry about it. I don't know what came over me. I must just be tired. Sleep deprivation and all that. Have a great time on your date!" Bridget says as she hangs up the phone.

I've still got about ten minutes to drive, and I contemplate turning around and going home. I also contemplate driving straight to Bridget's house to see if we can figure things out in person, but that seems to be exactly what Bridget doesn't want me to do. I need some time to absorb what she said and think about how much truth is behind it. The last place I want to be while this is on my mind is on a blind date, but I promised Zadie, and more importantly, I promised Bridget, so it seems like the least I can do right now.

We are meeting at a vineyard on the North Fork for a sunset wine tasting. My first reaction to the location was that it was a cheesy first-date option and lacked originality. After thinking it over, I decided to cut my date some slack. It can't be easy to think of unique ideas for dates, and wine-tasting may not be original, but it's popular, and it creates immediate interaction and conversation. I quickly chastise myself for my hasty judgment.

As I pull into the vineyard's valet parking zone, I try to remember what Zadie told me about Bob. She wanted to make sure that I was comfortable being matched with someone "well-known," although she was somewhat mysterious when I asked for more information on his potential celebrity status. Zadie was quick to remind me that I'm also "well-known," but I challenged her on this assumption. Although my name and business seem to be common knowledge, the average person couldn't pick me out of a line-up, so I have no problem walking down the street like anyone else. I got the sense that Bob might be more recognizable, but Zadie was tight-lipped with the details.

It's a beautiful late-July day, and even though it's almost five in the afternoon, it will be hours before the sun sets. The vineyard's back veranda overlooks acres of cabernet sauvignon grapes growing in meticulous rows for as far as the eye can see. I scan the crowd and see happy faces and young, lithe bodies gathered around the high-top tables. It reminds me of a magazine ad I saw recently for one of those new hard seltzers, but instead of inspiring me to join the party, it makes me feel old and single, and I desperately want to run back to the comfort of my couch. There doesn't appear to be anyone here under the age of thirty, let alone my blind date, Bob, who is in his late forties, according to Zadie. And then a man at the bar turns around, and I recognize Bob immediately. I'm sure everyone here has already recognized Bob since his picture was splashed all over the papers last weekend with rumors of his potential bid for governor. I start walking toward the bar and silently curse Zadie for casually throwing around "well-known" when Bob Elverson is a household name.

Bob stands up as I approach the bar and flashes me the gleaming white smile I've seen many times before, but never up close and personal. It's clear he knows I'm his date - either because Zadie gave him more information about *me* or because he deduced that I was the only person in here remotely near his age.

"It's great to meet you, Nora. I'm a big fan," Bob says as he shakes my hand and then pulls me in for a rough kiss on the cheek.

"You as well," I reply. I'm taken aback by his greeting and unsure how to reply. I don't know that I should describe myself as a "fan" of his, but it seems rude not to after his declaration. His background is certainly impressive. Anyone who can be called a mogul before the age of fifty, especially someone who started off at New York City public schools in the mid-seventies with a single mom in public housing, deserves immense credit. However, based on the bits and pieces I've seen in the news recently, I'm not sure how much I'm actually going to like Bob.

"Would you like a glass of wine?" Bob asks.

"Don't we have to wait for the official tasting to begin?" I chide.

"I decided it was easier not to do a tasting. We'll just order something, and if we don't like it, we can order something else. We don't have to waste our time with those tiny glasses and bullshit about the bouquet or notes of cedar or complex aromas," he grins.

Only an hour ago, I was annoyed at the prospect of having to find the right vocabulary words to accurately describe wine, but now that Bob unilaterally made the decision to cancel the tasting, I'm even more pissed off. I try to shake it off because it seems like a trivial thing to be annoyed about, and I told myself and Eva that I would give this a real shot.

"In that case, I'd love a glass of rose′," I reply, giving my best attempt at sounding breezy.

"The rose´ here isn't very good, I'm going to get you a glass of the Riesling," Bob says presumptively, signaling to the bartender before I have a chance to respond.

I hate Riesling. I do my best to smile at Bob and watch him sip from a glass of red wine while we wait for the bartender to pour mine. I wonder why he didn't order me a glass of whatever it is that he's drinking – it has to be better than Riesling! The bartender puts the full glass of sunny yellow liquid in front of me, and Bob raises his wine and indicates that I should do the same.

"To matchmaking," Bob says.

I offer a half-smile and clink my glass against his, but before I can take a sip of my vile drink, Bob continues his toast. "The only safe way to date anymore for people like us, am I right?" he laughs.

"I guess so," I reply half-heartedly. I take a sip of my wine, and just as I expected, it's disgusting. It's way too sweet, and it tastes and smells like flowers.

"I told you that you'd like that," Bob says, completely oblivious to my reaction. "All the girls like Riesling. It's a bit like a wine cooler, am I right?" he says and then laughs at his own dumb joke.

"What's going to be next, after sports bras?" Bob asks.

"What do you mean?" I ask him.

"You had that little company with all of the sports bras, and you just sold that, so what are you going to do next? Maybe try your hand with some sexier lingerie? I've got nothing against sports bras, but they aren't exactly the most flattering, am I right?" Bob chuckles.

My cheeks are burning with anger as I watch him laugh. I

ran the most popular women's athletic clothing company in the whole country! Limestreet Athletics is a household name because of me, and it is so much more than sports bras! Obviously, Limestreet *does* make the best sports bras in the world, I think to myself, but that's hardly the point.

My instinct is to throw this sweet wine in Bob's face and walk out, but I don't want to make a scene. Bob is famous enough that anything we do will likely be photographed and end up on *Page Six* tomorrow and a multitude of websites within a couple of hours. I'm mildly worried about upsetting Zadie and Eva, but I'm more concerned about what Bridget will think.

I remind myself that I've dealt with plenty of guys like Bob before, and I can handle him as well. I will end this date quickly without making a scene.

"I'm not sure lingerie will be my next move, but I'll definitely keep you in the loop," I say, giving him a smile as sweet as my wine. "Speaking of next moves, you've got some exciting things coming up, don't you?" I ask him.

"Those are just rumors," Bob says playfully, but I can tell from the glint in his eye that he wants to talk about it.

"You can tell me," I say conspiratorially.

"It's still early, but the numbers look like I would be a strong candidate," he says.

"Mm-hmm," I say.

"It's time to get some control back in New York," he says.

"What do you mean?" I ask innocently. I bought Bob's book at an airport news shop a few years ago, and assuming the memoir is true, I already know more about him than I knew about Mason after two months of dating. He's been more guarded in recent interviews, but if the shit from his book was accurate, I can wrap this up pretty quickly.

"The liberal elite have completely lost control of this state. New Yorkers who make a lot of money are tired of paying for all of the deadbeats who are too lazy to work. If you want a handout, you should move somewhere else. I'm going to lower taxes for the people who are working hard and really making the economy run, so they don't have to watch their hard-earned money go to those who can't be bothered to get a good job or a place to live," Bob says excitedly. It is easy to imagine him giving his speeches at rich white men's clubs across the state and getting privileged men all fired up. The press has already said that Bob could fund the campaign entirely from his own bank account, and although I don't know exactly how much a gubernatorial campaign costs to run, I've got to imagine Bob is first in line to protect his billions above all else.

"You know I'm on the board of The Bowery Mission, right?" I ask Bob.

"I don't think I knew that," Bob says, looking slightly uncomfortable.

"I started off volunteering there on the occasional weekend, but eventually I donated *so* much money that they gave me a seat on the board," I tell him and give him a coy grin,

"Hmm," Bob says through tight lips. "Good tax deduction, I guess," he says and raises his glass as if to toast me with his clever quip.

I don't return his toast, but I do take a hearty drink from my glass of wine before I remember that it's full of alcoholic grape juice, and I have to stop myself from spitting it back into the glass.

"That's another thing I'm going to fix once I'm elected," Bob says. "Charitable tax deductions," he continues as if I should have easily been able to follow his train of thought.

"What would you fix about them?" I question him.

"I think the definition of charity is simply too narrow," Bob says, using air quotes when he says the word "charity."

"I've never noticed that," I reply.

"I stroke a check for ten million dollars to the Metropolitan Opera, and that's tax-deductible, right?" Bob asks.

"Right..." I reply cautiously, feeling like I'm about to get caught in a trap.

"But let's say I don't give a shit about opera, and I want to support the New York Yankees. I write them a check for ten million, and I don't get shit," Bob says, looking at me for agreement.

"The Yankees aren't a non-profit organization," I reply. This seems so obvious that I can't believe I need to say it out loud.

"That's exactly what I'm saying!" Bob says and slaps his hand on the bar as if I've just made his point for him. "It's ridiculous that you don't get a tax credit for supporting great organizations like the Yankees, just because they want to make a little money," Bob explains.

I'm not sure there is a way to respond to him. We clearly have nothing in common, and this guy is a total scumbag, but it's not like he's going to have a change of heart based on anything I say to him – it's pointless to engage. I try another tactic instead while I decide how best to excuse myself *and* fire Zadie before I get to the car.

"Can the governor change the tax laws?" I ask him, looking as skeptical as I feel.

"Clearly not the federal tax laws," he says as if I'm the one who's being ridiculous. "But state tax laws will be under my jurisdiction," he says, and then unbelievably, he adds the words, "I think."

"Thanks for the wine," I say with an almost imperceptible eye roll. "But I think we both know that this is not going to work," I say bluntly.

"What are you talking about?" Bob asks.

"The fact that you don't know what I'm talking about says so much," I say to him, and I grab my bag and slide gracefully off my barstool.

"I could be a huge help to you. You don't know what you're giving up," Bob says angrily as I start to walk away.

"Oh, I think I do," I mutter to myself and walk out of the vineyard without even turning around.

Chapter 29

Courtney

"You missed a great party last night," Alyssa says when I walk out onto the patio the next morning and find her doing poolside yoga.

"I'm not so sure about that," I reply.

"What do you mean?" she asks. She raises her head from the downward dog position to catch my eye.

"I got home while the party was still happening, and I don't think it was so great," I say to her. During my restless night on the living room sofa, I kept trying to figure out how I should bring this up. I know that at some point in the early hours of the morning, I figured out the perfect thing to say, but of course, I've forgotten it now.

Alyssa unfolds her limber frame and rises to her full height with a look of bewilderment on her face. "What are you talking about?"

"You guys were all really high when I got home. I did come in and say hi, but you seemed really out of it," I say.

"Oh right, now I remember," Alyssa says as if thinking back on our encounter.

"Then I went to my room to go to sleep, and there were people having sex on my bed!" I try to keep the emotion out of my voice, but it's impossible. I'm just as angry as I was last night as I think back to the naked couple in my sheets.

Of all the reactions I expected, I definitely didn't expect this. "Oh my God, who was it?" Alyssa asks, clapping her hands together excitedly.

"I have no idea! And that's not the point. They were fucking in my bed! That's disgusting!" I yell at her.

"Oh, calm down; I'll make sure Linda washes your sheets today," Alyssa says casually. "Don't tell me that you and *Preston* never did it in some stranger's room during a party," she chides.

Hearing his name in her mouth makes me irrationally angry. It shouldn't mean anything, but something about the way she says his name and references our past sex life really pisses me off. "Of course not," I reply childishly.

I turn to walk away, even though I know I should try and smooth things over with Alyssa since we still have over a month left of the summer together. When I'm mostly out of earshot, I swear I hear her mumble, "That must have been when he was with someone else."

"What did you say?" I ask her.

"Nothing," Alyssa says, giving me the same cherubic smile that I've seen her use on countless guys this summer to get what she wants.

* * *

The next few days pass in awkward slow motion. Although Alyssa and I haven't been particularly close this summer, until a few days ago, we had been peacefully co-existing, and I think she thought I was having a great time. Now I am trying my best to avoid her, and since it's her house, it only seems fair that I spend most of my time in my room. I even took an Uber last night back and forth to work and then again this morning when I went to play basketball because I didn't want to have to ask her for the car keys.

I had no plans to run into Tucker at the courts, but I wasn't disappointed when he showed up shortly after I arrived. It was fun to have someone to shoot around with, as well as take my mind off my current predicament with Alyssa. There was a modicum of half-hearted flirting during our workout, but it's no surprise that someone like Tucker wouldn't be single for long, and during one of our water breaks, he told me about a dancer he had just started dating.

My muscles ache in a gratifying way on the Uber ride back to Alyssa's house. With a clear head and a renewed sense of purpose, I decide that I'm going to try to clear the air with Alyssa today and finally call Preston and be honest about my feelings. I'm tired of pretending that I'm okay with our breakup; I know that it will be hard to have a long-distance relationship, but I'd rather try to make it work than simply give up on the love of my life.

Excitedly I dial Preston's number and wait for him to pick up the phone. It rings five times and then goes to voicemail. Instead of hearing his deep voice, I hear the computerized message telling me that the person at this phone number is unavailable to answer the phone. I hang up and try again, but when I get the same recording, I leave a quick message for him to call me back and accept that there won't be instant gratification.

I can't find Alyssa when I get home, which means that the second part of my plan will also have to wait. Slightly deflated, I resolve to go to the beach and swim in the ocean. I've been in East Hampton for over a month, living on a private beach, and I've only been in the water a handful of times. I know that when I'm sitting in law school lectures this fall, I will be furious with my former self for not taking advantage of this living situation. With that in mind, I throw on a suit and grab a towel and beach bag, and head to the beach.

As soon as I spread my towel on the sand and grab my book and water bottle out of my bag, I realize that I forgot my phone back at the house. It's only a four-minute walk, and it would be easy to go back and grab it, but it seems like the perfect opportunity to unplug for a couple of hours.

* * *

After a chilly swim in the ocean and a fantastic nap on the warm sand, I feel calm and relaxed. As I make the short walk back to the house, I hope that Alyssa is home so we can get this conversation out of the way and go back to the normal level of awkwardness we had a few days ago.

My phone is sitting on the kitchen island, which must be right where I left it. On the lock screen, I see two missed calls from Preston but no voicemails. When I open the phone app, I notice that Preston is also listed under recent calls, and the timestamp is from forty minutes ago when I was at the beach. I immediately call him back and am comforted when he picks up after the first ring, but instantly on edge when I hear his tone. "What is it?" he asks angrily.

"Hey! I was just calling to talk. Do you have a minute?" I ask him.

"Not really," he says sharply.

"Is everything okay?" I ask. "We can talk later," I offer.

"I don't think there's any need for that," Preston says snidely.

"What's the matter?" I ask him. I'm confused by his angry tone and racking my brain to try to figure out the cause of it.

"I've got to go," Preston says, and then the line goes dead.

I'm just staring at the phone in my hand as if the blank screen can answer my questions when Alyssa walks into the kitchen. "Everything okay?" she asks in an upbeat tone.

"No. Not at all," I reply. "That was Preston, and he was acting so weird; I have no idea what just happened," I say to her.

"Huh," Alyssa says and shrugs her shoulders as she makes her way over to the fridge to grab a green bottle of Perrier.

I've virtually forgotten about our fight, and it seems that she might have as well because she's lost all of her hostility from the previous few days. "Did you talk to him by any chance?" I ask her. I know it seems crazy, but I'm trying to make sense of the recent call when I was at the beach, and this feels like the logical conclusion.

"Oh yeah, your phone was ringing earlier, and I picked it up," Alyssa says as if this is a totally normal thing to do.

"Did you talk to Preston?" I demand.

"Yeah, we chatted for a bit," she says while sipping her Perrier.

"What did you talk about? Was he upset?" I ask her, trying to keep my temper under control.

"Not that I can remember," she says nonchalantly while she dumps the remaining half of her sparkling water into the sink and leaves the bottle on the counter for Linda to recycle.

"Oh wait, he did mention something. Let me think if I can remember what it was," Alyssa says. While she is trying to recall this piece of information, she curls and uncurls a lock of hair around her finger, and it takes an insane amount of willpower not to completely lose it.

"Oh right, now I remember," she says casually. "He said that he has a few days off next week, and he was thinking about coming to visit, but he changed his mind," she tells me.

"What? Why would he say that? Is that literally what he said?" I throw all of these questions at her at once, trying to wrap my mind around Preston's angry tone and this bizarre piece of news.

"I don't know," Alyssa says, innocently shrugging her shoulders and jutting out her lower lip as if this is just as confusing to her. Something doesn't make sense, but I can't figure out what it is. The person I would turn to in this type of situation is Preston, and he's made it quite clear that he doesn't want to talk to me.

"I'm going to meet a few of the girls to go shopping; I'll see you later," Alyssa calls out. She walks past me toward the garage, but I barely notice her. I'm still trying to figure out what the hell just happened and what I can possibly do about it.

Chapter 30

Megan

I'm getting out of the shower when my phone starts vibrating on the bathroom counter, and out of habit, I lunge for it. Danielle makes fun of me for bringing my phone with me everywhere I go, and I suppose that this proves her point. Although I didn't bring it *in* the shower with me, so technically, I was unreachable for approximately eight minutes.

Courtney: Are you free? I've had a crappy few days - would it be okay if I came over?

I'm overly excited to receive this text because it feels like we've jumped a step or two in our friendship, and this makes me unreasonably happy. I miss Hope and my other close friends from school, and I miss how we were so entwined in each other's lives that I would send and receive texts like this multiple times a week. It feels like forever since I've been pulled in for some good drama (other than with Nora). I'm not happy that Courtney has had a crappy week, but I'm delighted to feel needed!

MEGAN: OF COURSE! COME OVER NOW

COURTNEY: LET ME PACK MY WORK STUFF AND CALL AN UBER – I HAVE TO BE AT DOCKERS AT FIVE

MEGAN: UBER? CAN'T YOU USE ONE OF ALYSSA'S CARS?

COURTNEY: LONG STORY – I'LL SEE YOU SOON

* * *

Courtney arrives an hour later, and I'm waiting for her out front. It's impossible to tell tone from text messages, and it wasn't clear what made her week so bad or what might have happened with Alyssa or with her car. I want to be there to greet her in case she's in bad shape. From what I know of her, she seems pretty strong and not the kind of person who would have epic meltdowns (like Hope) and need assistance with basic daily functions, but it's better to be prepared.

Courtney exits the black suburban carrying a purple backpack with a Northwestern basketball logo, and other than looking tired, she looks fine. "Thanks for letting me come over like this," she calls out as she slams the door of the oversized SUV.

"Of course!" I quickly reply. "Do you want a drink?" I offer.

"That would be great," she says, and she follows me down the sandy path to the property's back gate.

Once we are settled on the deck with chilled glasses of my best attempt at margaritas, Courtney relaxes and asks if

I'm ready to hear about the latest issues at Alyssa's house. I'm beyond curious at this point and wonder if the buildup will be worth it, but I quickly find out that it is.

"They were having sex in your bed?!" I practically shout at her after Courtney finishes telling me about the party from the other night.

"Exactly! That's the kind of reaction I would expect someone to have. But Alyssa acted like I was the one blowing things out of proportion, and then things were weird for days between us," she says. "It almost seemed back to normal today until Preston called..." she trails off.

Courtney has mentioned Preston briefly, but I don't know much about him or their relationship. I know they dated in college and know he is playing in the NFL or trying to play in the NFL, and he lives in Denver, but I don't know much else. "What did he say?" I ask.

"That's the crazy part! He called, and Alyssa picked up my phone, and then when I called back, he wouldn't even talk to me!" Courtney exclaims, gesturing wildly with her hands. "I hadn't talked to Preston for a week or so, and the last time we talked, it was strained, but I decided to call him this morning. I wanted to tell him that I was tired of pretending that I didn't miss him," she says.

"I hate to make you go through the whole thing, but I feel like I won't be any help if I don't have at least a little more background on you guys," I say to her, hoping that it isn't awkward to request their dating history in the middle of Courtney's story.

"Of course," Courtney says. She takes a long drink from her margarita and then puts the sweaty tumbler on the table and continues talking. "Preston was one of my best friends at school freshman year. I had a crush on him but pretended that I didn't because he dated a lot of girls, and I thought he wouldn't be interested in me. Then we got together in the middle of my sophomore year, and it was everything I thought it would be, or actually even better than I thought it would be. He was the best boyfriend, and we had the perfect balance of friendship and dating, and he got along really well with my family. Well, with my new family. I don't know if I told you about my sisters yet, but that's a whole other story for another time," Courtney laughs.

"He sounds perfect," I tell her. I think briefly of my high school boyfriend Ryan and how I thought he was perfect at the time. I've spent the past four years at Stanford dating a string of mediocre guys until I met Mateo. I thought he could be "the one," but that was before I found out that he is married. I attempt to put this out of my mind and focus on Courtney's issues.

"I honestly thought that we would get married someday, which must sound so stupid," Courtney says, and her eyes look like she might cry, but she rubs them quickly with the back of her hand and continues her story. "When he got drafted, and I got into law school in New York, we kept pushing off the discussion about what we would do after graduation. I kind of assumed that we would stay together, even though we both made comments about needing to 'figure things out,'" Courtney says, making air quotes with her fingers.

"What happened?" I ask although it seems pretty clear that they *didn't* stay together after graduation.

"We finally decided to sit down and talk about it right before graduation. We went to our favorite spot on campus by the library, and I thought we were going to talk about logistics of visits and FaceTiming while we were apart, and instead, we ended up breaking up!" Courtney cries.

"He broke up with you?" I question.

"Yes. No. I honestly don't know what happened – it all happened so quickly. I thought we were going to talk about one thing, and then he started asking if long-distance relationships made sense, and I got really upset and told him what he wanted to hear and agreed that we should break up," Courtney tells me.

"So, *you* broke up with *him*?" I ask her.

"No!" she says, shaking her head vehemently. "Well, I mean not exactly. It was "mutual," I think," she says, curving her fingers into air quotes again. "Even if I was the one who actually said the words, I only did it because he was about to say it, and it was easier than letting him do it," she says. By the way, she's biting her lip; it looks like she doesn't completely believe what she's saying.

I don't know her well enough to push her on this, and I certainly don't know anything about her relationship with Preston, so instead, I take another drink from my sugary margarita and wait for Courtney to continue.

"This just makes everything even more confusing," Courtney cries.

"What do you mean?" I ask her.

"Remember what I was telling you about before? I called Preston today because I was ready, to be honest with him. We've been texting off and on all summer, and I've been pretending that I'm happy being single and that I don't miss him, but clearly, I'm not. Then he called today while I was at the beach, but I left my phone at the house. Alyssa picked up my phone and talked to him, and then when I called him back, he said he didn't want to talk to me," Courtney says.

"Why did Alyssa pick up your phone?" I ask.

"I have no idea. It's weird. I haven't even stopped to think about how weird that is," she says.

"What did she say to him?" I demand. I'm now completely absorbed in this triangle.

"I have no idea! The only thing she told me is that Preston said he was going to come to visit for a few days, and then he changed his mind," Courtney says.

"What? Why would he tell her that? That doesn't make any sense," I reply. A few minutes ago, I didn't know anything about Preston, and now I'm secure in my beliefs about things he would or would not do.

"I know — none of it makes any sense! And Alyssa was being so weird and smug. I have no idea what's going on," Courtney moans.

"I'm so sorry," I tell her because that's all I can think to say at this point.

Courtney leans back in her lounge chair, and I do the same. We sit in companionable silence for a couple of minutes – I can only imagine what's going through her head, but my thoughts are jumbled between two very different places. The first is trying to understand Alyssa's motives, and the second is reassuring myself that the guy I saw on Dune Road this morning couldn't possibly have been Alex. Before my thoughts can get any more muddled, they are interrupted by Nora's cheerful voice. "Hi! Am I interrupting?" Nora asks as she pokes her head out of the sliding glass door.

"Oh my God! Of course not. This is *your* house!" I exclaim. "Do you want *us* to move?" I ask, sensing my cheeks blush. Suddenly I feel like I've gotten a bit too comfortable and should remember that I am lucky to be a guest here.

"Don't be silly," Nora says. "Can I join you?" She walks out onto the deck in a beautiful green silk kimono-style cover-up that is tasteful and revealing at the same time. It would look ridiculous on me, but it looks perfect on her.

"Hi, I'm Nora," she says, flashing Courtney a wave of her manicured hand.

"I'm Courtney," Courtney replies. "Your house is beautiful. The view is amazing!" she adds.

"Thank you," Nora says. "We bought the property years ago and spent a long time building this place. Who knew the house would be the only thing that met my expectations," she says while looking longingly at the sun glimmering off the waves of the Atlantic Ocean.

The three of us now sit in silence and look out over the dunes. There wasn't anything obviously inflammatory about Nora's comment, but I think we all know what she was alluding to, and now I'm not sure how to respond. I never mentioned anything to Courtney about Nora's background, but Courtney knew exactly who Nora was when I told her where I was staying. She knew about the public divorce, Nora's ex-husband's quick rebound, and the recent sale of Limestreet Athletics. As the common link between the two other women, I'm guessing that it is my role to keep the conversation going, although I'm not sure where to go on the heels of Nora's awkward comment and Courtney's puzzling roommate drama.

Thankfully, Courtney breaks the silence. "I should probably start getting ready for work," she says.

"You work at Dockers, right?" Nora asks.

"Yes. Just as a hostess a few days a week," she replies.

"How do you like it?" Nora asks.

"It's fine. It's better than going out to parties with my roommate," Courtney says. Understandably, Nora gives her a puzzled glance causing Courtney to expound on her answer. "I didn't know my roommate quite as well as I thought I did. We don't really like to do the same types of things or like the same people, but I didn't realize that until I got here for the summer," Courtney says.

"Good thing you met Megan," Nora adds.

"Exactly!" Courtney smiles. "Is there somewhere I can change?" she asks, looking in my direction.

"Sure, you can change in my room. It's over this way," I tell her, pointing toward the guest house on the side of the deck.

"I'll let you get ready. It was nice meeting you," Nora calls out. "Feel free to come over anytime," she adds.

"Thanks so much!" Courtney gushes.

"Nora is so nice," Courtney calls out from my bathroom while she is changing into her clothes for work.

"She is," I agree. "I didn't even see her the first couple of weeks that I was here, but since then, she's been great. I'm not sure I totally *get* her, but I definitely feel lucky that I ended up living here this summer," I say.

"You should! You could be living with Alyssa, and I

promise you don't want that," she says. Courtney comes out of the bathroom dressed in a short white sundress that shows off her tan and makes her legs look even longer than they already are. "Does this look okay?" Courtney asks.

"Yeah, it looks great," I tell her and nod my head effusively. "What are you going to do about Preston? And Alyssa?" I ask her, following up on our conversation from earlier.

"I honestly have no idea. I have to get to work now, so at least that will take my mind off it for a few hours. Are you free later? Do you want to come by the bar and help me try to figure out what's going on with my ex-boyfriend and my crazy roommate?" Courtney laughs, but she has a pained look on her face.

"Of course," I reply.

I contemplate how to spend the rest of the time before I meet Courtney at the bar, and I don't come up with many exciting options. I'm getting hungry, so I should figure out what I'm going to do for dinner. I don't have much in the way of groceries, and even if I did, I'm not very good at doing much other than boiling water, making toast, and frying eggs. I never realized how much I took the dining hall for granted at school. The food wasn't amazing, but it wasn't bad, and most importantly, it was always available, and all I had to do was show up! Suddenly I remember that there's still some leftover pizza in the fridge. I'm not sure if there is a limit to the number of times I can eat pizza in one week or how long pizza should be kept in the fridge, but neither seems that important.

After I wash my solitary plate and cup, I decide to call Hope and see what she's been up to – she is always a good source of interesting stories and good gossip. Just as I'm about to call, a text from Joel pops up on my screen.

Joel: What was the Greene girl's score on her last practice test? Please send it to me ASAP.

Megan: hello to you too

Joel: What does that mean?

Megan: sorry – nothing – let me check her score – one sec

Joel: Do you have it?

Megan: I'm looking – hold on – what are you doing later?

Joel: I'm working on the app tonight

Megan: I'm going to Dockers – that girl Courtney is working tonight

Joel: I'm sending my report to the Greenes right now, and I want to make sure that it has the most accurate information

Megan: omg hold on

Joel: Were the new geometry test tips helpful at yesterday's session?

Megan: one thing at a time – don't you want me to find the test score?

Joel: How long can it take to find a test score?

Megan: If you want the truth, I forgot my password on the site and had to reset it...

Joel: Are you serious? You use the test site

EVERY DAY. HOW COULD YOU POSSIBLY FORGET YOUR PASSWORD?

MEGAN: IT HAPPENS. WE CAN'T ALL BE PERFECT 😜

JOEL: PLEASE EMAIL ME THE TEST SCORE ASAP. I HAVE TO GO NOW.

I can picture Joel closing down the messaging app and putting his phone face down on a table in front of him. I know that it's hard to get a tone of voice through text messaging. Even in person, Joel isn't the best with tone, but still, he's the one who initiated the conversation, and *I* was just trying to liven things up a little bit. I shake my head in annoyance and use my newly reset password to access the test prep site. I know Joel asked for an email, but it's just because he wanted to "hang up" on me.

MEGAN: LATEST ACT SCORE WAS 33

I wait a few minutes to see if he'll respond, but the message isn't marked as read, and the three little dots don't appear. "Screw it!" I say out loud, even though there is no one around to hear me, and I put down my phone as well. I'm no longer in the mood to call Hope; maybe I should get dressed and go over to Dockers a little bit early. Courtney will still be working, but I can drink at the bar while I wait for her and hope that tonight is the night a cute, smart, *single* guy decides to come to the bar.

* * *

The tables at the restaurant look busy when I arrive, but there are only two other people at the bar. It's two women in their late forties or early fifties, and they are deep in conversation and also into their martinis. I don't think they even notice my arrival, but I take a seat at the opposite end of the bar to give them privacy. I order a glass of the Cakebread Sauvignon Blanc because I recognize it immediately as something that Danielle likes to order, and that makes the decision easy.

I drink the first glass way too quickly and realize why Danielle likes this wine. When the bartender comes back, I order a glass of ice water along with a second glass of wine and promise to pace myself as I wait for Courtney's shift to end.

Forty-five minutes roll by, and I've slowed my pace, but not before I manage to achieve a very pleasant buzz. Or, if I'm being honest, it's a bit more than a buzz. Courtney stopped by several times to apologize for making me wait, and I've assured her that I am genuinely having a good time. This is the most relaxed I've felt in months, and it's not like I have anything else to do right now. The bartender asks if I want another glass of wine. I can't be sure if I've had four or five glasses at this point (I think it's only been four), but in either case, I decline the offer and decide to go outside to the now-empty picnic tables to get some fresh air. A few hours ago, these tables were packed with tourists and locals eating lobster rolls from the Dockers' food truck while watching a picturesque sunset over Shinnecock Bay. But now that it's late and even the main restaurant and bar are getting close to closing, the outdoor area is deserted. The only sound is the din of conversation floating over from the remaining diners, and the only light is the glow from the security lights in the parking lot mixed with the glimmer from the waning moon.

I feel warm and fuzzy from the wine and decide to have a

seat in one of the Adirondack chairs overlooking the bay, even though at this hour, all I can see is inky black liquid. I'm lost in my muddled thoughts when I feel a hand on my shoulder, and a voice says, "Don't be scared. It's just me – please hear me out."

My heart practically jumps out of my chest, and the only thing I want to do is call for help, but the scream gets caught in my throat. I try to get to my feet, but my legs are too shaky. I'm not sure if it's from the wine or nerves, but I'm unable to steady myself. I've heard that in situations like this, the body is supposed to react with excessive amounts of adrenaline, and people can lift massive amounts of weight or run at tremendous speeds. It seems that my body did not get the memo, and it is completely failing me.

"What do you want from me? How did you know I was here?" I ask, trying to hide the panic in my voice.

"I only want to talk to you," Alex says.

"You followed me across the country for a quick little chat?" I ask with disbelief.

"No. Things have gotten out of control. It isn't supposed to be like this. Just hear me out," Alex says.

"I don't think so," I reply. Suddenly, my body finds the strength and reaction time it was missing moments ago, and I jump to my feet and start running back to the restaurant.

Alex catches up as we approach the parking lot and reaches for my upper arm. He's barely touching me, but just the shock of his hand on me makes me scream, "Get away from me!"

"Megan, please, let me explain," Alex says.

Before I can respond, and with Alex's hand still on my

upper arm, I see two figures walking toward us from the restaurant. As they make their way into the beam of the restaurant's outdoor light, I see that it's Courtney and Joel, and they seem to see me at the same time.

"Megan, are you okay?" Courtney yells to me. Simultaneously, Joel yells, "Get your fucking hands off of her," in a voice that sounds nothing like the socially awkward genius I've worked with the past few weeks.

"We're fine here. This is between Megan and me," Alex calls back to them. To me, he says, "Just come with me, and we can talk about this and figure it all out."

He's still barely holding on to me, but instead of pulling my arm away, I'm so flustered that I yell, "Alex, let go of me."

Before I know what's happening, Joel is right beside me. I hadn't properly registered his size until right now. He seemed smaller somehow when he was talking about coding or app programming, but now that he's inserted himself between Alex and me, it's clear that he's got several inches on Alex, and he's much broader as well. Apparently, Alex has also done this calculation because he seems to take a small step backward.

"This isn't any of your business," Alex says again to Joel.

"Megan doesn't want to be here with you, so you've made it my business," Joel says tersely.

"I just need to talk to her for a few minutes," Alex pleads, sounding desperate. His voice catches on the last word, and I begin to feel bad for him, but I'm so confused and upset by his sudden appearance and by this confrontation that I don't know what to think.

The next thing I know, Joel's fist flies through the air and lands squarely on Alex's nose, making a nauseating crack. Alex screams and releases my arm as both of his hands instinctively fly to his face, although the damage is already done. "You broke my nose," Alex screams.

Joel looks more surprised than Alex as if it wasn't *his* fist that caused the damage. Joel stares at me and Courtney and motions for us to walk up the short path back to the restaurant. I can't even begin to process what just happened, and the questions are popping up too quickly to keep track of. How did Alex find me here? What does he want? Why was Joel here? What am I supposed to do now?

Courtney runs the last few steps to me and envelops me in a hug. "Are you okay?" she asks in a shaky voice. "Who was that guy?"

Before I can answer her, we all hear Alex yell, "Shit!" and we turn at the same time to see him fall backward when his foot gets caught on the leg of one of the picnic benches. Then there is a sickening thud as the back of his head hits the table, and he slumps to the ground.

Chapter 31

Courtney

Megan is the first one to open her mouth after Alex hits the ground. I'm too stunned to speak, but Megan manages a gasp followed by, "Holy shit!"

"We've got to get out of here," Joel says hurriedly.

"We can't just leave him here," I argue, finally finding my voice.

"I can't be here," Joel says, and he starts to walk back to the parking lot. The confident bodyguard from only a few moments ago has disappeared and been replaced by an even more awkward version of the Joel I've met before.

"He tripped," Megan says. "He didn't fall because you punched him," she adds.

"It won't matter. I have to leave right now," Joel says urgently.

"What do you think?" I ask Megan. I feel completely out of my depth here. I don't think we should leave this guy lying on the ground, but he was threatening Megan, and I have no real desire to be here when he wakes up.

"Maybe we should check to make sure he's breathing?" Megan offers, but her feet remain firmly planted to the spot where she's standing.

"I'll check," I offer. I swear I didn't even know I was going to say this until the words were coming out of my mouth, and I certainly don't want to be the one to go and check, but now that I've made the offer, I have to follow through.

"Let's go, guys, we have to get out of here," Joel says, and I can hear the panic starting to rise in his voice.

"Just a second," Megan calls out to him.

Alex is only lying about twenty feet away from us, but it feels like it takes an eternity to reach him since I'm moving like my feet are stuck in syrup. When I reach him, I look back at Megan, and she waves her arm at me encouragingly but doesn't attempt to get any closer. Joel looks like he might break into a sprint at any second, and his behavior makes me wonder if I should be feeling a lot more concerned about my current predicament than I am right now. I crouch down next to him and suddenly have a flashback from an old-school horror movie. It's the one where the unsuspecting girl gets too close to a lifeless body, and then it pops up and grabs her while the audience screams and wonders why the dumb girl didn't realize what was going to happen. Thankfully, the body doesn't jump up and grab me, *and* from what I can tell, he is still breathing. I run back to Megan and Joel before my luck runs out and report the news. "I think he's breathing," I say.

"You *think*?" Megan questions, her voice rises sharply on the second word.

"I took a CPR class in high school, and I'm pretty sure he was breathing," I reply.

"Oh my God. What are we supposed to do?" Megan says, looking back and forth between Joel and me.

"We have to get out of here," Joel says firmly, and he turns and starts walking toward the parking lot.

"What do *you* think?" I say to Megan. I have zero connection to this guy and essentially no connection to Joel, but Megan is caught in the middle, and I want her to feel okay with whatever we decide to do.

"It doesn't feel right to leave, but I also don't want to be here when Alex wakes up," she says.

Just then, Joel pulls up in his car. I didn't even notice that he had left to get his car, but it appears that he wasn't kidding about his desire to leave. "I'm going now. If you want a ride, get in," he says. His deadpan tone almost sounds like he's trying to be funny, but based on my limited exposure, this is likely just Joel being himself.

I look at Megan, and she shrugs, then sighs and proceeds to open the front passenger door of Joel's BMW. I certainly don't want to be stuck here by myself, so I follow her lead and get in the backseat. Joel drives out of the lot, and we sit in deafening silence as he makes his way down Dune Road to Nora's house. I don't want to be the first to speak, but I feel like I have to say something to Joel about where I need to be dropped off. I'm pretty sure he has no idea where I'm staying, and I haven't a clue where he lives. I don't imagine he signed up to drive me all the way back to East Hampton at this hour, but I'm not sure what else I'm supposed to do about a ride.

"Hey Joel," I croak. My voice sounds hoarse and almost unrecognizable. I swallow and try again. "The house I'm staying at is out in East Hampton," I say.

"That's fine. I'll take you," Joel says, his voice devoid of emotion.

Megan turns her shoulders and glances at me over the seat. We share a look that seems to acknowledge that it isn't an ideal situation but certainly seems like my only option.

"Thanks," I say. I try to picture the long drive alone in the car with Joel and wonder if it could possibly be any more awkward than the evening has been up until this point, but I fear that it might be.

The little white pebbles crunch under Joel's tires as he pulls into Nora's driveway and stops in front of the imposing gate. "Thanks," Megan says awkwardly to Joel as she slides out of the car.

"Do you want me to drive you to the Levy's for their session tomorrow?" Joel asks Megan.

"No. I'll bike. Thanks," she says.

To me, Megan says, "Text me tomorrow, okay?"

"Of course," I reply.

Megan starts to close her door but then sees me still sitting in the back seat and raises her eyebrows, and lowers her chin as if asking, "Are you really going to stay in the back-seat?" I think this trip is going to be weird no matter what, but I actually wonder if it will be slightly less weird if I stay back here, so we don't have to pretend to engage in conversation. I quickly reconsider and decide that it will violate too many social norms to have Megan's friend and boss chauffeur me home, no matter how awkward it is.

We pass the first fifteen minutes of the drive in complete silence. I contemplate turning on the radio, but I don't have the audacity to do it. Instead, I stare out the window as we drive east along Route 27 and try and make sense of the evening. A few hours ago, I was seating tourists for their overpriced seafood dinners, eagerly anticipating a post-shift drink with Megan. Now I feel like I might be fleeing a crime scene, and that may mean that I'm with the criminal.

"I'm sorry about tonight," Joel suddenly says. It's been quiet for so long that the sound of his voice takes me by surprise, and I jolt in my seat.

"It's okay," I say reflexively because that's my stock response to an apology, but I'm not sure that it *is* okay.

Thankfully, Joel reaches over and switches on the music after that. The car immediately fills with the sound of classical music, which isn't what I was expecting, but it certainly beats the silence. When we pull onto Alyssa's street, Joel lets out a long whistle, and I laugh. I've already gotten so used to the absurdity of these houses that I've forgotten how ridiculous they are – even to Hamptons' residents who are accustomed to impressive houses; these estates are something to behold.

"I know, right?" I reply.

"I really am sorry about tonight. Maybe I can try to explain," Joel says, but his voice trails off.

"It's fine," I say again and quickly wonder why I keep saying things I don't mean. "Thanks again for the ride. I know this was totally out of your way," I say, and I definitely mean that.

Joel gives me a quick wave as he turns around and drives down the street. I watch his taillights drive away and start to walk up the long driveway, shaking my head at the absurdity of the night. That's when I hear the loud music coming from the house, and I fear that my night is about to get even worse.

* * *

The house feels different from the moment I open the door. Alyssa has had people over all summer, and I have been here for several parties, but something about the music and the smell and the high-pitched voices coming from the other room gives this place an entirely different vibe. Alyssa practically tackles me when I walk into the living room. She is bouncing on the balls of her feet and pokes me repeatedly in the shoulder. "You're back. You're back. You're back," she says over and over again. Previously, Alyssa has been passed out from drinking too much or blissfully high from pot or edibles, but this is a different side of her.

"Are you okay?" I ask Alyssa, trying to get her to look me in the eye.

"I'm great," she giggles and starts bouncing again.

"It's been a long night. I'm going to go to bed," I tell her.

"Did you talk to your boyfriend?" she says in an odd babyish voice before erupting into laughter.

I decide to ignore her and get myself a glass of water and go to bed. I know if I say something, I'll regret it, and it's not like she's in any state to reason with me right now. As I pass by the kitchen island, I notice a girl leaning over a marble cutting board snorting a fine line of white powder through the cut-off end of a striped plastic straw. I feel naïve that I didn't put the pieces together until just now. I know people did coke in college, I mean, they must have, but those weren't the people I hung out with. Honestly, I've never even seen it up close before.

I forget about the water and turn around to go to my room. The sooner I can go to sleep and forget about this night, the better. Alyssa jumps in front of me as I leave the kitchen, and I've had about all I can take. "What's with you?" I say tersely.

"I talked to Preston," she chuckles.

"Yeah, I know," I reply, trying to push my way past her.

"No. I mean, I talked to him *again*," she says. "He called me this afternoon," she adds.

At this, my head snaps back, and I stare directly at her. "What are you talking about? Why are you screwing with me?" I spit at her.

"You do know Preston, and I used to have a *thing*, right?" Alyssa says, doing her best to look earnest.

"That's a lie," I say.

"It's true. We fucked all through freshman and sophomore year, and then I got tired of him. I guess you two started dating after that. But he never *really* got over me," she says, batting her eyelashes.

I rack my brain, trying to determine if there could be any truth to what she's saying. Preston did sleep with quite a few girls before we got together. He was one of my best friends from the beginning of college, so, unfortunately, I heard all about that. But I didn't think Preston and Alyssa even *knew* each other, except through me, and he always seemed to dislike her. My head is spinning as I try to figure out what's really going on.

"Now that he knows the truth about you, he probably doesn't even want to be friends with you anymore," Alyssa says triumphantly.

"What are you talking about?" I yell at her. Everyone in the kitchen is staring at me, and either someone turned down the music, or my voice has gotten so loud that it can be heard above it.

As if her behavior weren't maddening enough, instead of responding to me, Alyssa turns back around to the counter and does another bump off the marble cutting board and then vigorously rubs her hand underneath her nose. "I guess you'll just have to ask Preston about it. If he's even willing to talk to you," she smirks. And with that, she walks out of the room, leaving me speechless behind her.

Chapter 32

Nora

I set my alarm for eight o'clock, although I'm not sure why I ever think I'll be able to sleep that late. When Mason and I used to stay out late or drink too much, I would barely be able to sleep until nine (if afforded the luxury). But now that I go to bed early and rarely have more than one drink, my eyes pop open at six-seventeen every morning as if they were spring-loaded. Today I decide not to fight it, and I put on workout clothes immediately after I brush my teeth — I'm determined to get a run in on the beach while it's still mostly deserted and not too hot.

I glance quickly at the coffee pot in the kitchen and then force myself to power through without caffeine. I tell myself that coffee will be my reward after my run, but honestly, it's really because I'll have to pee in twenty minutes if I have a cup before I go.

I open the sliding door to the deck to do a few quick stretches by the pool before I head down the bridge to the beach, and that's when I see Megan's friend Courtney. She's asleep on a lounge chair with a beach towel draped over her body, and there are two giant suitcases on the ground next to her chair.

I sigh and accept that I'm not getting my early morning run in today. I don't want to scare her, yet it seems irresponsible to leave her here and either continue on my run or go back inside. There could be a simple explanation for why she's sleeping on my deck, like Megan and Courtney had too much to drink last night, and she passed out here. Although I know that doesn't make sense. Why wouldn't Courtney be in the guest house with Megan? And why does she have suitcases? Something's very off.

Courtney must sense my presence, or the morning light has gotten to her because she shifts in her sleep and opens her eyes. "I'm so sorry!" Courtney says the moment we make eye contact. She scoots back in the chair until she is sitting in an upright position. She clutches the navy and white towel around her body as if she needs to cover herself, although she is fully dressed in her hostessing clothes from the night before.

"Don't apologize," I say. "Are you okay?" I ask and gesture to the suitcases.

"I didn't know where else to go," she says grimly, and it looks like she's about to cry.

"What happened?" I ask cautiously. I take a seat on the chair right next to where I'm standing, but I'm careful to leave space between us, so I don't scare her away.

"Things blew up with the girl I'm staying with, and I had to get out of there. It was already after two in the morning by the time I packed my bags, and I couldn't wait until the morning to leave, but it was too late to call anyone. I happened to see Megan enter the gate code when we came in before, so I knew how to get in. I'm so so sorry," she says and buries her face in her hands.

I'm not upset that Courtney chose my deck as a safe haven, and I'm relieved that the gate code and alarm are working properly, but I am wondering what I'm supposed to do or say next. This feels like a job for a mom, and I have no experience with that. I don't like to admit it, but other than sending outrageous birthday gifts and the occasional Face-Time, I barely even have experience as an aunt.

"Maybe it will look better in the light of day?" I suggest, but I cringe as my mother's words come out of my mouth.

"I'm not sure," she says, trying to cut my stupid suggestion some slack.

Thankfully, Megan picks that moment to emerge from the guest house. She's dressed in light pink floral pajama pants and a hot pink tank top, and she's carrying a mug with steaming hot coffee. I chastise myself for the thought, but I can't help but wonder if it would be okay to run inside and get my own cup of coffee now that Megan is here.

"Courtney?! What are you doing here?" Megan says, clearly shocked to see her friend.

"I'm sorry," Courtney says again. "I didn't have anywhere else to go."

"What happened?" Megan cries. She practically sprints the ten feet over to Courtney's chair and miraculously doesn't spill a drop of coffee as she does it.

"It was awful!" Courtney exclaims. "I got home, and

everyone was doing coke, and Alyssa was being crazy! She told me that she and Preston used to sleep together and made it seem like she told him some terrible secret about me, but I have no idea what she meant!" Courtney moans.

From the way Courtney is sharing, I think she's forgotten that I'm even here. At this point, it feels more like I'm eavesdropping than providing any real assistance. I'd be lying if I said I wasn't intrigued about Courtney's story, yet it doesn't seem to be any of my business. I slowly stand up and start to back toward the door while the girls are talking, trying not to draw too much attention to myself; Megan calls to me just as I reach the sliding door.

"Nora, can Courtney stay here?" she calls out. "Just until she figures out what to do? She'll stay with me in the guest house," Megan adds.

Before I can answer, Courtney, says, "I'll just go back to Chicago. Please don't worry about it."

"It's completely fine," I hear myself say. "Courtney, you can stay for as long as you want. There's plenty of room."

"Thank you so much!" Megan says, at the same time Courtney asks, "Are you sure?"

"When one door shuts, another opens," I say to the girls and then open the door to head inside. But first, I pause briefly to look up, as if I can see my mom smiling down on me repeating her corny proverbs.

* * *

I wrap my hands around the ceramic mug, inhale the freshly brewed coffee, and try not to think about the day that Mason and I got these mugs. We were at a resort in Aspen, and when we came in from a day on the slopes, they served us hot cocoa in these striking black and white mugs. I made such a big deal about them that Mason asked the manager where we could buy them. He was told that a local artist made them exclusively for the resort, and they weren't for sale. Mason doesn't take no for an answer, and two weeks later, six of the mugs were delivered to our apartment in Manhattan with a handwritten note from the artist. I attempt to brush away the memory to enjoy my coffee *and* my mug.

I grab my iPad to scroll through emails, morning news, and social media while sipping my coffee. I'm still in my running gear, but at this point, I've determined that I'll skip the run and either go for a bike ride later this morning or work out in the gym – I've lost the necessary motivation. I quickly scan the headlines and determine that there's no "new" bad news this morning that can't wait to be read later. Social media provides a similar vibe, and it's the same old thing on repeat – vacation pics, family shots, photos of last night's dinner, humblebragging about life in general. I honestly can't remember if this is the type of crap I used to post as well, back when I wasn't just a voyeur, but I swear I wasn't this annoying.

I close out of the offending apps without liking or commenting on a single post and finally turn to my email. I don't know why it's taken her this long, but Zadie has replied to my email.

Dear Nora,

I'm so sorry that Bob wasn't a good fit for you. I know that he isn't everyone's cup of tea, but I

THOUGHT THAT WITH BOTH OF YOUR BIG PERSONALITIES AND SUCCESSFUL CAREERS, YOU MIGHT BE A MATCH. I GUESS NOT. I DO HAVE ANOTHER MAN THAT I'D LIKE FOR YOU TO MEET. HE LIVES IN ALABAMA RIGHT NOW, ALTHOUGH I BELIEVE HE IS OPEN TO RELOCATION. HE'S BEEN RELUCTANT TO TRY MY SERVICES AFTER HIS WIFE PASSED AWAY A COUPLE OF MONTHS AGO, BUT HE FINALLY AGREED TO GIVE IT A GO! PLEASE LET ME KNOW WHAT YOU THINK.

BEST,

ZADIE

I can't keep from laughing out loud at her response. I know that Bridget meant well when she suggested a matchmaker, but where did she find this nut-job?! And more importantly, what was I thinking when I agreed to it? I quickly realize that I know exactly what I was thinking – I was tired of feeling lonely. My finger hovers over the delete key as I contemplate whether I should even continue with this exchange, but I hate loose ends, so I have to wrap this up.

DEAR ZADIE,

I BELIEVE THAT I HAVE GIVEN YOUR SERVICES A FAIR TRIAL. I KNOW THAT MY SISTER WILL BE DISAPPOINTED, BUT AT THIS POINT, I DO NOT WISH TO GO ON ANY MORE DATES, NOR DO I WISH TO BE INTRODUCED TO ANY MORE OF YOUR CLIENTS.

THANK YOU AND BEST WISHES,

NORA

I quickly re-read my email before hitting send. The language doesn't match my feelings, and I'm tempted to add harsher wording, but it doesn't seem worth the effort. I press send and close my laptop with a flourish, which gives me some small satisfaction.

I need to text Bridget to tell her what's happened so she doesn't hear it first from Zadie. We've texted a few times on meaningless topics since her explosion the other day, but true to her word, she doesn't seem ready for a call or to talk about what happened. Before I can write to her, a text from Eva pops up on the messenger app.

EVA: I HAVE A HUGE FAVOR TO ASK YOU. ARE YOU AROUND?

NORA: SURE! WHAT IS IT?

I have no idea what Eva is about to ask, but I've already decided that whatever she asks, I'll do. I'm so happy to have Eva back in my life, and if she feels close enough to ask me for a favor, I'm not going to let her down!

EVA: WE HAVE THE CHANCE TO GO TO ITALY FOR TWO WEEKS FOR FREE (LONG STORY) – BUT WE CAN'T TAKE PENNY, AND SHE ISN'T SPAYED YET, SO I CAN'T BOARD HER. IS THERE ANY CHANCE THAT YOU WOULD TAKE HER WHILE WE'RE GONE?

It takes me a second to remember that Penny is their massive untrained Labrador retriever puppy. I always wanted a dog when I was little, but I also wanted a pony and a unicorn – I never truly had any expectation of having one, nor did I ever think about how I would take care of one. Maybe Eva senses my hesitation because I see the three dots indicating that she is typing again.

Eva: Don't worry about it – it was a long-shot – I know it's too much to ask

Nora: I'd be happy to take Penny!

I type the words before I can give it any more thought. I said I was going to help Eva with whatever she asked, and that's what I'm going to do.

Eva: Really? Are you sure?

Nora: Yes! I might need a few tips about puppy care, but I'm happy to help. Can't wait to hear about the trip to Italy!

Eva: Thank you so much!!!!

Nora: 😀

Eva: First tip – you might want to hide your favorite shoes 😜

Nora: 😂 hmmm...when do you leave?

Eva: That's the other thing – our flight leaves from JFK at ten tonight. It's so last minute, I know! We just found out this morning and are

SCRAMBLING TO TRY AND MAKE IT WORK. I KNOW IT'S REALLY SHORT NOTICE

I reset my thoughts from moments ago when I envisioned spending the next couple of days puppy-proofing the house and reading up on dogs to prepare myself for Penny's arrival. A tiny part of me is tempted to tell Eva that it's too much and I can't handle the dog with such little preparation, but I don't want to be that kind of friend.

NORA: IT'S TOTALLY FINE. WHEN DO YOU WANT TO BRING HER OVER?

EVA: IN ABOUT AN HOUR, IS THAT OKAY?

NORA: I'LL SEE YOU THEN!

I glance around at my immaculate living room, and I'm not sure what I've signed up for, but I think I'm about to find out.

Chapter 33

Megan

"Are you sure it's fine if I stay here?" Courtney asks, looking equal parts worried and exhausted. The dark circles under her eyes, instead of her usually flawless skin, are a clear sign of the limited hours of sleep she got on the lounge chair.

"Nora said that it was fine," I tell her.

"I know, but she was just being nice. She probably felt like she didn't have any other choice," Courtney says.

"She's really nice. I honestly think she's fine with it. She doesn't use this space anyway, and I get the feeling she likes having the company," I say.

"I can't believe what a disaster my summer has turned into," Courtney groans.

"Think about how much closer you'll be to work now?" I offer.

Courtney offers a partial smile, but it quickly fades. "I should just go back to Chicago for the rest of the summer.

This was supposed to be my summer to relax and have fun before law school. It was going to be the first summer that I wasn't training or studying or working, and now everything's a mess!"

I try not to take any offense at her comments since I know they aren't aimed at me, but I can't help feeling that my summer has only improved since I met Courtney, and if she leaves, I'll go back to having no friends here. "It doesn't have to be all bad," I suggest. "You still have most of August, and this could be the relaxing part of your summer. I'm sure we could find a ton of fun things to do," I offer.

"I guess so," Courtney says, but she doesn't seem convinced.

"Do you want to talk anymore about the whole Preston thing?" I ask her.

"Not right now," Courtney says. "I'm too tired."

"That's okay," I reply. "Do you have to work today?" I ask her.

"Thankfully, no. I'm not on again for the next few days," she says.

"Actually, I have to get to work soon," I say to her, glancing at my watch to check the time. "Are you going to be okay if I go?" I ask her.

"Yeah, sure. I think I'm just going to take a nap if that's okay," Courtney says.

"Of course! I think the couch has a pull-out sofa, but the double chaise over there is huge, and honestly, it's more comfortable than the bed. I've fallen asleep there several nights," I confess.

"I'm so tired I think I could fall asleep right here,"

Courtney says, gesturing to the backless bar stool she's sitting on.

"There are extra sheets and blankets and pillows and pretty much anything you could need in the linen closet," I say. It feels weird to play the role of hostess since this isn't my house, and it also feels overly formal with a girl my own age, but I've watched my mom and Danielle perform this role so many times over the years that I can't help but slip into it.

"Don't worry about me; I'll be fine," Courtney says. "Are you planning to see Joel today?" she asks, suddenly perking up.

"I told him that I didn't want a ride, but I'll see him at the house for tutoring," I say. "I've been trying not to think about what happened last night, but I need to talk to him about it."

"I've been so absorbed in my own drama that I didn't even ask you how you were doing after last night. I'm so sorry!" Courtney exclaims.

"Don't worry about it. I'm honestly not even ready to think about Alex. I don't think it's hit me yet that he was here – it's all such a blur," I say to Courtney, and I realize as I'm talking just how true these words are. I'm pretty sure I was in shock after Alex showed up last night, and then when Joel punched him, and he fell down, I went through the motions on autopilot, but I didn't truly absorb anything. I took an Ambien with a glass of wine when I got home to make sure I went straight to sleep, and then Courtney was here when I got up this morning, so I haven't had time to process anything.

"Let me know when you *are* ready. And let me know if Joel says anything. He was silent the whole drive home last night, and then right when we got to Alyssa's house, he said he wanted to explain, but I told him it wasn't necessary," Courtney says. "Although he acted pretty weird about the whole thing, so clearly I'm curious about what happened too," she adds.

"You think Alex is okay, right?" I ask her. This thought has run through my head on a loop since last night, even though I claim not to be thinking about Alex, but it's the first time I've been able to say it out loud.

"Yeah, totally. He probably has a killer headache, but other than that, he's fine," Courtney says, and I desperately want to believe her.

"Okay, I've got to go to tutoring. I'll be back later. Text me if you need anything," I say.

Joel's car is parked in front of the Levy's house when I arrive. My back is soaked in sweat from the long trip, and I ride my bike up the long pebble driveway and park it in the shade near the garage. It's only the third day of August, but the weather feels entirely different from the mild July heat. The temperature seems to have risen twenty degrees in the past three days, and the humidity has almost doubled. I'm sure that this is what summer was like in Rye and in Manhattan, but having spent the past several summers in Palo Alto or on Cape Cod, I've completely forgotten about the possibility of swamp-like heat.

I let myself in through the back gate and then the unlocked back door, which is what Joel instructed me to do on my first visit. I thought it was odd that we wouldn't ring the doorbell but rather just let ourselves in – especially when the family hadn't even met me! But Joel assured me that we should behave exactly the same as all the other "help" and that we should be invisible.

I can hear Joel's voice from the rear sun porch, where he is already reviewing Twin A's errors from last week's test. I check my watch again and see that I still have two minutes before our lesson is officially set to begin. I breathe a small sigh of relief; I guess Joel is simply overzealous today.

There is no sign of Twin B yet, and I hope that he appears soon. I've never been further into the house than the kitchen or the sun porch, and I get the feeling that I'm not welcome in any of the front rooms of the house. At times like these, I wonder how the Levy's would treat me if they met me under other circumstances? I don't know if they are the kind of people who measure worthiness based solely on wealth or if there is more to their equation. I'm sure that Danielle and Ted would be too average for their tastes, but I find myself wondering if the Levy's would offer me a drink and a seat in the living room if they knew my father. I quickly shake my head as if to physically dislodge that idea from my brain. I never want any association with my father, so what would possibly make me want that now? Thankfully Twin B walks into the kitchen at that moment, so I don't have to think about it any longer.

"Are you ready to go over the writing section from last week?" I ask cheerfully.

"Whatever," he grumbles, sliding into his seat at the kitchen table. He's wearing a rumpled Princeton lacrosse t-shirt that I'm sure he slept in and low-slung athletic shorts that reveal three inches of navy-blue boxer briefs with Paul Smith printed across the waistband. It's obviously unfair to make judgments based on the twins' appearance, but after a few sessions getting to know them, I feel relatively confident saying that I *know* these boys. I went to middle school and high school and, unfortunately, even college with these boys. Clearly, I don't know these two seventeen-year-old privileged brats from Long Island, but there are so many boys just like them that they all blend together.

I slap a smile on my face, since for some crazy reason I decided to take this job, and try again. "I've got a few suggestions for expression of ideas," I say to him.

"Whatever," he replies again and reaches for his phone, which is currently face down on the table next to his laptop.

I resist the urge to smack his hand since I know that wouldn't go over well, but I definitely think it's called for. "We have an hour, and I know your parents want to see some progress," is all that I can manage to say.

"Look, I know it's not your fault, but I'm really not up for this today," he says.

Based on how I'm feeling, it's hard to argue. I'm also not up for this today, and I'm about to tell him that I understand exactly how he feels when he becomes a far less sympathetic character.

"I know my parents want us to get our scores up, but we all know it's bullshit," Twin B says.

"Really? Why is that?" I ask.

"We're quadruple legacies at Princeton, and our grandfather donated the new science building two years ago," he bluntly states.

I try to keep a neutral expression on my face, but it's hard. I know that college acceptances are never guaranteed, but if what he's saying is correct, it's almost impossible that Princeton wouldn't accept them. "So why am I here?" I ask him.

"My dad doesn't think we should expect things to be *handed to us*," he says, using air quotes to mock his father. "Which is pretty fucked up considering everything he's gotten from my mom's family," Twin B says.

I feel like we are getting off-topic and into some serious family issues, so I try to recover. "Remind me, what's your current score?" I feel like I should know this, but now I'm wondering if I ever even got this information. Looking at him now, I can barely remember what we are trying to achieve.

"I have a fourteen ninety, and my brother has a fourteen eighty," he says, rocking back in his chair and looking much younger than the man-child that he is.

I'd gotten so wrapped up in my own issues and somewhat overwhelmed with the different stories for the different students that I had forgotten that Joel initially told me that these were just crazy parents who were paying us a lot, and we didn't need to be here. It was all so new at the time that I didn't think to ask any more questions.

"What score does your dad think you need to have so Princeton isn't being *handed to you*?" I ask him, stealing his air quotes from earlier.

It's small, but something changes in Twin B's tone when he responds, and I think we both know something has shifted in how we view one another. "He says that we don't deserve to go to Princeton if we can't get over fifteen hundred. Of course, that's what he got like thirty years ago or whatever, so he's decided that anything below that isn't *worthy*," he says, curving his fingers around the last word.

I wish I could go back and change my previous impressions of these boys. I'm sure there are several things I could still find to dislike about them, but some of my judgments from earlier are certainly unfounded. I know it's not appropriate to gossip with this rising high school senior, but I have a feeling we would have a lot in common if we started to swap stories about our respective fathers.

It isn't really my place, but before I completely abandon my role as his tutor, I want to make sure I have the full picture. "I assume you have a good GPA?" I ask him.

"Unweighted it's a four-point zero, weighted it's four-point four five."

"Got it. And your activities?" I continue.

Twin B sighs, but I think he knows where I'm going, so he's willing to play along. "I'm captain of the baseball team, which went to the state championships last year, and I'm also nationally ranked as a junior squash player. Princeton wants me to play there, but I'm not sure that I want my whole college life to be about squash," he says. "Oh, I also started a local charity that provides children's books in Spanish to pediatricians' offices across Long Island," he adds.

"Do you want an iced coffee?" I ask him.

"What?" he says, looking at me like I'm crazy – which I probably am.

"I'm sorry about your dad. If he makes you take the test again, I'm sure you'll get those ten points on your own. There's nothing I'm going to do here today that's going to help you with that. And it certainly doesn't seem like you need my help getting into Princeton." Twin B looks at me and shrugs, so I continue. "But I could desperately use some coffee, and it's really hot out, so I thought an iced coffee sounded good," I tell him.

"Are we going to ride your bike?" he smirks.

"That's currently my only option," I say to him, but I find his jab endearing, whereas ten minutes ago, I would have wanted to slug him.

"We could take *my* car," he offers.

"Now you're being helpful," I tell him. "Let's go."

My phone buzzes as we are heading toward the garage, and I glance down and see that it's from Joel.

JOEL: WHERE ARE YOU GOING?

MEGAN: STUDY BREAK

JOEL: YOU CAN'T DO THAT

MEGAN: DON'T WORRY – I QUIT

JOEL: YOU QUIT????

MEGAN: NOT ALL TUTORING, BUT I DEFINITELY QUIT WORKING FOR THIS FAMILY. THESE BOYS ARE FINE. I'M NOT GOING TO TAKE THEIR MONEY AND TORTURE THESE KIDS

JOEL: YOU CAN'T DO THAT!

MEGAN: WE'LL TALK LATER. WANT ANY COFFEE?

* * *

When Twin B and I arrive back at the house forty minutes later with our iced lattes, Joel is standing next to his car waiting for me, and he looks crestfallen. I thank Twin B for the ride and wish him luck with his applications, and it *almost* feels like we should hug goodbye – but not quite.

I hop out of the car at the end of the driveway, and I start talking while I'm still fifteen feet away from Joel. I already feel guilty, and his puppy-dog look isn't helping, so it feels like the best course of action is to jump right in before giving him a chance. "I can't help him. He's got everything he needs, and he certainly doesn't need my assistance to get into Princeton. He doesn't want to spend his time doing SAT prep to get ten stupid points," I explain to Joel.

"That's not the point," Joel says through tight lips. He doesn't raise his voice, but I can tell that he's upset.

"Of course, that's the point," I reply.

Joel audibly exhales and runs his fingers through his shaggy hair. He is badly in need of a haircut, but the way his hair flops over his eyes is surprisingly cute. I also realize that he isn't wearing his glasses today, and his eyes are almost the same brilliant blue color as the sky. I try to clear these thoughts from my head so I can hear what Joel is saying *and* because it's unnerving to look at him this way. "Half of my business is funded by demanding parents who have unrealistic expectations for their children," Joel says.

"Well, that sucks," I state emphatically. "And you're fine taking their money and making these kids sit through weeks of tutoring for no real reason?" I ask him.

"Yes. And no," Joel sighs. "When I started, most of the kids I tutored legitimately needed help. Then word spread, and I got a lot of parents who just wanted to push their kids to be perfect, even though it wasn't necessary; it didn't seem like my place to turn them down. You knew this when you started. Why did you get so upset today? What happened?" Joel asks.

"I *may* have overreacted. Twin B told me something about his dad, and I kind of lost it. My dad is a complete asshole, and I may have misplaced some of my anger today," I say to Joel and then continue, "I guess I knew that we weren't doing missionary work or anything, but somehow I lost track of how absurd this tutoring really is," I sigh.

"It's not *all* absurd," Joel says defensively.

"Yeah, okay," I say, fighting the urge to roll my eyes.

"Most of the families aren't this bad. And I've helped several students improve their scores and get into colleges they wouldn't have been able to get into otherwise, which statistically gives them a chance for higher earnings upon graduation," Joel says. His tone reminds me of the arrogant robot I met back at the beginning of the summer, and suddenly he looks a lot less cute than he did a few minutes ago. This seems like the perfect opportunity to change the topic and ask about last night.

"What was that last night?" I say to Joel. The initial look of surprise on Joel's face shows that I caught him off guard, but then his features shift, and it's obvious that he knew this was coming.

"Do we *have* to talk about it?" Joel asks halfheartedly.

"You showed up out of nowhere and helped me, and then you totally lost your shit and ran away. Yes, we have to talk about it," I say to him.

Joel leans uncomfortably against his car just as Mr. Levy's vintage Aston Martin pulls into the driveway. Mr. Levy glances at us but doesn't even bother to give a cursory wave. "Can we do this somewhere else?" Joel asks.

As much as I don't want to delay the discussion, I have to agree with Joel – this isn't the place to have it. "I have to take my bike anyway. Can we meet back at Nora's house?" I ask him.

Joel tugs on the collar of his turquoise polo shirt, and I think he's going to make up an excuse for why he can't do it, but then he agrees to meet me there.

I'm about to get on my bike when my phone rings, and an unfamiliar number with the local area code pops up on my caller ID. I almost never answer if I don't know who it is, but I have a weird feeling about this call, and I pick up.

"Hello, is this Megan Walters?" the voice on the other end says before I can even say hello.

"Yes. I'm Megan," I reply.

"This is Grace; I'm a nurse at Stony Brook Southampton Hospital. We have a patient here named Alex who's asking to see you."

Chapter 34

Courtney

I'm in the middle of one of those dreams where I have to use the bathroom but can't seem to find one. I finally think I've found the toilet, but when I start to pull down my pants, I realize it's a giant toadstool. When I open my eyes, I realize that I desperately need to pee, but then it takes me a minute to figure out where I am. The vaulted ceiling above me is alarmingly unfamiliar, but then I roll on my side and look over at Megan's stuff on the coffee table, and it all comes back to me. I groggily make my way over to the bathroom, and I'm highly disturbed when I catch a glimpse of my reflection in the mirror. My hair hangs limply past my shoulders, and instead of looking like the pretty shade of dirty blonde that it usually does, it looks like dirty mop water. There are faint purple circles under my eyes, which I imagine must look slightly better than they did before my nap, and somehow, I look pallid, even though I've spent almost every day in the sun, and yesterday I swear I had a tan.

I'm eyeing Megan's fancy bath products and contemplating a shower while wondering if Megan really *did* mean to make myself at home when I hear the front door open and a man's voice. I briefly worry that Megan forgot I was here and brought some guy home with her, but then I realize it's only Joel.

"Courtney?" Megan calls out, and I can hear the concern in her voice.

"I'm in here. I'll be out in a second!" I yell back. I run the cold water from the tap and splash some on my face and run my wet fingers through my hair; unfortunately, it doesn't seem to make things any better. I note my ratty NU basketball shirt and tiny green plaid pajama shorts in the mirror as I turn the door handle. I still don't know Megan all that well, and I barely know Joel, so this wouldn't be my first choice of outfit to wear around either of them, but it doesn't look like I have much of a choice.

When I emerge from the bathroom, the scene at the kitchen counter is not at all what I expect to find. Joel and Megan are sitting side by side on the barstools with a bottle of vodka and a carton of orange juice in between them and appear to each be halfway through their screwdrivers. Megan must see the surprise on my face because she is quick to address my unspoken question. "We needed a drink. You'll probably need one too. It still felt early for straight vodka, so we decided to add a little OJ," she says before taking a large swallow from her cocktail.

"What's going on?" I ask. I cross over the sun-filled room and stand across from them on the other side of the counter. Other than for about three minutes this morning, I haven't seen the guest house during daylight hours, and then I was way too tired to notice anything. Now I can see that the back wall is floor-to-ceiling windows with stunning views over the dunes and out to the water. The house is *relatively* small, compared to Alyssa's monstrosity or even Nora's main house, but it is perfectly decorated in beachy whites and blues. If I weren't so freaked out about what Megan is going to say *and* I could forget about what Alyssa told me about Preston last night, I might really be looking forward to staying here.

"I got a call from the local hospital this morning. Alex is asking to see me," Megan says.

"Oh wow," I reply. "Is he okay?" I add.

"The nurse wouldn't say over the phone. He didn't call me directly, so I don't know if that's good or bad news," Megan says while draining the rest of her drink.

"Are we going to talk about what happened last night?" I ask, trying to catch either Joel's or Megan's eye.

Megan opens her mouth to speak, but then Joel cuts her off. "I can't have anything else on my record," he says matter-of-factly.

This is the last thing I was expecting Joel to say, and from the shocked look on Megan's face, it seems she feels the same way. "You have a *record*?" I blurt out like the word tastes terrible on my tongue.

"I'd prefer not to talk any more about it," Joel says. He splashes more juice and vodka into his glass and then stares down into it without taking a sip.

"I don't mean to pry, but we might *need* to hear more about it," Megan says. "I have no idea what's going to happen when I go to the hospital, but I think I should have some background and maybe be able to explain why we ran away," Megan says with a raised voice.

"You're going to go see him at the hospital?" I ask in disbelief.

"I don't think I have much of a choice," Megan answers.

"He attacked you!" Joel says loudly.

"Yeah, maybe we should talk more about *that* before we get into Joel's criminal history," I offer. I mean it as a joke, but my attempt to break the tension falls flat.

Megan takes a deep breath and pulls her blonde hair into a messy bun as if this will help her prepare to tell us the story. "Here's the abbreviated version. Alex is my ex-boyfriend from Stanford. We were friends up until the beginning of our senior year, and then we started dating. Although we barely did anything more than kiss, so I don't know how serious our relationship really was. After winter break, he got really weird and jealous. I tried to break up with him, but he didn't seem to accept that we were broken up. Then he found out that I was seeing my TA and things went downhill," Megan says.

"What do you mean when you say that they went downhill?" I ask her.

"I haven't told anyone else about this," Megan says quietly.

"What did he do to you?" Joel utters with a mix of anger and concern.

"It's not what you think. It doesn't even make sense," Megan says while shifting uncomfortably on her stool.

"Try us," I say.

Megan sighs again and then continues. "When he realized that Mateo was my TA, he knew that he had leverage over me. He threatened to tell the department about us, which would mean Mateo would lose his position and I might lose my place in the graduate program," Megan says.

"He blackmailed you?" I ask.

"Not really. I mean, I don't know that it's the right word. In exchange for his silence, I had to pretend to keep dating him," Megan says.

"What do you mean, *pretend*?" I ask her.

"Exactly that. We told everyone we were still together and occasionally went out on dates where people would see us and we acted like everything was fine, but unless we were in front of people, we didn't come within ten feet of each other," Megan says.

"I don't get it," I say.

"What's wrong with him?" Joel interjects.

"Honestly, I have no idea. We used to be friends, and he used to be a nice guy. Or at least I thought so," she says.

"So that's it? You had to pretend to date him? Then he showed up here last night and grabbed you?" I say, trying to connect the dots.

"That's not quite the whole story. I kept seeing Mateo, which pissed Alex off because he was worried someone would find out that I was *cheating* on him. At first, he decided there wasn't much he could do about it, but then he found out that Mateo was married," Megan says, and her words hang in the air. The stunned look on Joel's face would be priceless if I wasn't convinced that mine was a mirror image.

Megan ignores our shocked responses and plows ahead.

"If it helps, I had absolutely no idea that he was married when I started seeing him," Megan says earnestly.

"That definitely makes a difference," I quickly say and hope that it doesn't sound too judgmental. "If you broke up with the married TA, then why was Alex still bothering you?" I ask her.

"I didn't stop seeing him right when I found out," Megan says sheepishly, "Anyway, once Alex knew about Mateo's wife, he confronted us both and threatened to tell her," Megan says.

"Why did you care?" Joel says angrily, speaking up for the first time in several minutes. "This guy lied to you about being married and took advantage of you."

"He *hardly* took advantage of me," Megan says. "It was definitely consensual," she adds, and by the pained look on Joel's face, it seems like an unnecessary addition. "Mateo got married when they were both nineteen, and he's not really in love with his wife anymore. But she wants to come live and work in California, and if he divorces her, she'll have to stay in Venezuela, where her options aren't nearly as good," Megan tells us.

"Just so you know, that's basically the same lame line that every scumbag uses when he cheats on his wife," Joel says.

"*Anyway*," I say loudly, trying to lighten the mood. "Let's get back to Alex. Explain what he's holding over you. And why he showed up last night!" I exclaim.

"Right. I was getting to that," Megan says. She refills her drink with equal parts vodka and orange juice and wanders over to the opposite end of the white linen sofa. The contrast of the bright liquid against the pristine backdrop of the couch makes me nervous, but I suppose that's not my place. "Saying this out loud is going to make me sound ridiculous," Megan says.

"No, it won't," I assure her. However, this is clearly impossible since I have no idea what she's going to say. What I do know is that my levels of impatience and curiosity are both about to peak – I try to refrain from yelling, 'Just spit it out!'

"Alex said he was going to tell the school and tell Mateo's wife about us. I wasn't sure he was going to follow through with it, but Mateo was freaking out. I know this doesn't make any sense, but Alex said he would drop the whole thing if I agreed to do something for him. So, I agreed," Megan says. By this point, she has finished her second drink and is now chewing on the cuticles of her left hand.

"What did you agree to do?" Joel asks.

Without answering the question, Megan gets up and walks to her bedroom. Joel and I stare at each other in disbelief. I'm not sure what's running through his slightly eccentric mind, but I know that my head is spinning with all of the potential options.

I'm surprised when Megan emerges from her room less than a minute later and comes back to take her seat on the couch. I almost wonder if I imagined the whole thing. But then she holds out her hand and opens it up so we can both see what she's holding.

"Is that an engagement ring?!" I exclaim.

"It is," Megan says softly.

"You're engaged to the guy that I punched last night?"

Joel asks as if he's trying to wrap his head around this possibility.

"I guess technically I am..." Megan trails off. "I *told* you that it would sound crazy. Alex said that he would leave Mateo alone and would never say anything to the school or anyone else if I agreed to get engaged," she says.

"You're going to marry this guy?!" Joel cries out.

"No. No, of course not. I'm not actually going to go through with it. Or at least, I never imagined it would ever be a possibility when we made the initial deal. I told him that I wouldn't tell any of my friends or family and that it had to be a very long engagement, and we wouldn't even talk about it until after I finished grad school. He was planning to go back to the east coast for work, and I was planning to stay in Palo Alto for school, so it seemed outrageous, but also somewhat harmless to pretend to have a long-distance engagement," Megan says.

"Seriously? Why would he even want to get married if your relationship isn't real?" I ask. I'm trying to give my new friend the benefit of the doubt, but her story is absurd.

"I know, I promise you, I know how this must sound," Megan says.

"So, what happened? How did we end up here?" Joel asks, cutting to the chase.

"Right before finals, Alex changed his mind and said that we had to get married this year. He said we needed to set a date, and he wanted to do it before the end of the summer," Megan sighs.

"Oh shit," I reply. I can't help but get sucked into the farce.

"I didn't know what to do, so I ran away for the summer and didn't tell him where I was going," Megan confesses.

"And what about Mateo?" Joel asks with a little too much interest.

"That was never going to work out. He's still married, and his wife is moving to California. *But* I do think that he's in a bad marriage and that he did have real feelings for me," Megan says.

"I get that you like this guy. And maybe he is a great guy in a bad situation, but at this point, isn't it worth it to throw him under the bus so you can move on?" I ask. I no longer care that my exasperation is evident.

"That's what I was planning to do. I was about to tell Alex that I didn't care anymore, when I found out that his grandmother sent out invitations to our engagement party!" Megan says, burying her face in her hands.

"That sucks," I say.

"I let it get so out of control that I don't know how to stop it now," Megan says.

"So, you're just going to marry him? Is that your solution?" Joel asks.

"No! Of course not. But I don't know how to fix it. I'm going to look like a complete moron if I try to tell the truth. Look at the way you guys are responding. Imagine how other people would react?" Megan asks.

I don't want to make her feel any worse, but she has a point. She definitely doesn't come off well in this story. "Does your family know? Any of your friends at school?" I ask her.

"No one knows right now. This is one blessing of my totally fucked up family. I guess I haven't given you guys any of the details, but to make a long story short, I have almost no contact with my parents. I lived with my dad's much younger ex-wife for most of high school, and then she got remarried and had two kids. They are kind of my family now, but they have a lot going on," Megan says.

I might have had a lot of questions about Megan's unique situation a few years ago, but given the situation with the recent discovery of my birth father and two half-sisters, I'm certainly in no place to judge someone else's family. "What about your friends?" I question.

"That was a little harder. At Alex's initial request, I pretended that we were still together. But I never told anyone we were engaged. When I decided to move out here for the summer, I told my closest friend, Hope, that I wanted some space over the summer, but that everything was fine," Megan says.

"What happened last night?" Joel asks. His patience seems to be wearing thin as well.

"I'm not sure. He got there right before you did. He said that we needed to talk and begged me to listen to him, but before he could say anything else, you showed up," Megan says, pointing at Joel.

"Was he trying to hurt you?" Joel asks.

"I don't think so. I was frightened because I wasn't expecting to see him, but I think he honestly just wanted to talk – although I don't know what he wanted to say. I've messed this up so badly," Megan moans.

"What are we supposed to do now?" I ask, posing the question to both of them. "And we still haven't gotten back to

Joel's whole criminal record. Don't think we've forgotten about that," I say, staring straight at him.

"I think I have to go see him in the hospital. I can't hide from this anymore," Megan says.

"What are you going to say?" I ask her.

"I'm not sure. I'll figure it out on the way over there," she says. "Can you drive me?" she asks Joel.

"Two years ago, I punched a guy in a bar," Joel says, which definitely does not answer Megan's question but are presumably the words he's been trying to get out since last night.

"Who'd you punch?" I ask.

"Rich Michaelson," Joel replies without missing a beat.

"Who's that?" Megan asks.

"He was just some asshole in the bar who was bothering the waitress. She repeatedly asked him to leave her alone, and he was drunk and wouldn't listen, so finally, I punched him," Joel says.

"Sounds like he deserved it," I say.

"It turned out his dad is a lawyer and didn't see things that way. He pressed charges, and I ended up with an assault charge. I paid a fine, and I just finished my community service hours," Joel says.

"Wow," I say, looking at Joel in a whole new light.

"I have no idea what would happen if anyone found out about last night, but I can't imagine it would be good," he says sadly.

"But you thought I was in danger," Megan says.

"That's what happened last time, and it didn't seem to matter," Joel reminds her.

"You shouldn't go to the hospital," I tell him. I have no idea what the legal implications are for Joel or if he is in any trouble, but this seems like the right thing to say. "Megan, I'll come with you."

"Thanks, Courtney," she says. "Joel, why don't you go home, and we'll text you later."

Joel is quiet for a minute like he's not sure he likes this plan but then nods his head in agreement.

"Let me get changed," I say as I look down and realize that I'm still in my tattered pajamas.

"Sure," Megan replies. "I'll walk you to your car," Megan says to Joel. This seems out of character, but maybe Megan wants to give me some privacy, or maybe she wants a few minutes alone with Joel. That would also seem unlikely, but after the revelations of the past thirty minutes, everything feels upside down.

Joel opens the door to let Megan walk out ahead of him. Before any of us realize what's happening, a giant black dog runs into the room, followed immediately by Nora, who is waving a leash in her hand and yelling, "Come back here!"

The black dog jumps up on the sofa, twirls around in a circle, and plops down as if he (or she) owns the place. Nora sighs and says, "Everyone, meet Penny."

Chapter 35

Nora

"Sorry about that," I say sheepishly to Megan and her friends as I chase Penny into the guesthouse.

"She's adorable!" Courtney gushes.

"It's your house. You don't have to apologize to me," Megan says. "Whose dog is it?" she asks.

"She belongs to my friend Eva. I said I would watch her for the next two weeks," I tell them.

"I love dogs!" Megan says. She sits down on the couch next to Penny and starts stroking the dog's back, and Penny quickly rolls over onto her back and snorts in delight. "Okay, I'll rub your tummy," Megan says in a silly voice that I've certainly never heard her use before.

"You're so good with her," I comment.

"My ex-boyfriend from high school had a yellow lab, and I adored him. I always wanted a dog, but my parents didn't want one, and Danielle said she couldn't manage one in the city," Megan says.

Penny has only been in my care for twenty minutes, and I'm already feeling overwhelmed. I debate whether it would be shirking my responsibilities if I ask Megan if she wants to help with Penny or if I should simply offer that she can play with the dog whenever she would like. Thankfully, Megan beats me to it. "I'm happy to help you take care of her. I can walk her or whatever you need me to do. Just let me know," Megan says.

"That would be great," I say, but what I really want to say is 'Thank God!'

"We're actually on our way out right now; I'll stop by when I get back, okay?" Megan offers.

"Sure. Have fun!" I tell her.

Courtney gives Megan a look that I can't quite interpret, then they both turn to me and simultaneously say, "Thanks."

"I was just leaving," Joel says. Megan offers to walk him out, but Joel declines and picks up his backpack, and walks to the door.

"I'll text you later," Megan calls after him.

"I'll get out of your way," I say to the girls, suddenly feeling awkward. "Let me just get Penny on her leash while she's sitting still." I take a few steps toward the couch to attach the leash to Penny's collar, and before I can reach her, she jumps off the couch and runs into Megan's bedroom. "Oh shit," I mutter as I chase after her. It only takes seconds, but by the time I reach the bedroom, Penny is sitting in the closet with a third of a sandal firmly between her jaws and the rest of the shoe trapped underneath her oversize puppy paws. I lunge for the shoe, but the dog is faster and far more agile than I am and runs back into the living room. She stands in front of the sofa with the torn shoe in her mouth, staring proudly at Megan and me.

"I'm sorry, Megan, I'll pay you back for those," I say to her.

"Don't worry about it; those are super old," Megan says casually; I'm pretty sure she's lying to make me feel better.

"My ex-boyfriend's dog loved shoes too. You'll learn quickly not to leave them on the floor," she says.

"I think I'm going to learn a lot of things. I'm worried that I won't learn them quickly enough," I sigh.

"Courtney and I have to run out quickly. I'll come by as soon as we're back, and I'll take Penny for a long walk. That will help her burn off some energy," Megan says. "Right puppy?" she says in the same sing-song voice, directing the statement directly toward the dog.

"I'll try to survive while you're gone," I say.

Penny and I go back inside the main house, and she instantly lies down on the cool, tile floor, so close to me that her hind leg is on top of my bare foot. She looks up at me with her expressive dark, brown eyes and soft, floppy ears, and I can't help but fall a tiny bit in love with this dog that I've just met.

Unfortunately, it seems that short rest was all Penny needed to recharge, and before I know it, she is up and running down the hallway toward the front stairs. I chase after her, and it seems that she is delighted with the game and continues running right up the stairs. While she ducks into the first guest room on the right, I take the opportunity to close the rest of the doors on the second floor, saving countless pairs of shoes, and Lord knows what else, from their demise.

It only takes me a second to understand why there are tiny feathers floating in the air when I walk into the guestroom. Penny is curled up in the corner with her latest trophy – a down pillow. She has managed to rip through the pillowcase, pillow protector, and the actual pillow and is pulling out tufts of feathers as quickly as she can. She looks up at me, but instead of looking guilty, she seems proud of her accomplishment. I'm sure I shouldn't encourage this behavior, so I get down on my hands and knees and crawl over to her to try and wrestle the pillow away from her powerful jaws. At that exact moment, my phone rings, and without looking at the caller ID, I pick it up and breathlessly say, "Hello?!"

"Hey, it's me," Bridget says. "Both of the girls are actually taking a nap at the same time. Can we talk now?"

Penny loosens her grasp on the pillow, and I declare victory as I pull the ruined item into my lap. Unfortunately, the victory is short-lived since Penny only gave up so she could move on to her next target – the silk damask throw pillow. I reach up to pull it away from her before she can get a firm grip on it. "I'm sorry, Bridget, now isn't a good time. It's total chaos here," I say and hang up the phone. The irony isn't lost on me as I chase Penny back down the stairs, but I don't have the capacity to think about it now. As my mom would probably have said – don't judge a man until you've walked a mile in his shoes.

Chapter 36

Megan

The Uber drops us off at the main entrance. The hospital is bigger and more basic than I thought it would be. I had a vision of it being elegant or exclusive, like so many other places in the Hamptons, but this looks like an ordinary hospital.

"Are you ready?" Courtney asks.

"Not really," I reply. I move away from the automatic doors to let an elderly couple shuffle inside, and Courtney follows my lead. "I have no idea what to expect when I see Alex. I don't know what condition he's in, and I assume he's upset, but it's so hard to know," I sigh.

"Let's just get it over with. The faster you get in there, the faster you can leave," Courtney offers.

"You're right," I agree and slowly follow Courtney into the hospital. As soon as we are through the second set of doors, goosebumps break out all over my body. The temperature is at least twenty-five degrees colder than it was outside and my tank top and shorts, which were perfect for ninety degrees, are definitely inadequate in the sea of air conditioning. We walk up to the registration desk, and for a moment, I contemplate finding the hospital gift shop to buy a sweatshirt but quickly dismiss that as an absurd idea – I'll just have to be cold.

Courtney must sense my hesitation and thankfully strides straight up to the desk and begins asking for help. She doesn't get very far before she turns to me and says, "What's Alex's last name?"

"Oh, right. It's Beaver," I tell her.

"Seriously?" Courtney says. "So, your name could be Megan Beaver?" she laughs.

"This is not the time," I say to her. Although, it's hard not to smile. Alex has always been a good sport about it, but everyone gives him shit about his name.

Courtney turns away from the desk, clutching a small scrap of paper in her hand. "He's in room 232," she tells me. "Do you want me to come with you?" she asks.

"Yes, that would be great. Maybe you can wait outside in case I need you?" I suggest.

"Of course," she replies.

We ride up the elevator in silence and then walk side-by-side down the sterile hallway, which smells like a mixture of Clorox and artificial citrus meant to cover up something the bleach couldn't kill. I am prepared for someone to stop us on our way to Alex's room and ask where we are going or demand to see credentials, but the scrubs-clad men and women walk by without giving us a second look. As we pass room 231, we are less than four feet away from Alex's door. I realize now that I was planning for someone to question our motives, and I didn't expect to actually make it all the way here.

"I'll wait right over there," Courtney says, pointing to a cluster of chairs near the nurses' station.

"Got it," I tell her. I take a deep breath and brace myself for whatever awaits me in room 232. I'm practically sweating from nerves as I approach the door and wonder how I could have been cold only moments earlier. The door is open halfway, but the bed that I can see is neatly made and empty. Either Alex is in the bed by the window and doesn't have a roommate, or they gave Courtney the wrong room number.

I jump when a hand lands firmly on my shoulder. "The doctor is in with him right now; you'll have to wait until she's done," the gruff voice says. I spin around and find a tall, heavyset man in pink scrubs with a name-tag that says "Leonard."

My breathing rate begins to return to normal, and I thank the nurse and head over to the visitors' chairs to join Courtney. She must not have seen what happened because she seems shocked to see me. "Are you done already? What happened?"

"The nurse told me that I couldn't go in yet. At least I think he was the nurse," I say, pointing in Leonard's direction. "I need to wait until the doctor is done with Alex, and then I can go in," I tell her.

"Sorry," Courtney apologizes.

"Let's talk about something else while we wait. Have you heard anything from Preston? Did Alyssa say anything when she realized you moved out?" I ask.

"Nothing from Alyssa, which is not a shock. Nothing from Preston either," she sighs. "But I did get a weird text this morning from someone claiming to be Alyssa's friend. I was going to see what you thought earlier, but then all of *this* happened," Courtney says, indicating our surroundings.

"Let me see it," I say to her.

Courtney turns her phone over in her hand and holds it up to her face to open the screen. She quickly navigates through her texts to find the one she is looking for and then hands me the phone.

Hi Courtney – this is Serena – we met a few times through Alyssa. Up until now, I've felt bad going behind her back, but after watching how she's treated you, I have to say something. Give me a call on this number, and I can tell you more.

"Holy crap – that's so cryptic," I say, looking up from Courtney's phone.

"I should just ignore it. Right?" Courtney asks cautiously.

"Probably," I say at first. "But what if she can help you figure out what's really going on with Preston? And maybe she can explain why Alyssa's turned into such a bitch," I suggest.

"What if she's just as crazy as Alyssa. Or even worse! What if this is some weird trick and Alyssa put her up to it?!" Courtney hypothesizes.

"I guess that's possible," I wonder aloud. "Can I see the text again?" I ask her. But as I extend my arm to take her phone, I feel a firm hand on my shoulder yet again. I'm startled, but it's not quite as surprising as the last time, and I do a better job of composing myself.

"The doctor is all done. You can go in now," Leonard says.

I find it mildly disturbing that he hasn't asked for my name or my relationship to Alex. It seems like he's fine letting anyone into a patient's room, but perhaps they don't pay him enough to care about things like that, or maybe things like that don't happen in Southampton. "Thanks," I say to Leonard. To Courtney, I say, "Hopefully, I'll be back soon. I'll think about the mysterious text."

I brace myself for the unknown as I enter Alex's room. He's propped up against a pillow on the bed by the window, and other than the bandage on the back of his head and bruising on his nose, he looks exactly the same. His tall, muscular body barely fits on the narrow hospital bed. Alex's legs are folded up into an awkward-looking yoga pose because his six-foot-one-inch frame is no match for the rigid, plastic footboard. Even though it's apparent that he could use a shower, and his nose is banged up (but clearly not broken), he still looks good, and I hate myself for thinking this. His bleach blonde hair is slightly longer than when I saw him last, but the highlights are even more pronounced and somehow seem wasted on a guy. He stares at me with his mocha-colored eyes, and I don't see any of the rage I've been anticipating, but then again, he's never *been* an angry guy – that's always been one of the things that's so hard to reconcile about this ludicrous situation.

"Hey," Alex says quietly.

His soft tone throws me, and I'm unsure how to respond. I had run through multiple scenarios, but all of them began with Alex yelling obscenities (even though he's never once done that). "Hey. How are you doing?" I ask.

"I have a bit of a headache, and my nose hurts. But other than that, I'm okay," he says.

My instinct is to apologize, even if it's just on Joel's behalf, but I decide against it. Instead, I get right to the point. "What are you doing here? How did you find me?" I'm not sure that the second question matters, but I still want to know.

Alex sighs and says, "Hope told me that you were in the Hamptons."

"It's a pretty big place! How did you know that I was in Westhampton? How did you know I would be at Dockers?" I probe.

Alex's cheeks flush, and he looks embarrassed, which is not an emotion I'm used to seeing on him. "I called Danielle at work and told her that I couldn't remember where you were staying and wanted to surprise you. I didn't have a plan when I got here, but then I got lucky and saw you in town on your bike a few days ago. And then I followed you the other night," Alex says, hanging his head with shame.

"Oh my God – this all has to stop. I don't care what happened back at school or what I said I would do. You can tell Mateo's wife, or you can contact the public policy department – I don't care anymore!" I shout.

"I know," Alex says, shaking his head.

"Exactly," I reply. "Wait, what did you say?" I ask him.

"That's what I came here to tell you. But then I totally

fucked that up too," Alex sighs. He rests his face in his hands and then says "Ow!" and quickly jerks his head back up. "Forgot about the nose for a second," he says.

"What did you come here to tell me?" I ask. My tone is still severe, but I've managed to lower my volume, which hopefully means I won't attract attention from Leonard or anyone else outside of the room.

"I wanted to apologize. And I wanted to try to explain everything to you. Although, I understand you may not want to hear me out," he says miserably. Alex may be four years older and may have put me through hell this past year, but suddenly he looks exactly like the timid boy I met freshman year.

"Try me," I say. I pull the vinyl visitor's chair from its position against the wall and move it next to Alex's bed to take a seat.

"Where do I start?" he asks, although I'm pretty sure it's a rhetorical question, so I keep my mouth shut. "My grandmother has a lot of money," he says, nodding his head as if this will help me comprehend her level of wealth.

"That's definitely not where I thought you were going with this," I say, shifting in my seat.

"Sorry, it's all related, I promise," he says and takes a deep breath.

"I mean a *lot* of money," he emphasizes.

"Okay. Your whole family has a *lot* of money," I reply, starting to lose my patience with him.

"Not really; the money is all hers. My grandmother is also a total bitch. She controls all of it, and everyone else is essentially on an allowance and waiting for her to die," he says.

"Gotcha," I reply.

"Last winter break, she got sick. She revised her will and the terms of all of our trusts," Alex says.

I nod my head to show him that I'm listening. I feel like I might be able to see a relevant thread in his story.

"She changed the terms of my trust so that I only get the money when I get married," Alex says.

I leap out of my chair, fueled by newfound fury. "You've been blackmailing me into marrying you so you could get your money a few years early!" I yell. I've forgotten my previous goal of keeping my voice down, and I'm sure people can hear me all over the hospital.

"I know that's what it sounds like, but please listen to the rest of it," he pleads.

I perch on the edge of my chair, but I'm no longer committed to this conversation. "Fine," I say tersely, crossing my bare arms over my chest.

"I know what I did was wrong. I promise that I never meant for things to happen the way that they did or for things to get so out of control, but once it got going, I didn't know how to stop it," Alex claims.

"What are you talking about?" I ask, although it's hard not to relate to his feelings of being out of control. "Here's what happened. We started dating – although you barely ever wanted to come near me, so I don't know if it really counted as dating. Then I tried to break up with you since you had no interest in me, but you got all weird about it. I started dating Mateo. And I know that was wrong, but we can come back to that later. Then, you totally freaked out and blackmailed me. Does that about sum it up?" I ask snidely.

"Yes. But also no," Alex says quietly. "You were the first person that I ever dated," Alex tells me.

"That can't be true," I quickly reply. Although thinking it through, I can't remember any of his past girlfriends or anyone he's ever talked about.

"It is," Alex says. "After I came back from summer break, I decided that I was going to give it a try. If there was anyone I would ever want to date, it would be you, Megan," Alex says sincerely.

"What is that supposed to mean? You never wanted to touch me. I felt like I repulsed you. That hardly seemed like I was the only person you wanted to date," I tell him.

"Megan, I'm asexual," Alex says quietly.

"Oh!" I reply. I'm taken aback by this news. Even though the Stanford campus is wildly progressive and bursting with LGBTQ+ groups, I don't know too much about being asexual. I'm racking my brain to recall something Hope's friend told me a few years ago about asexuality. I remember she said that it is a spectrum and interest in sex varies widely across the spectrum and also that many people have romantic relationships, while some prefer close friendships. I try to remember anything else she told me, and the last part I recall is that she said she felt very misunderstood. "I had no idea," I mutter.

"I know you didn't," Alex says. "I spent most of high school knowing that I was a little bit different, but I couldn't figure out what it was. I assumed that I just hadn't met the right person. Then I got to college, and I slowly figured out that I was ace – that's what we call it," he explains. "And then I spent the next three years hoping that it would change because I just wanted to be like everyone else. You were the final *test*, for lack of a better word," Alex says.

"I'm so sorry," I say, wishing I could take back the horrible things I'd just said.

Alex shifts in the narrow bed and then continues. "Anyway, after my evil grandmother made that ridiculous rule, I kind of lost it. I was furious with her and mad at my family in general. I wanted to talk to you about it when I got back to campus in January, but I didn't know what to say. At first, I was going to see if you would agree to elope so we could get the money and then get a quick divorce, or something equally stupid," he says.

"Why didn't you just ask me? If you had asked me and told me everything, I'm sure I would have gone along with it," I tell him.

"Don't say *that*," Alex moans. "I was trying to figure out the best way to tell you about my asexuality and propose this scheme, and then you said you wanted to break up with me. Then I found you with Mateo, and I snapped. I can't really explain it because it's not like I wanted to have that kind of relationship with you. But at the time, I was jealous that you had that with him," Alex admits.

"I guess I can see that," I say, although I'm still trying to process everything he's saying.

"I can't fully explain the rest of my behavior. It's pretty much indefensible. I told my grandmother that I was engaged, hoping that it would pacify her and maybe even get her to change the terms of the trust again since she knew I'd be getting married in the future. Unfortunately, she made it her mission to have the wedding before she died, and as I said before, it spun out of control," Alex says.

"What changed now?" I ask. "Did she change the trust?"

"No. Nothing like that," Alex says. "I got the dose of reality I needed when you ran away this summer. I was finally able to look at the mess I'd made, and I was appalled," Alex says, looking me straight in the eyes. "I found a support group out near school and met other aces and learned that I'm not alone and that there's nothing wrong with me. I also learned that I might very well get married someday and have a wonderful relationship that doesn't include sex, but I'm not in any rush for that."

"That's great," I say to Alex, looking at him and seeing the same person I've known all these years but also noting new quiet confidence when he talks about himself. "So, what about the money? What happens with your grandmother?"

"I went to see her in Connecticut before I came out here. I told her that she could keep her money if it was dependent on marriage. I also told her that I'm asexual, but I don't think she understood what I said," he tells me.

"Wow. That takes a lot of courage," I say. "I'm glad you stood up for yourself."

"I'm still kind of hoping she changes her mind," Alex laughs. "But it's so much better this way," he says. "I'm really sorry about everything," he says.

"Me too," I say. I stand up and take a step closer to the bed and grab hold of his hand to give it a squeeze.

"Think we can be friends again?" he asks.

"Definitely," I reply.

Chapter 37

Courtney

Megan is quiet on the ride home from the hospital. She's adamant that things are 'all good' now with Alex, and she'll explain it all later, so it doesn't feel right to push her, but I'm dying of curiosity.

We find Nora sitting on the deck with Penny standing in front of her, happily wagging her tail. Nora is holding a near-empty bag of baby carrots and looks exhausted. She's still in the same running clothes she had on when I saw her first thing this morning, but they are covered with feathers and a pink sticky substance. Her ponytail has come loose, and her hair is hanging in front of her eyes, but she barely seems to notice.

"I'm almost out of baby carrots," she says, sounding somewhat worried.

"What happens when you run out?" I ask naively.

"I have no idea!" Nora exclaims. "Eva said that Penny

loves carrots and can have them as a treat. I've been able to keep her distracted out here with the carrots, but I'm not sure what she'll do when they're all gone."

"We'll take her for a walk," Megan offers. "She probably just needs to burn off some energy," she says confidently.

"That would be wonderful," Nora replies. "I think I've given up any chance at exercise today. But I do need to clean up inside, and I've got some phone calls to return. I'd also love to take a shower without worrying that Penny's going to destroy something while I'm locked away in the bathroom."

"Did your friend tell you where Penny sleeps?" Megan inquires.

"Huh?" Nora says, staring at Megan like she has three heads.

"Like in a dog bed or a crate? My ex's lab slept in a crate even when he got to be older because he loved it so much, but I feel like a lot of puppies have crates," Megan says.

"Oh my God, I'm such a moron!" Nora cries out as she slaps her own forehead. "Eva dropped off Penny and then said she would run back home and return with the rest of her stuff. I was so busy chasing Penny around the house that I ignored the doorbell, and I don't even know where my phone is!"

"We'll grab the leash and take her out for a bit now. Maybe you should see what your friend dropped off while we're gone?" Megan suggests.

"Thank you both!" Nora says. She hands Megan the leash and is already rushing inside toward the front door while we make our way toward Dune Road.

* * *

We mostly talk about dogs for the first few minutes of the walk. Megan tells me a little bit about her high school boyfriend Ryan's dog, and I tell her about a crazy but lovable German Shepard that my neighbor had while I was growing up. Eventually, she starts telling me the details about her visit with Alex at the hospital. I make her repeat the story twice because I want to be sure I don't miss anything. Then we're quiet for a bit as I absorb everything that has happened over the past twenty-four hours, and I assume she is doing the same.

We reach the parking lot of the Quogue Beach Club and decide that it is time to turn back to Nora's house. We've walked almost two miles, and Penny is finally starting to lose a little steam; if the distance Penny's tongue is extending out of her mouth is any indication, she's also quite thirsty.

"One of the girls on my basketball team is an ace," I tell Megan.

"Really?" she asks.

"She was a freshman my senior year, so I didn't know her very well. She was really involved in the Rainbow Alliance, which is the LGBTQIA group at school. She seemed really comfortable and confident about the whole thing. She mentioned it one day in the locker room like it was no big deal, it was just who she was, and then that was it," I tell Megan.

"Unfortunately, I don't think Alex has had quite the same experience," Megan says.

"It doesn't sound like it," I agree.

"I'm going to try and put this whole crazy thing behind us and be super supportive," Megan says.

"Speaking of being supportive," I say, deciding to change the topic. "What do you think I should do about Serena? Do you think I should call her?" I ask.

"Yes. Definitely call her. Let's call her right now!" Megan says excitedly. "Put your phone on speaker," she instructs.

I pull my phone out of my back jean shorts pocket and squint at the screen in the bright afternoon light. I find the text from Serena, and before I chicken out, I press the call icon and hold the phone up so Megan can hear too. It rings five times, and I'm about to give up when a female voice answers in a clipped tone, "Hello?"

"Hi, is this Serena?" I ask.

"Yes. Who is this?" she asks sharply.

"It's Courtney. You told me to call you?" I say and phrase it in the form of a question.

"Oh right! Hi Courtney," Serena says, her tone now much friendlier. "I can't talk now, but do you want to meet me later for a drink?"

I look at Megan for support, and she nods her head and mouths the word 'yes.' "Um, yes. Sure. Where should we meet?" I ask.

"Let's not go anywhere in East Hampton. Who knows where Alyssa will be tonight," Serena says. "Where are you staying?" she asks.

"I'm in Westhampton Beach," I reply. I'm genuinely surprised that she thought to take my location into account.

"Southampton Social Club! It's in between us, and we

can sit outside. I'll make a reservation for eight," Serena says confidently.

"My friend Megan will be with me," I blurt out. I'm not sure if it's proper social etiquette to bring a plus-one when someone's going behind another friend's back, but I don't really care.

"Okay. I'll make it for three. See you later," she says casually and ends the call.

Chapter 38

Nora

While the girls were out walking the dog, I got Penny's crate set up in the laundry room. I spread her toys out in different rooms so that she wouldn't have to go far to find one. My theory is that this will discourage her from chewing pillows and shoes, but I'm not sure if that's true. I also put the enormous, immaculate dog bed, with Penny's name embroidered on it, in the living room, but Eva's post-it note said, "Penny doesn't use this, but we're trying!"

I showered, cleaned up the rest of the dog damage from the morning, and felt refreshed when Courtney and Megan returned. Penny came inside, drank almost her entire bowl of water, and then miraculously went straight to her crate to lie down. Apparently, Megan knows what she's talking about.

An hour later, Penny doesn't seem quite as exhausted as she did immediately after the walk, but her demeanor is still a far cry from what it was earlier today. I'm sitting on the couch skimming through news highlights on my phone. Penny has jumped up, and I've pushed her back down at least a dozen times, and I finally give up. She's compromised and agreed to lay beside me on an old beach towel, so I consider this to be a huge win. She must shift over slowly because I don't notice it while it's happening, but suddenly, Penny's black, furry muzzle is resting on my thigh. Instinctively, I reach down to rub the top of her head and scratch behind her ears, and I'm shocked at how wonderfully soft her fur is, especially her silky ears. She lifts her neck to press her head into my hand, encouraging me to keep going. Before I know it, Penny is up on all fours, and I think she's going to jump down to the floor, but instead, she twirls in a circle and then crawls into my lap and sits down! Penny is perched precariously on my thighs, completely unaware that's she's a seventy-pound Labrador and not a lap dog. It's not entirely comfortable to have her there, but there's also something wonderful about the closeness and the body heat and security I feel from the weight of her muscled body. I know this is Eva's dog, and Penny will probably soon realize that she's in the wrong lap, but I put my arms around her anyway, and she snuggles closer.

It's only when Penny is safely in her crate for the night, after another long walk down Dune Road, that I remember Bridget's call from earlier today. It's only a little past nine, even though I'm exhausted from the day and heading up to bed, but I have no idea if that's too late to call. I can't imagine that she would already be asleep, but I have to admit I don't have a good sense of what Bridget's days or evenings look like.

I shoot off a text to Bridget to see if she's awake and then do a quick check of the doors, turn off all the downstairs lights and pour myself a glass of water. She texts back as I'm brushing my teeth.

BRIDGET: I'M STILL UP – WATCHING REAL HOUSEWIVES – DON'T JUDGE ME

NORA: HAHAHA – CAN YOU TALK? OR WANT TO DO IT TOMORROW?

The three dots pulse and then disappear and then pulse again and disappear for a second time. It seems that Bridget is struggling over whether she wants to talk to me. I'm going to write back and tell her not to worry about it, but my phone rings before I can do that and it seems Bridget has made her decision.

"Did you pause the real housewives?" I joke.

"It just ended," Bridget replies, and I'm weirdly hurt that she didn't have to choose me over the show.

"I'm sorry that I couldn't talk earlier," I say. "There were feathers flying everywhere. It's hard to explain," I say.

"Sounds like it," Bridget says.

"I got a dog," I share with her. "I mean, I didn't actually get a dog. My friend had to go to Italy at the last minute, and I'm watching her dog for two weeks, and the dog just got here this morning. I was having a bit of a tough time getting her to listen to me," I try to explain.

Bridget laughs uproariously, and I hear her move the phone away from her mouth to try and catch her breath. "What's so funny?" I ask.

"I'm just trying to picture you with a dog. Trying to picture you working with something that doesn't do things the way you want," she says.

"Ouch!" I reply. "What do you mean by that?" I question.

"Sorry, Nora, but you have to admit that you like everything to be a certain way, and you *always* like to be in control of, and at the center of, the situation," she says bitterly. "That's not how it works with dogs. Or with kids," Bridget adds.

Before I reply, I pause to think about what she just said. It's not that I don't have any self-awareness. I know that I'm type-A, and I like to have control; this is one of the reasons the past several months have been such a disaster with Mason leaving me and relinquishing my company. However, I had never stopped to think that this had any impact on Bridget.

"I am quite particular, aren't I?" I venture, trying to find my footing.

"You could say that," she replies.

"I haven't meant to be so self-absorbed," I say.

Bridget sighs at the other end of the line. "Everyone's self-absorbed; it's human nature," she says.

"You're not," I say. "You always put other people first - Patrick or Colleen and Quinn, or even me! You went out of your way to get me a matchmaker, so I wouldn't be alone; there's no way you have time to be doing things like that. You always put everyone else before you," I tell her as if I'm realizing this for the first time. Bridget doesn't respond, so I go on. "I'm sorry if I haven't been a very good aunt or sister," I say.

"Don't be ridiculous," Bridget says, but I think I can hear a smile in her voice.

"I don't think I have a good appreciation of what your life is like. If I'm being honest, I haven't spent much time thinking about it, and that sucks," I say to her.

"Don't feel too bad for me. I *love* my life. I wouldn't trade Patrick or the girls for anything. This is exactly what I always wanted," she says, letting out a heavy sigh. "But sometimes it's really hard. Patrick has to work longer and longer hours with his new position, and it's just a lot to do on my own."

"Is there anything I can do to help?" I ask her. I am appalled as I realize this is the first time I have genuinely asked her this question. I've made several suggestions of what I thought she needed or what would work well for *me*, but I haven't asked with only Bridget in mind.

"Let me think about it," Bridget says.

My instinct is to start making suggestions of all the ways I could help, but I fight it and merely say, "I'll be here."

"Thanks, Nora. That means a lot to me," Bridget says. "Oh, and I should probably apologize to *you* about Zadie," she says.

"Why?" I ask.

"I wasn't completely forthright about how I found her," Bridget admits.

"So, she didn't come as a recommendation from one of your good friends?" I ask.

"Not quite," Bridget says sheepishly. "I found her on some website when I was searching the internet."

I should be mad, but instead, I find this incredibly funny and start to cackle. "That would explain why she's such a wacko!" I say between giggles.

"It seemed like a good idea at the time," Bridget says. "But at four in the morning, there are a lot of things that seem like good ideas."

"You're right about that," I agree, finally able to catch my breath.

"Are we good? Bridget asks.

"Yes. Very good. I'll call you tomorrow?" I suggest.

"I'd like that," Bridget says.

"I love you, Bridget," I say. I can't remember the last time I said this to my sister, other than in a half-hearted casual way.

"I love you too, Nora," she says. My heart is full as I hang up the phone.

Chapter 39

Courtney

Nora graciously let Megan borrow her car to drive to Southampton. It's probably less expensive than Alyssa's top-of-the-line Mercedes, but I still feel nervous borrowing her new Porsche Boxster for the evening. I rarely think about it, but the money I received from my biological father's family after his death would certainly allow me to buy a car like this. However, my first nineteen years were spent in a comfortable but solidly middle-class upbringing, and I haven't changed many of my actions or my thought process since inheriting the money.

Megan pulls the car onto Elm Street, and I worry out loud about the ability to find a place to park, but she quickly reassures me. "They'll have valet. I haven't been here before, but I'm sure somewhere like this has valet." As she pulls to a stop in front of the restaurant, a uniformed parking attendant materializes beside her door, proving her right.

The place is packed with beautiful women in teeny

sundresses that show off their tans and overconfident men in white linen pants and pastel shirts. I barely remember what Serena looks like, and as we start to push through the throng of bodies, I can't imagine that we'll actually be able to find her. I respond to my phone's vibration in the back pocket of my tight, white jeans.

Possibly Serena: I have a table on the back patio – I'm wearing an orange dress

It's eerie that she texted at the exact moment I thought I wouldn't be able to find her, but it's certainly helpful. I nudge Megan's shoulder and point her toward the rear exit. I spot Serena as soon as we emerge onto the patio. I've only met her a few times with Alyssa, and those have either been at the pool or the beach, but now I remember her jet-black hair and flawless olive skin. She is wearing a bright orange strapless mini dress that would look terrible on ninety-nine percent of women, but it looks stunning on her. She waves as soon as she sees me, and I wave back.

"Wow," Megan whispers as we approach the table.

"I know," I reply. "I think she's a model," I whisper back, vaguely remembering something Alyssa told me earlier this summer.

Serena has already ordered a bottle of champagne for the table and pours us each a glass as soon as we sit down. I blunder the introductions, but no one seems to notice. We all sip champagne and talk about nothing for at least fifteen minutes as if we're simply friends catching up. When Serena beckons to the waiter to order another bottle of bubbly, along with tuna tacos and two rainbow rolls, I determine that it's time to get down to business.

"Can we talk about Alyssa now?" I ask bluntly.

"Sure. Of course, we can," Serena says. She polishes off her glass and dabs at her lips with the white linen napkin. Her shiny lip-gloss is somehow untouched, while my Aveda lip moisturizer has left a waxy residue on my glass. "As I said before, I generally wouldn't do anything like this. Alyssa and I grew up together out here during the summer, and she *is* a good friend," Serena says.

I nod in agreement to show that I understand this is out of character for her; hopefully, I also convey that I won't judge her, no matter how much she tells me.

"Alyssa has always been a bit wild. I mean, I'm sure *you* know that." Serena says, but thankfully she doesn't wait for me to agree. "But something has changed this summer, and I feel like she's taken everything too far. I know that she's pissed off at her parents, and she doesn't want to go to Juilliard," Serena says, rolling her eyes as if this is totally normal. "But there have to be some boundaries, and it's no excuse to fuck with your life."

"Can you say more about that?" Megan asks.

"Oh right. Yes. Where should I start?" Serena asks.

"If you could tell us as much as you know, that would be great," I say. "I know she said something to Preston, but I didn't think she even knew him. Other than through me," I add.

"Oh shit," Serena says. The waiter appears right then, and she grabs the bottle and fills all of our glasses. I'm about to protest, but she says, "You're going to need this."

"I'm driving," Megan informs her.

"That's fine. Courtney will probably need yours too," she says, moving Megan's glass beside mine.

I'm trying to be patient, but I don't know how much longer I can wait for Serena to get to the point. "So, what did Alyssa do?" I ask naively.

Serena exhales and elegantly folds her long arms in front of her on the table. "Let me start at the beginning. I'll try to tell you everything I've heard from Alyssa," she says.

I nod for her to begin and then look down and see that I'm clutching the picnic table as if physically bracing for the news.

"Alyssa met Preston at a party the first night of freshman year," Serena begins.

"What?" I ask, immediately interrupting her.

"This is going to take a long time if you already have questions," Serena comments.

"Right. Sorry. Go on," I instruct her.

"They slept together a couple of times that first week and the way Alyssa described it, he wasn't interested in anything serious after that, but she was. Actually, I think she described him as quite the player," Serena says.

I don't interrupt her this time, but I nod along. I had no clue that Preston and Alyssa had ever slept together, let alone at the beginning of freshman year. Preston's description is accurate, or at least that was his reputation. He wasn't a saint, but from what he told me, people thought he slept around a lot more than he did, and he didn't bother correcting them.

"She moved on and dated other guys, but she always liked him. I remember her talking about him the summer before her sophomore year, and she was convinced that she would change his mind that fall. Apparently, that year, she ran into him at a party, and he was drunk and really upset, and they hooked up again. She was sure they were going to get together - but it turned out that he was only upset about a fight that he had with *you*." She says with a strong emphasis on the word, and she gestures in my direction in case I don't understand.

"That would have been the middle of sophomore year," I say, more to myself than to either Serena or Megan.

"I guess shortly after that, you and Preston started dating, and then you've been together ever since," Serena says with a flourish.

"Alyssa has been interested in Preston the entire time we've been friends, and she's never said anything?" I say with disbelief.

"What's she supposed to say? I want to screw your boyfriend?" Megan suggests.

I ignore her comment. "And what about Preston? He had this history with Alyssa, and he obviously knew that she liked him, and he just let me come live with her for the summer?" I cry.

"Didn't you say that he thought it was a really bad idea?" Megan asks.

"Well, yeah, but I thought it was just because Alyssa and I didn't know each other that well. I didn't realize it was because he knew she was his stalker!" I moan.

"In his defense, I'm not sure Preston knew that Alyssa was still interested," Serena offers.

"I'm not sure I'm looking to defend him right now, but thanks. So, what is going on now? Has she been talking to him? Oh my God – are they together?!" I ask, the thought just occurring to me.

"I'll tell you what I know based on what she told me at the beginning of the summer. She said that when she initially asked you to come to stay with her, she didn't know you guys were going to break up. I think there was still something twisted about her wanting to spend the summer with Preston's girlfriend, but that's another issue. Then you guys broke up, and she told us that she was finally going to be able to go after him," Serena says. She pauses and waves to a pair of beautiful women making their way toward our table, and I worry that they are going to come to join us, and I'll have to wait to hear how this story ends. But then they veer off toward another crowd, and Serena is free to continue.

"Shortly after you arrived, she got the idea that you weren't happy about the break-up and that you were going to get back together. She started by posting a few pictures on Instagram of you with other guys and making sure that Preston saw them. Then she texted pictures of you and Tucker at that bar and playing basketball to show Preston that you had moved on," she says.

"This is crazy," I say.

"Apparently, it wasn't having the desired effect because you guys were still talking, and she felt like you were probably going to get back together. In my opinion, that's when she crossed the line," Serena says.

"What does that mean?" I demand. I've got both palms on the table, and I've pushed my body aggressively toward Serena in what is decidedly a hostile posture. Megan places a hand gently on my back, and I try to relax my stance – after all, it's not Serena's fault.

"Alyssa picked up your phone when you left it on the counter. I think you were at the beach? Anyway, she talked to Preston, and he told her that he had a few days off and he wanted to come and visit you. I'm not sure if it was supposed to be a surprise or not. That was the last straw for Alyssa because she knew that meant you would get back together. She told Preston that you were dating Tucker," Serena says.

"Didn't you say he was furious?" Megan asks. "Why would he have gotten *that* mad if you two were already broken up and you started dating someone?"

"That's not all she said," Serena says contritely. "Alyssa told him that you had been cheating on him the last two years at college. She made up an elaborate story and said that she knew everything because she lived down the hall from you at the Kappa house and used to see you sneak guys in and out of your room," Serena says.

"She's such a fucking liar! I'm going to kill her!" I cry out.

"I know. It's pretty awful," Serena says. "I was at that party with all the blow, the one where she told you that Preston called *her*, but that was also a lie. As I said, I've known *her* for years, and I just met *you*. I was going to stay out of it, but then she took it too far. She's been bragging about messing up your life ever since she talked to Preston, and it doesn't seem right." Serena says pragmatically as if all of this is normal.

"What am I going to do?" I wail, at the same time that Megan thankfully has the presence of mind to say, "Thank you so much for telling us – that was really kind of you."

"Yes, thank you," I add. "I know you didn't have to do this."

"You're welcome," Serena replies. "I would appreciate it if you keep me out of it," she says. "Alyssa has a lot of issues, but we grew up together, and she's still my friend," she says.

"Sure," I reply automatically. Honestly, as much as I want to murder Alyssa, I mostly never want to see her again. My primary concern is if I'll ever be able to get Preston to talk to me again.

Chapter 40

Nora

Penny is snuggled next to me on my bed. I wanted to relax upstairs, watch TV and look through emails in my room. It seemed too early to put her in her crate, so I didn't object when she followed me up the stairs. Now her warm body is pressed tightly against my legs, and I can't bear the idea of waking her up and taking her downstairs. I tell myself that she'll probably wake up and need to go outside to pee anyway, so she won't be here for too long.

With an old episode of *Modern Family* in the background, I open my iPad and return to the document I'd been working on earlier today. It's nothing remarkable, but for the first time in months, I've been jotting down notes about ideas for potential ventures. I'm taking the often-used approach that there are 'no bad ideas' in brainstorming, but I'm seasoned enough to know that's absolute bullshit. I read over my list and chuckle as I notice that at least a third of the ideas are dog-related. I absentmindedly rub my hand down my muse's back and find it hard to believe that Penny has only been here for six days – it feels like a lot longer.

There are a couple of decent ideas on my list. I've got nothing worth sharing with investors yet, but it feels amazing to be working again. Or at least doing something that could *lead* to working again. I developed the idea for Limestreet Athletics so long ago that I'd almost forgotten how exhilarating it was at the very beginning when it was just an idea.

When I wake up in the morning, I realize that Penny is no longer curled against my legs. I have no idea what kind of trouble she's gotten into during the night, but I hope that it isn't too awful. I should jump out of bed and start to assess the damage, but I want to relish my ignorance for a few more minutes.

I roll over in my king-sized bed toward the window and am shocked and delighted at what I see. Penny may have left her spot as my leg warmer, but she only did it so she could rest her head on the pillow next to mine. She is fast asleep in what would have been Mason's spot, fully stretched out with her broad head resting right on top of the down pillow. I slowly reach for my phone on the night table because I have to get a picture of her like this. As my mom used to say – a picture is worth a thousand words.

All of my recent photos are now pictures of Penny, but what else am I supposed to take pictures of? I've sent several of them to Eva over the past few days to let her know that Penny and I are surviving, but I decide against sending this one. I'm not sure that Penny sleeping in bed with me will be well received.

Penny wakes up as soon as my feet hit the floor. Her internal clock must alert her that she's been asleep too long, and she bolts out of the room. I can hear her nails click-clacking on the hardwood floor all the way down the stairs. I also need to pee, but it seems wise to run after her and take care of her needs first since I likely have better bladder control. Blessedly, Penny makes it to the driveway and drowns the patch of grass next to the fence before looking up at me and bounding back up the deck stairs.

After I barely make it to the bathroom, I put a pot of coffee on for myself and then feed Penny while I wait for it to brew. I marvel at our little morning routine and how it can already feel habitual after barely a week. I spread peach jam on a slice of sourdough toast and sit down at the kitchen table to read over an email from my financial advisor about his increased fees. Penny is by my side as soon as my butt is in the chair. She sits patiently next to me and looks up at me with what can only be described as 'sad puppy dog eyes.'

"I let you sleep in bed with me last night. I can't start feeding you from the table now, can I?" I ask Penny before I realize that I'm engaged in a conversation with a dog. Penny continues to stare at me, and if it's possible, her big brown eyes look even sadder than before. I tear off a piece of the crust and look around as if someone is going to catch me, and I toss it to Penny. She jumps up and gracefully grabs it out of the air and then rubs her nose against my pajama-clad leg – I think it's her way of saying thank you.

I check my personal email and am elated to see new

emails from three college friends. The four of us were inseparable at Duke, and we stayed in touch for the first several years post-graduation even though we were scattered across the country, but then I let the group slip away. I've reached out to each of them a couple of times over the past few weeks to apologize for my behavior and see if they would be interested in reconnecting. To my delight, they were all surprisingly understanding, and we exchanged a mix of individual and group emails. I reply to the group email and suggest a virtual happy hour for later in the week. I know that I can't make up for lost time, but it's never too late.

I've left the last bite for Penny, and I try to make her sit before I toss it to her. She almost complies, and I give it to her anyway; I'm definitely a terrible dog trainer. Just as Penny catches the toast, I hear the sliding glass door open behind me and footsteps on the tile floor.

"I saw that," Megan laughs.

"Oh shit," I laugh. "No one was supposed to see me," I reply, embarrassed.

"It's okay," Megan says. "I'm pretty sure most people give their dogs table scraps. Ryan's dog used to lick all the plates before they went into the dishwasher," Megan adds.

"Really?" I ask.

"Yeah, it was pretty weird. But that dog could eat anything; he was like a walking trashcan," she jokes. "They never had a single crumb on the floor."

"I guess so," I say, still trying to figure out how I feel about a dog licking all of the dishes.

"I just came in to see if you wanted me to take Penny for a walk?" Megan asks.

"That's so nice of you. I'm going to go for a run in a bit, and I'll take her with me," I say. "Maybe later this afternoon, if you're around? But don't worry about it if you're not."

"You're really taking to the whole dog thing," Megan comments.

I hesitate slightly before I reply. "It's just a favor for my friend," I say, downplaying it. "Although it is nice to have a little bit of activity in the house," I admit.

"You could get a dog!" Megan squeals.

"What?" I question.

"I know that you are just dog-sitting right now, but you could get a dog of your own!" She says excitedly.

"Oh, I don't think so," I reply. "This has been fun, but I don't think I could actually have a dog," I tell her.

"Okay," Megan says, shrugging her shoulders and retreating back through the glass doors. "Courtney and I are going to go to the beach before I have to go tutor if you want to join us," she says.

"Thanks, maybe," I reply, although I didn't entirely hear her. I'm too busy thinking over what she said about another dog, and that as crazy as it is, I *could* imagine myself with a dog, but only with *this* dog.

Chapter 41

Courtney

It's a stunning August day on the beach. Cerulean blue, cloudless skies, and a soft, warm breeze that makes the temperature feel around eighty, even though it's probably ten degrees warmer. Yet, I'm not able to enjoy this perfect morning on the beach; I'm too preoccupied with what Serena told me last night and stressed that Preston won't return my calls, texts, or emails.

"What am I supposed to do?" I ask Megan. She is lying on the striped towel next to me, trying to read her book and likely wanting me to stop pestering her.

"I don't know," Megan says. "Maybe try him again in a little bit?"

I flop back down on my towel and groan. "I've left a dozen messages and sent about a million texts."

"Maybe give him a day and see what happens?" she suggests.

"I'm going to fly out there," I say, as soon as the idea occurs to me.

"To Denver?" she asks.

"Yes! I'll go find him at training camp. I don't know if our relationship is salvageable, but I can't have him thinking that I cheated on him like that. Before we were a couple, we were best friends, and I can't lose that," I tell her.

"Can you just show up at an NFL training camp? How will you find him if he isn't responding to you?" Megan asks.

"I've actually got an answer to that," I tell her. I quickly grab my towel and beach bag and throw on my cover-up. "Sorry, I've got to go," I say to Megan.

"Are you leaving now?" she asks, sounding shocked.

"I have to make a few phone calls, and I'm going to book my flight and get packed. I can't just sit here," I say, already walking toward the wooden stairs.

"What about your job?" Megan asks.

"I'll call them once I figure out my flights. I only have a few shifts left there anyway. I'm sure I can get someone to cover for me," I tell her.

"Okay," Megan calls out, sounding unconvinced. "Good luck!"

* * *

I debate whether I should buy my plane ticket or call Mark first, but decide it's a little too risky to buy the ticket before I talk to him. Mark picks up on the first ring. "Hey, Courtney! How's everything going? Jennifer showed me some of the pictures you sent. The beach looks gorgeous out there. Although it's no Lake Michigan," he laughs.

Hearing his friendly voice makes me regret that I haven't been better about keeping in touch this summer. Mark is part of the family I inherited overnight when I found out about my birth father, and he's an amazing brother-in-law, or maybe half-brother-in-law if there is such a thing.

"It's pretty nice out here," I tell him. I haven't filled anyone in my family in on the commotion with Alyssa or that I'm living with Megan now. My parents are still away in Australia, and both of my half-sisters have busy lives, and it didn't seem worth it to bother them. I continued to reply to their texts with emojis, one-liners, and pictures of the scenery, and everyone seemed satisfied. My goal now is to get Mark's help while still keeping him in the dark to the full extent of the drama.

"Jennifer's at the office," Mark says. He must assume that I'm trying to reach my half-sister but couldn't get in touch with her and that's the reason I called him.

"Actually, I wanted to talk to you," I say to him. "I was hoping you could help me with something," I say.

"Sure, what is it?" he asks jovially.

"Who do you know at the Broncos?" I ask.

"Other than Preston?" he jokes. Although the majority of people don't know one player on an NFL team, it's highly likely that Mark knows multiple players and, ideally, some of the coaches. Mark knows Preston because he's my boyfriend (well, ex-boyfriend), but he also knows him because he's the offensive coordinator for the Northwestern football team. Before he met my half-sister, Mark used to play for the

Chicago Bears and then went back to coaching a few years ago. I usually tuned out the conversations when Mark and Preston talked NFL connections, but now I wish I'd paid more attention.

"Is Preston okay?" Mark suddenly asks, sounding worried.

This is a tricky question to answer because, as far as I'm concerned, he's definitely *not* okay, but in the greater sense, he's fine. I also don't want Mark to worry, and I really don't want Jennifer to worry, so I have to massage the truth. "Yes, Preston is great. I want to go to Denver to surprise him, and I want to make sure that it's okay. He mentioned that he had a few days with some downtime, but I'm not sure what that looks like," I explain.

"I'm sure he'll love that," Mark says. "Let me think about it for a second." I can picture him standing in their gorgeous white kitchen drumming his fingers on the island while he flips through his mental Rolodex of past contacts. "Larry's out in Denver now," he exclaims as soon as he remembers.

"Larry?" I ask.

"I can't even remember where we met, but he's a good guy. He's their new special teams coordinator. He may not be working directly with Preston, but he generally makes it his business to get to know all the new guys," Mark tells me.

"Could you check with him and see what he thinks about the idea of a visit?" I ask. "Make sure he knows that it's supposed to be a surprise."

"Of course," Mark replies.

"I know I'm already asking a big favor, but could you try and get an answer quickly?" I ask. "This is kind of last-minute on my end. I have a couple of days off work, and I'd have to leave today," I explain.

I hear Mark's big booming laugh and wonder if he's going to tell me that my request is ridiculous, but instead, he says, "I'll call him right now. I'll text you as soon as I hear back."

"Thank you!" I say, feeling an iota of relief that I am making forward progress.

"Anything for family," Mark says sweetly. "Tell Preston we miss him. Pre-season isn't the same without him."

"I will," I reply, but what I'm really thinking is that nothing is the same without him.

True to his word, Mark talked to Larry and gets back to me fifteen minutes later. However, he exceeds my wildest expectations when he sends over a detailed schedule of Preston's activities for the next three days! Luckily, Megan comes back from the beach in time to rescue my attempt at packing. I'm so nervous that when she finds me, all I have packed is underwear and bathing suits.

* * *

The only seat left on the six o'clock flight is in first class, and I decide to splurge. The balance in my bank account says that this isn't a big deal, but it definitely feels like one. It's the first time I've ever sat on this side of the curtain. I've walked through the first-class cabin dozens of times and seen travelers casually enjoying pre-flight cocktails while trying to avoid eye contact with those of us stranded in the aisles. I never thought I would be one of those privileged passengers enjoying warm nuts while debating how far to recline my seat.

First-class is *almost* enough of a distraction to keep my mind off of Preston, but not quite. Although it's almost a five-hour flight, we land at eight-forty-five due to the two-hour time difference. According to Preston's schedule, his practice ended at seven tonight, and then he doesn't have anything scheduled for the next forty-eight hours. I talked it over with Megan, and we decided that I should go straight to my hotel from the airport and get a good night's sleep and go see him in the morning. This is still my plan when the plane lands. But while I'm walking toward the airport exit and I give the Lyft driver my destination, I put in the address for Preston's apartment.

The building itself is unremarkable, but the neighborhood looks like one big party. I've never been to Denver before, and I'm not sure what I was expecting, but it isn't this. Foolishly, I thought it would be all mountains. But Denver doesn't look that different than parts of Chicago. Preston lives in the Lower Downtown neighborhood, which apparently some people call LoDo. There are several high-rise apartment buildings on this block and bars with patrons spilling out onto the street enjoying the warm summer night.

Standing in the lobby of Preston's building, clutching my suitcase, I begin to regret my impulsive decision. A middle-aged woman let me into the lobby while on her way out. If there is a doorman, he seems to be on a break, leaving the elevator ride as the only thing that stands between Preston and me. I try to picture his face when I knock on his door, and all I can see is anger and hurt. In the worst version of the scenario, Preston answers the door half-naked, and there's an equally naked woman in the apartment behind him.

I laugh out loud at the stupidity of my plan and am fortunate that no one is there to hear me. I open the Lyft app on my phone and enter the hotel as my new destination because it's too late to get a flight back to New York tonight. I'm relieved to see that I'll only have to wait three minutes for my driver, Harriet, to arrive. I know Megan is waiting for an update, but I don't think I have the energy. I told her that my flight had landed safely, and she assumed that I was already at the hotel, which is where I'll be soon.

I see Harriet's teal Toyota Camry pull up outside the building and give the lobby a quick once-over before I leave. This is the closest I'll ever get to Preston's new apartment, so I want to absorb it in case I ever want to picture him here.

The elevator doors open behind me right as I push open the doors to exit. It's a massive building, and the odds are small, but I just know that it's Preston in the elevator. "Courtney?!" the familiar voice says as if he's not even sure that's my name.

"Hey," I say self-consciously as I place my duffel bag on the floor by my feet.

"What are you doing here?" Preston asks, his southern drawl achingly familiar. He doesn't sound as angry as I thought he might be, but he certainly doesn't seem pleased to see me. The last time I saw him, his short hair was dyed blonde, but it seems he's shaved it again (which is actually my preference), and the sparkle of his hazel eyes against his light-brown skin is quite a sight for sore eyes, as corny as that may sound.

For a split second, I think about lying and saying that I'm in town to visit a friend and had no idea he lived here. However, that would likely make things even more awkward than they are right now. "I came to see you," I say quietly. "You wouldn't return my calls or texts," I add by way of an explanation.

"I don't think we have anything to talk about," he says, folding his arms across his chest. It's at this point that I notice how much more muscular he is than he was just six weeks ago when I last saw him. I wasn't sure it was possible for him to be in better shape, but clearly, I was wrong. There are sculpted peaks and valleys visible through his t-shirt that I want to reach out and touch, although that certainly wouldn't be welcome given what he thinks of me right now.

Harriet honks her horn and simultaneously texts me to tell me that she started the wait time two minutes ago. I take the gamble that Preston will hear me out and text back to cancel the ride and accept the cancellation penalty, then watch her drive away.

"Will you please hear me out?" I ask. "I know you're upset, but Alyssa was lying to you," I say.

"Why would she lie to me?" he asks.

"Because she's in love with you. Or she is obsessed with you. Or perhaps something in between. Apparently, she has been ever since you slept with her freshman year. And sophomore year," I add with a caustic tone.

"What are you talking about?!" he asks, looking at me like I'm a lunatic.

"It's fine. I mean, I wish you had told me about it before. And I *really* wish you had told me about it before I went to live with her this summer," I say.

"I never slept with Alyssa," Preston says.

"But she told her friend..." I say, trailing off.

"We met at a party that first week of school. She flirted with me the entire time. I'll admit that I thought about it, but then she got shit-faced and was still acting like she wanted something to happen. I would never hook up with a girl in that condition," Preston says, and of course, I know that's true.

"So, nothing happened?" I ask him. "What about later freshman year? Or sophomore year?"

"Nothing ever happened. I swear," he says. "I saw her at some parties, and I know that she was popular with a lot of other guys on the team if you know what I mean, but I really didn't know her that well," he says.

"She feels otherwise," I say, but it's more to myself than to him. "Alyssa told all her friends in East Hampton these elaborate stories about you over the past few years. Basically, you're the *one that got away*, and I'm the one that's keeping her from you," I tell him.

"That's absurd," he says. "Like I said, I barely know her."

The elevator opens again, and this time it's a group of men and women a little bit older than we are heading out to a bar. We stop talking to let them go by and wait in silence until they are out on the street. I hadn't planned to do this in the lobby of Preston's building, but it seems that I'm not going to have another option. As succinctly as I can, I give Preston a rundown of my summer with Alyssa. I watch his face go through stages of indifference to confusion to anger to sadness as he tries to take it all in.

When I've finished retelling everything Serena told us last night (was it really only last night?), I look at him expectantly. He's quiet, as if he needs more time to digest all the craziness. I was secretly hoping that the minute I finished my story, he would hug me and say something like, "Good thing that's all settled," even though that's not something he would ever say.

What he does say is, "What about those pictures she sent of you and those guys?"

"Tucker?" I question.

"I don't know names," Preston replies. "And there was more than one guy," he says crossly.

"Tucker's just some guy that I met playing volleyball on the beach. He's nice, but that's it. He had a connection to help me get a summer job, and we ran into each other and played basketball twice," I tell him. "I know she posted a picture of me on Instagram early in the summer with one of her friends, and I was basically just sitting next to him, but from the angle of her photo, it looks like I'm on his lap. From what Serena told me, I'm guessing she did a lot of shit like that," I tell him.

"I don't get it. I thought you and Alyssa were *friends*," Preston says sarcastically.

"I thought so too!" I exclaim. "I mean, I knew we weren't great friends, but we had always gotten along. She's a completely different person at school than she is out in the Hamptons," I say.

"How so?" he asks.

"All she does is party. She drinks all the time and is always hooking up with different guys, and the other night everyone at the house was doing coke," I tell him.

"That doesn't sound so different from how she was when I saw her at school," Preston says.

"Are you serious?! She always seemed quiet and mellow around the Kappa house. She was serious when we took that class together," I add, trying to form an accurate picture of Alyssa in my mind.

"I'm not sure what she was like at the house, but she definitely knows how to party," Preston says. "It's like you went to spend the summer with someone you barely knew," he accuses.

"That's because you broke up with me, and I didn't know what else to do," I yell back at him, surprised by the tone of my own voice.

"I didn't break up with you," Preston says vehemently, looking straight at me. I have no idea if he believes that Alyssa lied to him and we're past that topic or if we've merely pressed pause. However, this feels like the issue that's been brewing under the surface for both of us all summer long.

"Yes, you did. Even if you didn't say those exact words, you made it quite clear that you didn't want a long-distance relationship," I say.

"That's not what I said. And that's not what I meant. All I wanted to do was talk about what things would be like when you were in New York, and I was in Denver, and the next thing I knew, you said we shouldn't bother trying," Preston says, rubbing his hand across his chin the way he does when he's distressed.

I think back to that day on the bench outside Deering Library when Preston initiated the discussion. My mind basically went blank as soon as he said he wanted to talk about how things would be after graduation. I assumed I knew what he was going to say next, so I decided to beat him to it and suggested we break up at the end of the year. "I only said that because you were *about* to break up with me," I say.

"Seriously?" he asks. And my face grows hot with embarrassment from the way he looks at me. "What is this, middle school?" Preston asks, sounding both amused and annoyed.

"I was protecting myself," I admit, although it feels foolish now.

"I get that. But you didn't even give me a chance. You didn't give *us* a chance," Preston says sadly.

From the way he says it, I'm quite sure that I've lost all of my chances, but I can't leave without knowing that he doesn't believe all of the crap that Alyssa told him. I may have ruined my chance for a future with Preston, but I'm not willing to ruin how he thinks of our past. "I'm sorry. I'm really sorry that I didn't have enough faith in us," I say. "At least tell me that you don't believe what Alyssa told you," I say.

"I don't," he says. "And I'm sorry that I ever believed any of it for a minute. I was just hurt."

"Okay," I say quietly, bending down to pick up my bag. I should probably arrange for a ride before I go outside, but I need fresh air, and I don't want Preston to see me cry. I turn around to push the door open again, back to where I was merely half an hour ago before Preston came out of the elevator. I wonder if he'll continue on his way out for the night or if he'll at least wait until I'm gone...

"Where are you going?" Preston asks as I'm halfway out the door.

"I don't remember the name of the hotel. I'd have to look it up. I think it's a Westin," I say wearily.

"I meant, why are you leaving?" he asks.

I turn around to look at him and see a hesitant grin on his face. "I thought that's what you wanted?" I say, phrasing it as a question.

"I think we both have some work to do. And we both need to do a better job of saying what we mean and not jumping to conclusions. That's what I think," Preston says with a smirk.

My heart skips a beat. "What do *you* want?" I ask him.

"I want you," he says, walking toward me and picking me up in the bear hug that I've been longing for. He doesn't know his own strength, but I wouldn't trade the intensity of his hug for anything in the world. When his lips meet mine, it's almost as if no time has passed. We both know what it's like to think we'd lost each other, which makes this even more extraordinary.

"I want you too," I reply without hesitation.

Chapter 42

Megan

Although I usually ride my bike when I tutor for this family in Quogue, Joel offered to drive me today, and I accepted. He said he had another session with a student close by, around the same time, and he could drop me off and pick me up. I usually enjoy the exercise and solitude that my bike ride provides, but with another day of temperatures in the mid-nineties, the air conditioning is quite appealing.

As always, it's quiet in the car with Joel. As we near my stop, I try to make small talk and ask Joel a few questions about progress on his app, but he doesn't have much to say. In a business-like tone, he tells me that he will be back to get me in ninety minutes and drives off.

Today is one of my last tutoring sessions of the summer. My classes don't start for a few weeks, but I'm leaving to go back to Stanford next week to move in with Hope. Most of the students will leave right after Labor Day anyway, and they will be taking their next (and hopefully last) SAT or ACT in a couple of weeks. Time goes quickly today, and I feel unusually pleased with the progress that we have made. Unlike some other students, this girl got a mediocre score on her first two attempts, but she's clearly very bright. She gets nervous with the pressure of the test and needs some tools to help her succeed – in other words, she is the ideal tutoring pupil, and I'm thrilled to be able to help her and her parents.

Joel picks me up exactly ninety minutes later. I'm waiting outside the beachfront Quogue home, scrolling through texts from Courtney. She's decided to stay for an extra week in Denver, and the smile on her face in the adorable selfies of her and Preston is evidence enough that things are going well for the happy couple.

"How was it?" I ask Joel when I get in the car.

"How was what?" he asks.

"Your student. Tutoring?" I ask, looking at him quizzically.

"Oh. Right. I didn't have anyone to tutor today," he replies.

"Did they cancel?" I ask.

"No," he says.

"Then why did you tell me you did?" I ask.

Joel doesn't turn his head even the slightest bit away from the road to look at me when he says, "I told you that so I would have an excuse to drive you."

"Why would you do that?" I ask. I assume that he'll shift his gaze now to look in my direction, but he continues straight down Old Country Road without taking his eyes off the street.

"I wanted to talk about what happened the other night," Joel says.

"It's fine," I say quickly, glossing over it. It already seems like so long ago, but it's been less than a week. I think back to the afternoon when Courtney and I got home from the hospital. I texted Joel to explain as much as I could about what Alex told me and to assure him that he had nothing to worry about; Alex had no interest in pressing charges or even finding out who hit him.

"It's not fine with me," Joel says. In an uncharacteristic move, Joel makes an un-signaled left turn into the parking lot of the Quogue Wildlife Refuge and turns off the engine. Fortunately, he also opens the car windows, so we don't melt.

"I promise it's not a big deal," I say to Joel, but he cuts me off.

"This isn't easy for me to say. You probably know that about me by now," Joel begins.

"Okay," I say with a slight smile. I have no idea what he's about to say, but I do know that many things don't come as naturally for him as others, while some things come way more easily – that's one of the things I really like about him. I try to take time to digest this thought, but Joel keeps going.

"Aren't you curious why I was at Dockers that night?" he asks.

"Oh yeah," I say. "I guess I am. Why *were* you there?" I ask. I did wonder about this, but there were too many other more pressing issues, and eventually, I forgot about it.

"It was a crazy idea, but I came to ask you out," Joel says shyly.

"Huh?" I say, trying to make sense of this.

"I told you that I'm not very good at this," Joel says.

"Wait. I remember that night. You had just yelled at me about test scores and forgetting my password," I recall. "And then you wanted to ask me out?" I question.

"I'll apologize for that as well," Joel says. "I was having some technical issues with my app and was agitated. I had also been planning on asking you out, and then I got flustered over our text exchange," Joel says.

"And then your solution was to come to Dockers and beat up my ex-boyfriend?" I offer.

Joel blushes, and it's hard not to find it adorable. I honestly can't remember at what point during the summer I went from finding him to be haughty and self-righteous to kindhearted and unique.

"I came to talk to you, and then I saw that you were in trouble, and I reacted badly," Joel says solemnly.

"You were trying to help me," I say hurriedly, reaching over and placing my hand on his arm.

"I should have learned my lesson last time. Adrenaline took over and got the best of me," Joel says.

"I really appreciate it," I say. "I know now that I was never in danger. But you had no way to know that. And at that moment, I was scared, and I'm glad you were there," I tell him.

"I'm lucky. I could be in a lot of trouble," he muses.

"Thank you for taking that risk for me," I say. My hand is still on his bare arm, and we both look down at it simultaneously.

"I know it was an outlandish idea to ask you out. I'm trying to do a better job communicating my feelings. I know you're leaving to go back to California, and I wanted you to know before you left," Joel says and exhales. "You probably think I'm crazy for telling you about it at all." He's back to staring out the windshield – across the street; there are groups of little kids haphazardly lined up, waiting in the heat to enter the wildlife refuge. I stare at them for a minute and think about all that's transpired this summer. It's hard to believe everything that's happened in the past two months. It feels like I arrived on Dune Road only yesterday, but so much has changed since then. I only came here to run away from my problems, but I feel like a light has been turned on, and I can see everything so much more clearly now.

"I don't think it's crazy at all," I say meaningfully, as he shifts his gaze back towards me.

Chapter 43

Nora

I always thought this house would be an amazing place for a Labor Day party. I envisioned at least a hundred people spread out all over. Some would be inside the house, which is beautifully designed in an open style to allow for such a party, while the rest would spill out onto the deck, gathering around the glowing turquoise pool. Everyone would be dressed in resort wear, sipping chilled cocktails and dancing until sunrise.

While I still maintain that this house would be a great venue for a party, this Labor Day, I will be here all alone. I've been trying not to think about it, but today is Sunday, and it's difficult not to dwell on it. I hadn't realized how nice it was to have company here until Megan arrived. I thought I was doing Danielle a favor, but really, she was the one who helped me. Megan brought much-needed energy, and for the time Courtney was staying here, it was practically like a slumber party. At almost twice their age, I know they didn't consider me to actually be part of their *group*, but even to occasionally be included was enough for me.

If I'm being honest, the biggest adjustment will be when Penny leaves later today. I certainly never thought that I lacked a dog in my life. However, Penny has filled a void that none of those ridiculous blind dates ever could. The phrase that keeps popping up in my head is one of my mom's favorites – you never know what you've got until it's gone. Although in this case, Penny is sitting right here next to me with her magnificent head in my lap, and I don't think I have to wait until she's gone to realize what I have.

I've thought about Megan's suggestion, and I've looked at a few local rescue sites, but I can't think about running out and adopting another dog. I know I've only been taking care of Penny for two weeks, but I feel like I have a special bond with her. I check my watch again, and my chest grows even tighter. Eva's flight landed a few hours ago, and she could be here any minute. I rub Penny's silky ear like it might be my last chance to do so, and she briefly looks up at me, lets out a heavy breath, and continues her nap.

* * *

Penny and I are sitting on the deck when Eva arrives. I texted her to tell her that we are out back, and Penny jumps off the chaise when she hears footsteps.

"There's my girl!" Eva says when Penny comes over to greet her. I fight back the absurd feelings of jealousy that are bubbling up and tell myself to get a grip as I watch my friend pet *her* dog.

"Welcome back!" I say, walking over to give Eva a hug. "How was your trip? I want to hear all about it!"

"It was amazing!" she gushes. "Although the flights were excruciating. The kids didn't sleep at all," she sighs.

"Come sit down," I say, motioning to the lounge chair next to the one where I was sitting. "Can I get you something to drink? Eat?"

"I'd love some water," Eva says. "I can't stay too long, but I'll stay for a few minutes to catch up. And maybe that means Chloe will start unpacking without me," she jokes.

I grab glasses of water for both of us. When I sit down, Penny hops right back up on my chair and curls her body against my legs even though she's too big for the spot and her hind legs are hanging over the edge.

"It looks like she's right at home," Eva laughs. "Was everything okay? It sounded like things were going well from your texts," Eva says cautiously.

I hesitate before I answer, unsure what to share. "It was fine," I finally decide to say.

"Oh good," Eva says. "I can't thank you enough," Eva says.

"No problem. She's a great dog," I say.

"I know she can be a handful," Eva says. "It was really great of you to do this for us."

"Honestly, once I figured out that she needed multiple walks a day, she was great," I tell Eva.

"Really?" Eva says, looking surprised. "It's been hard to manage a dog with work and the kids," Eva sighs.

"What do you mean?" I ask.

"Don't get me wrong. Of course, we love her. Look at that

face; who wouldn't love her? There just aren't enough hours in the day to get everything done. You know what I mean?" Eva says.

I laugh in spite of myself and shake my head. "I used to know what you meant, but at the moment, I do not."

Eva smiles tiredly and continues, "I thought the kids would love the dog. And they do, but only for about ten minutes, and then they are interested in something else. And of course, they don't do anything to take care of her – although they're still probably too young to do much," Eva sighs.

"What about Chloe?" I ask.

"I had to talk Chloe into getting the dog in the first place. She said we weren't ready, and I told her that we would be fine. So that's another source of tension. Anyway, it was just really nice these past two weeks not to have to worry about Penny. I mean, of course, I missed her," Eva says, reaching over to give Penny a quick pat, "But it was a lot less stressful," she groans.

"Hmmm," I say, wondering if I could actually say what I'm thinking out loud.

"Oh well, I guess that's why they call it a vacation, right? Now it's back to reality and all the hassle that comes with it. Thanks again for doing this. It was a huge favor, and I owe you big for this," Eva says, pulling herself to her feet.

"What if Penny stayed here?" I blurt out before my brain can stop my mouth from talking.

"What?" Eva asks, looking incredibly confused.

"I love her," I say, no longer caring that I am unabashedly declaring my love for my friend's dog. "I have the room and the time, and I would love it if she kept staying with me." I gauge Eva's face for a reaction and plow ahead. "She'd obviously still be your dog, but I could take care of her," I say. This last part is a bit harder to think through, but my offer is ridiculous enough.

"You would do that?" Eva finally says. She'd been quiet for so long that I had no idea what to expect when she finally spoke.

"You'd be doing me a big favor," I say to her. "I'd bring her by to see you guys or the kids whenever they want, or you could come to see her over here?" I suggest.

"I'd love to come to visit her, and then I'll get to see you as well," she says happily. "I'm sure the kids may want to see her occasionally, but the last two weeks, all they've talked about is wanting to get a goldfish and a frog. They haven't mentioned the dog once," Eva laments. "I think this might be a much better environment for Penny."

At the sound of her name, Penny's ears perk up, and she lifts her head and looks around as if assessing her surroundings, and then she snuggles even closer to me and sighs contentedly. Penny and I have both found our home.

Epilogue

The Following Summer

Nora

"This is a great house for a party," the caterer says as he sets up the temporary bar on the deck.

"Thanks," I reply casually. But what I really want to say is, "I know, right?!"

"You couldn't ask for better weather on Memorial Day weekend," he comments.

"Nope. It's pretty much perfect," I say. I don't particularly want to get sucked into a conversation about the weather, so I excuse myself and walk back inside. The kitchen and most of the first floor are swarming with the rest of the catering staff, so I make a beeline for the stairs.

I knock lightly on one of the guest-room doors and wait for a response. "Come in," Bridget calls back. I slowly open the door, and a smile spreads across my face at the scene in front of me. Colleen and Quinn are lying on the floor with Penny, all tangled up together – it's unclear which of the three of them is having the most fun.

"How's it going?" I ask her.

"The girls are having a great time with Penny," she says, gesturing to the trio on the floor. "Penny has been such a good distraction that I was able to get ready in peace. Maybe we should get a dog," she says.

Just then, Patrick walks out of the bathroom, freshly showered and dressed in blue linen pants and a loose white button-down – this may only be his second time in the Hamptons, but he sure looks the part. "You cannot be serious?" he says to Bridget, looking terrified at the idea of another living creature in their home.

"Of course not, calm down," she laughs, playfully swatting him on the arm as he walks by and kisses her cheek.

"I love your dress," I tell Bridget.

"Are you sure?" she questions. "Sophia helped me pick it out, and I think I'm a little too old to wear it," she says, looking at herself again in the mirror.

"You look amazing! Sophia has great taste," I assure her.

"I have no doubt that she has great taste, but my concern is that she only knows what teenagers should wear," Bridget says.

"You look great," Patrick assures her. "Speaking of Sophia, is she ready yet? The party starts soon, right?" he asks me.

"I'll text her right now," Bridget says. "But she's always on time," she reminds him.

"I'm going to go downstairs in case people start arriving," I tell them. "I can go check at the guest house as well and let Sophia know to come upstairs."

"Don't worry about it. She just texted back. She's coming up right now. I can't remember what we did before her," Bridget says and laughs in a breezy way that fills me with joy.

I decide that this is a rhetorical question, and she doesn't want me to remind her that she was overwhelmed and sometimes miserable up until last winter when they hired Sophia to help part-time with the girls. I certainly can't take a lot of credit for their improved situation, but I feel like I can take a little. During the fall, I started spending one day a week with Bridget and the girls. I showed up one day and figured out how to make myself useful. The small relief gave Bridget enough room to figure out what she needed and to hire someone to help her part-time with the girls and around the house.

By five o'clock, the party is in full swing, and it's better than I'd ever imagined it could be. I step away for a moment to survey the scene and take it all in. There are approximately seventy-five people laughing and talking and dancing. Almost all of them are squeezed onto the deck, as the weather is so spectacular that only a few have opted to stay inside. I'm proud of the work I've done over the past nine months to reconnect with friends and colleagues – so many of whom are here tonight. Naturally, not all of my attempts were successful. Some friends weren't as forgiving of decades of silence and had no interest in reconnecting, or some of those who wanted to only did so for selfish reasons.

I think almost everyone that RSVP'd yes is here, and at this point, I feel like I've made the rounds and at least said hello to each guest. Although there are two people that I haven't seen and thought should have been here by now. Before I can get too worried, Joel and Megan walk out onto the deck; Joel is clutching a bottle of wine or champagne wrapped elaborately in shiny foil and ribbons.

I slide my way past a few guests and give Megan a hug. "I'm so glad you could make it!" I say to her.

"Of course! We wouldn't miss it," she says.

"How was your flight?" I ask, wishing I had a more original question.

"It was fine. I got in yesterday, and Joel picked me up," she replies.

"How long are you staying?" I ask her. I'm not sure why I'm asking her this since I already know the answer. Joel and I talked about it a few days ago, but it's the first thing that pops into my head.

"Only for a few days. I still have a few more weeks of classes," Megan says.

"Then Denver or Vegas, or is it New York?" I ask, although again, I know the answer.

"First we go to Denver to see Courtney and Preston. She finished classes at NYU last week and has a few weeks off before she starts her summer internship. Although she's interning at a firm in Denver, so she'll be living there for the summer," Megan says.

"That's great. How are they doing?" I ask. I never got to

know Courtney that well, but I feel a connection with her from the short time she was here, and Megan did a great job of filling me in, so I'm invested.

"They're doing really well. I think they might get engaged soon. Courtney says it's way too soon, but I'm not sure I believe her," Megan chuckles.

"Then you go to the tech conference?" I ask.

"First New York for a few days to see my family and Alex, and then the tech conference," Megan says.

"How's Alex?"

"He's doing great. We text all the time and talk on the phone a lot. He loves his job, and he's found a great group of supportive friends in New York. He even has a girlfriend," Megan adds.

"That's wonderful. I'm so happy for him," I reply. "So Vegas after New York?"

"Yup. Vegas for a few days at the end of June should be interesting," she says. "But after Joel sold the first app last year, there's a lot of interest in the next one," Megan beams.

"There's a moderate amount of interest," Joel says, his cheeks flushing slightly with Megan's praise.

"Don't be modest," Megan says, wrapping her arm protectively around his bicep.

"I'm well aware of how talented he is," I nod in agreement. "He's been instrumental in helping me get ready for my meetings next month," I say.

"It's not that big of a deal," Joel says. "Just some simple coding."

"I couldn't have done it without you," I say, although I don't want to further embarrass him.

"Is Penny ready for her big debut?" Megan asks playfully.

"Hardly," I laugh. "Thankfully, I only needed a few pictures of her for the mockups. I think that's about her limit."

Eva walks over right then to join the conversation and puts her arm around me. "Are we talking about my famous former dog? Or the new line of pet supplies and clothing that's going to make my famous friend even more famous?" she asks, taking a sip of her Bellini.

"Hardly!" I say to her, squeezing her shoulder. "Penny isn't your *former* dog," I say, but we both know that's not true. With the exception of offhand comments like these, we don't talk about it, but it's pretty clear that Penny is all mine. "And I have no idea what's going to happen with this new venture," I protest.

"We all know that if you're behind it, it's going to be a success," Eva says.

"Thank you," I say to my friend.

Eva raises her glass, and Megan and Joel quickly follow suit with the glasses of rum punch they took off the server's tray. "To Nora!" Eva says.

It's slightly weird to toast myself, so instead, I raise my glass of champagne, and surrounded by friends, family, and loved ones, I say, "To another amazing summer on Dune Road!"

THE END

Acknowledgments

Once again, I must thank all of you first. Thank you to my readers for buying, reading, downloading, and reviewing my books. I hope that you enjoyed reading this book as much as I loved writing it.

I want to thank my early readers and wonderful friends for their insightful feedback and helpful comments – Aimee Kaplan, Erin Ginsburg, and Kathy Soderberg. You three are amazing to make time for me and to continuously cheer me on – thank you!

Thank you to my sister, Sarah Nelson, for reading as a I write. You provide endless support for my writing.

Thank you to my parents, John & Vicki Nelson. Thank you for all the encouragement you provide for my second career. I greatly appreciate your unwavering support even though I know it's not quite how you pictured me using my MBA. Thank you as well to my mom for a last round of proof-reading – your attention to detail is appreciated!

I don't know how I got so lucky to have such wonderful children, but I certainly would not be able to do what I do without you. Morgan, Samantha, and Lexi - you are my world and I love you more than you will ever know.

Last, but certainly not least, I am indebted to my amazing husband, Doug. You are the best partner and friend I could ever ask for. Thank you for your constant love and support.

About the Author

Rachel Cullen is a graduate of Northwestern University and NYU Stern School of Business. She worked in consulting and marketing in San Francisco, London, and New York and currently lives in Westchester, New York, with her husband and three children, and her two large dogs. *Summer on Dune Road* is her sixth novel.

www.rachelcullenauthor.com

 facebook.com/RachelCullenAuthor

 instagram.com/RachelCullenAuthor

Also by Rachel Cullen

The Way I've Heard it Should Be

Second Chances

Only Summer

First Came Us

The Last Summer Sister

Made in the USA
Middletown, DE
21 April 2022